**The Flight
of the Silver Turtle**

Before starting to write and illustrate his own children's books, John Fardell has been working as a freelance cartoonist, illustrator, and occasional designer of puppet theatre shows. A regular contributor to *Viz* (he is the creator of 'The Modern Parents' and 'The Critics' amongst others), his work has also appeared in the *Independent*, the *List*, the *Herald*, the *New Statesman* and the *Evening Standard*. He is married with two boys and lives in Edinburgh. *The Flight of the Silver Turtle* is his second book for Faber and follows *The 7 Professors of the Far North*.

by the same author
The 7 Professors of the Far North

THE FLIGHT OF THE SILVER TURTLE

JOHN FARDELL

ff

faber and faber

First published in 2006
by Faber and Faber Limited
3 Queen Square London WC1N 3AU

Typeset by Faber and Faber Limited
Printed in England by Bookmarque Ltd, Croydon

A CIP record for this book
is available from the British Library

ISBN 978-0-571-22691-7
ISBN 0-571-22691-4

10 9 8 7 6 5 4 3 2 1

To Mum and Dad,
with love

Chapter One

BANG! A loud explosion erupted from the kitchen, rattling the open French windows and jingling the milk-bottle chandelier. A cloud of smoke plumed out from the kitchen doorway, engulfing the sunlit dining table and the five people sitting at it.

Marcia Slick, the brown-haired thirteen-year-old sitting nearest to the kitchen, suppressed her instinct to run from the house and phone the fire brigade. The three other children at the table – Ben, Zara and Sam – seemed quite unperturbed and were laughing as much as they were coughing. Marcia had discovered during her brief previous visit to 12 Pinkerton Place that minor technological mishaps were a normal part of everyday life here.

The large woman at the end of the table, who wore a flower-covered straw hat, seemed similarly unfazed. But Marcia knew it took a lot to faze Professor Petunia Hartleigh-Broadbeam.

The gangly figure of Professor Alexander Ampersand emerged from the kitchen. His pink, beaming face was blasted with soot, and the white hair that surrounded his bald head stuck out even more wildly than usual. He was wheeling a trolley supporting a large metal box, whose burnt and buckled sides emitted a few last trickles of smoke. Arriving at the table, he lifted the box's lid, revealing a smouldering heap of slightly scrambled

eggs, very scrambled bacon and completely scrambled sausages, all jumbled up in a sizzling puddle of boiled orange juice. 'Breakfast is served,' he announced.

'Do you not think your auto-breakfast-preparer might have somewhat *over*-prepared the ingredients, Alexander?' asked Professor Hartleigh-Broadbeam.

'Maybe just a wee bit,' admitted Professor Ampersand, shovelling the charred and juice-sodden debris onto six plates. 'And the separate drink-cooling compartment seems to have malfunctioned. But I think the invention's sound in principle. An ideal labour-saving device for busy families.'

Sam tried a mouthful. 'It's actually quite nice if you imagine it's *meant* to be all mixed up like this,' he said.

'It's not *too* bad,' agreed Zara, 'but it would be better without the hot orange juice.'

'The juice takes away some of the burnt bacon taste,' Ben pointed out. 'What do *you* reckon, Marcia?'

Marcia tasted some of the odd but surprisingly edible mixture. 'It's fab,' she said, smiling at her friends. 'Totally fab.'

Marcia had first met Ben, Zara and Sam only a few months before. Although their time together had been short, the perilous events they had been through had made them the closest of friends. Zara and her brother Ben, twelve and eleven respectively, lived here in this Victorian terraced house in Edinburgh with their great-uncle, Professor Ampersand. He had adopted them as babies when their Tanzanian father and Scottish mother had been killed in a car crash.

Living with a sixty-eight-year-old eccentric inventor might not be some people's idea of a perfect upbringing, but Marcia knew of no happier family. Her own parents had been obsessed with creating a perfect family, and their desire to turn Marcia into their idea of a perfect daughter had led them to get involved with a sinister and illegal medical research organization. They were now in prison.

The Ampersands would have loved to have Marcia join their family. But, after some consideration, she had decided to accept an offer of a new home from Professor Hartleigh-Broadbeam, another inventor, who had also been caught up in their adventure. It had turned out her flat was in the same part of London as Marcia had lived before, and after everything Marcia had been through, she'd liked the idea of staying somewhere familiar.

Professor Hartleigh-Broadbeam was also in her late sixties and could rival Professor Ampersand when it came to being eccentric – she gave each one of her many hats names and tended to talk to them – but Marcia found her to be a kind and considerate guardian. For the first time in her life, Marcia felt loved and valued for who she was.

And at last Marcia could attend the local school instead of the horrible private establishment her parents had sent her to. It was great to be at school with her footballing friends from the park, the friends her parents had always despised.

The one thing that troubled Marcia was that she hadn't felt able to explain her situation honestly to these school friends. She referred to Professor Hartleigh-Broadbeam as her great-aunt and gave the impression that her parents were working abroad. She knew it was wrong to lie, but she couldn't face telling people that her parents were in prison, and were there because of what they had tried to do to her. Just thinking about it brought back bad feelings that it was *her* fault her parents couldn't love her, that she wasn't good enough. She knew that such feelings were irrational, but they were lurking inside her all the same.

Now though, Marcia was back in Edinburgh for the summer holidays, with friends who knew her whole story and needed no explanations. She and Professor Hartleigh-Broadbeam had travelled up by train the previous evening, accompanied by eleven-year-old Sam Carnabie, who lived near London. The two professors planned to work on some projects together, and Marcia and Sam could look forward to four whole weeks in this extraordinary house.

Chapter Two

'That's the post,' said Ben, hearing the letterbox clattering. He ran to the front door and brought a postcard and an envelope back to the table. The postcard had a photo of a huge vertical fountain in front of a lakeside city, with the caption *Jet d'Eau* beneath it.

Jet d'Eau

'That's Geneva, isn't it?' said Professor Ampersand. 'Must be from Ivy and Adam.' Professor Ivy Sharpe, another old colleague of Professor Ampersand's, was an environmental biologist who worked for the United Nations in Geneva. Adam was a young parentless boy they'd met during their recent adventure, whom Professor Sharpe had now adopted.

'You're right,' said Zara, turning the postcard over. 'It's from Adam.' They all read it:

Dear Everyone,
  I'm really looking forward to coming to Edinburgh in three weeks' time. I can't wait to see you all again!
  Professor Gadling, Professor Gauntraker and Professor Pottle are staying with us at the moment, planning a short expedition into the mountains to look for the rare Alpine tumbling snail. Afterwards, they're going to come to Edinburgh with us. Mum says perhaps we'd better all find a hotel to stay in!
  See you soon.
  Lots of love, Adam x x x x

Éditions Le Giraffe

Jet d'Eau, Genève

To   Zara, Ben,
   Marcia, Sam,
   Prof. Ampersand and
   Prof. Hartleigh-Broadbeam,
   12 Pinkerton Place,
   Edinburgh,
   Écosse, U.K.

'That's excellent,' said Professor Ampersand, 'but I wouldn't dream of letting my old friends and colleagues stay in a hotel. I'm sure we can squeeze them all in here somehow. Now, what's this other letter?' he went on, scrutinizing the envelope. 'Ah. Looks like it might be a reply from Globewide Automobiles.'

'Uncle Alexander's invented a new electric motor,' explained Zara, as her great-uncle ripped open the envelope. 'He's been trying to find a car manufacturer to take the invention on.'

'Yes, you mentioned this new motor in your last e-mail, Alexander,' said Professor Hartleigh-Broadbeam. 'I've been looking forward to seeing it.'

'What does the letter say, Uncle Alexander?' asked Ben.

'Same as all the others,' said Professor Ampersand, frowning: 'Very sorry, but not something we'd be interested in . . . too radical for today's market . . . we're already working on our own electric-vehicle projects . . .'

'They've all said they've got their own electric-vehicle projects,' said Ben, 'but Uncle Alexander's motor is far more advanced than anything the car companies are producing.'

'We've just put the prototype motor into our motorbike,' Zara told Sam, Marcia and Professor Hartleigh-Broadbeam. 'Come and see.'

The entire ground floor of the Ampersands' house consisted of a single open-plan room. As they all walked across to the front of the space, Sam looked around him, taking it all in again: the high metal walkways along the two side walls, with bookshelves above them, spanned by a narrow metal catwalk; the bushy, plant-covered spiral staircase in the centre of the room; the workbenches beneath the walkways, spilling over with half-finished inventions of every description. Sam loved inventions, and had notebooks full of his own. His easy-going parents, former students of Professor Ampersand, were more than happy to let him spend most of the summer holiday here. It was great to be back.

Over by the old sofa at the front of the room, the Ampersands' bright yellow motorbike-and-sidecar stood poised on its round metal platform, facing a large window in the centre of the house that looked out onto the street. The long, torpedo-shaped sidecar was much as Sam remembered it. The huge bike was still festooned with lamps, dials and gadgets, but several new bits and pieces had been added, and its overall shape was different.

'This is my new motor, down here,' said Professor Ampersand, pointing to a bulky cylindrical device at the bottom. 'Though I say it myself, it really is a radical improvement on traditional electric motors, giving massively more power for the same amount of electricity.'

'Is it powered by a big battery?' asked Marcia.

'Or by hydrogen fuel cells?' asked Sam, who'd seen something on TV about new electric vehicles.

'Actually, I've also invented a new kind of energy cell which combines the technology of batteries *and* fuel cells, and is more compact and efficient than either,' said Professor Ampersand. 'After just ten minutes plugged into the mains electricity, my energy cell contains enough power to keep the motor running for several hours.'

'Wow!' said Sam.

'Of course, the system will only be *completely* environmentally friendly when all our mains electricity is generated in renewable-energy power stations,' added Professor Ampersand. 'But even so, electric vehicles are a huge improvement on our highly polluting and ludicrously inefficient petrol-engined cars. I'd hoped that the car companies would at least take a *look* at my invention.'

'Couldn't you start making and selling electric cars yourself?' asked Marcia.

'I really should,' agreed Professor Ampersand. 'But it would take a fair bit of money to set up a proper manufacturing business and I'm afraid I'm down to my last brass farthing. Well, almost,' he added hurriedly, forcing a chuckle.

Zara and Ben glanced at each other, neither child convinced by their great-uncle's attempt to make light of his financial difficulties. While helping to keep his office upstairs in some sort of order, they had both seen enough of his business paperwork to know that they really were completely broke, even more so than usual. Zara just couldn't see how they'd be able to pay all the monthly bills for much longer. Even Ben, normally less inclined to worry about such things than his older sister, knew that things were serious.

'I'd fund your electric vehicles like a shot, m'dear,' said Professor Hartleigh-Broadbeam, 'but, as you know, I haven't a bean. Maybe you'll be able to catch the eye of a financial backer now that you've got your motor fitted to an actual vehicle. Does the bike go well?'

'Really well,' said Ben, 'though it's only had a short test drive so far. We just finished fitting the motor yesterday.'

'Hey, why don't we give it another test drive now, Uncle Alexander?' suggested Zara.

'Yeah!' said Ben. 'And we could have the sidecar canopy off. It's really hot and sunny out there.'

'Excellent idea,' said Professor Ampersand, genuinely beaming once more. 'Let's forget about Globewide Automobiles and take a spin out to the seaside.'

'That'd be brilliant!' said Marcia, who had never ridden in the sidecar before, and had been longing to. 'But will we all fit?'

'Just about,' said Professor Ampersand. 'Petunia can ride on the back of the bike and you four can squeeze into the sidecar. Round up your swimming stuff and I'll pack a wee picnic.'

In less than ten minutes they were all aboard, Professor Hartleigh-Broadbeam looking very dashing in Professor Ampersand's spare bike helmet (which she christened Orlando). It was a tight fit in the sidecar, with Ben and Sam both squashed onto the toolbox between the front and back seats, but nobody minded. Marcia had been given the front seat and her skin tingled with anticipation as Professor Ampersand pressed a button on the bike's headlamp and the house's large central window slid upwards. From the outside window sill, a metal ramp unfolded itself over the pavement and down to the edge of the road.

The bike's motor started with a bright whirring buzz, a considerably quieter noise than the throaty rumble Sam remembered the old engine making, but an equally exciting one. Professor Ampersand eased the vehicle down the ramp and out into the July sunshine.

Chapter Three

Half an hour later, the motorbike-and-sidecar was buzzing through the East Lothian countryside, beneath a cloudless sky. The ride had been every bit as exhilarating as Marcia had dreamed. The road was almost following the coastline now, and through gaps in the hedges and trees to their left, they could see the nearby sea, a deep inviting blue, sparkling in the glorious sunlight.

'There's a lovely wee beach just around here somewhere,' said Professor Ampersand. 'Not many people know it. Ah, I think this is the turning coming up.'

The professor steered the bike into a narrow dusty track, marked by an overgrown wooden signpost which read PETTICRAIG BAY. The track twisted through a copse of trees and brambles down towards the sea. They passed an elderly woman on a bicycle, but saw no other people or vehicles. After a couple of hundred metres, the track forked in two. The foliage and undergrowth made it impossible to see where either track led. 'I *think* the beach is this way,' said the professor, taking the right-hand fork.

A short distance on, the track emerged onto a dusty patch of ground. An old open-backed truck stood parked outside a large building whose walls and curved roof were an orangey-brown patchwork of completely rusted corrugated iron. The wall facing them was windowless but had a battered plywood door in the centre.

Next to the door hung a hand-painted sign that looked newer and brighter than everything else about the building. It said:

A pebbly beach was visible beyond the building, but Professor Ampersand shook his head. 'This isn't it,' he said, starting to turn the motorbike-and-sidecar round.

At that moment, the plywood door opened and a young woman stepped out. 'Can I help you?' she said, giving them a quizzical but friendly smile. She was about twenty, short and slightly stocky, with a pleasant, round face and pale hair, tied back in an untidy ponytail. She wore blue mechanic's overalls.

'We were looking for the wee sandy beach,' explained

the professor. 'Did we take the wrong turn on the track?'

'Aye,' confirmed the woman, 'but you're no far off. Nice machine,' she added, studying their vehicle admiringly.

'Uncle Alexander built it himself,' said Zara, proudly. 'We're testing the new pollution-free electric motor he's invented.'

'I was just thinking how quiet it was,' said the woman. 'That's really impressive.'

'Och, well, thanks,' said the professor, blushing.

Sam pointed to the sign by the door. 'Is this an aircraft hangar?' he asked.

'It is,' said the woman. 'I'm Amy McAirdrie, owner and managing director of McAirdrie Aviation.' She grinned. 'And sole staff-member: designer, mechanic and pilot. I'm just building my first aeroplane. Come in and take a wee look, if you like. Unless you're in a hurry tae get tae the beach . . .'

'Not *that* much of a hurry,' said Zara, eagerly scrambling out of the sidecar, followed by the others.

'No, indeed,' said Professor Ampersand, as he and Professor Hartleigh-Broadbeam dismounted the motorbike. 'It's not every day you meet someone who's building their own aeroplane. I'm Alexander Ampersand,' he added, shaking Amy's hand, 'and this is Professor Petunia Hartleigh-Broadbeam, Zara, Ben, Sam and Marcia.'

They followed their new acquaintance inside. At the front of the hangar, a pair of big doors had been opened wide onto the sunny pebbled beach. The space had a wonderful combined smell of summer seaside and welding.

The hangar's concrete floor was strewn with tools, plans, aluminium tubing and sheeting, steel cable, tables and stepladders. In the centre of it all, facing the hangar's open front doorway stood Amy McAirdrie's aeroplane.

Its design was unorthodox. The tailless body, supported on three wheels, resembled a small motorboat, and was topped with a Plexiglas canopy. Two wide, streamlined struts thrust forwards and outwards from the rear of the body to support a swept-back crescent-shaped wing. The two wing tips each ended in a sleek vertical fin.

Sam could see that the plane was unfinished – several panels were missing from its silvery surface, wires and cables were trailing loose everywhere, and there was no sign of an engine or propeller – but even in its incomplete state it looked somehow eager to be zooming up into the sky. But from where would it take off? Sam could see no runway outside. However, there was a wide concrete slip-way leading from the front of the hangar, over the beach and down into the sea.

'Is it a seaplane?' Sam asked.

'Aye,' confirmed Amy. 'Tae be specific, she's an amphibious flying boat. Amphibious because she'll be able tae operate from both land and water, and a flying boat because she'll float on her fuselage hull, rather than on separate floats like a float plane. The wheels will fold up when she's flying and the bases of the two wing-tip fins will fold down on struts to act as stabilizer floats when she's landed on water.'

Sam had a closer look at the ingeniously engineered undercarriage legs and wing-tip floats, working out how all the moving parts would operate. 'Brilliant!' he said. 'How many people will she carry?'

'She'll seat five in the cockpit itself,' said Amy. She slid back the middle section of the Plexiglas canopy so they could have a closer look. 'See – two in front, with dual controls, and three behind,' she pointed out. 'And I'll be putting another seat intae the nose hatch here.'

Sam looked at the open hatch in the plane's stubby curved nose. That would be the best place to sit, he thought, feeling excited just at the thought of it.

'She's beautiful,' said Zara. 'Did you really build her all by yourself?'

'I did,' said Amy. 'My father's a boat builder, so I grew up learning all aboot that, but I've always been mad aboot planes. I spent my teenage years saving up for flying lessons, and got my pilot's licence at eighteen.'

'Goodness, you must have been keen,' said Professor Hartleigh-Broadbeam.

Amy shrugged. 'I could never understand why *everyone* wasnae desperate tae fly,' she said. 'We're able tae do what oor ancestors could only dream of being able tae do: tae fly like the birds. For the thoosands and thoosands of years we've been aroond, humans have been a flightless species. Now we've finally cracked the secret of powered, controlled flight. Yet most people dinnae even consider becoming a pilot or owning a plane. It's seen as too expensive, too dangerous, too complicated, too impractical – not something that ordinary people do. I wanted tae design and build a plane tae change all that: a plane that's fast, long range and able tae land and take off from almost anywhere, but cheaper than a small car, completely safe and so simple that a beginner can learn tae fly her in a few hours.'

'How long has it taken you to build her?' asked Zara.

'Oh, a guid couple o' years,' said Amy. 'Tae be honest, I didnae know whether it'd really be possible but I decided tae make a start anyway. I heard that East Lothian Cooncil were selling off this old hangar for next tae nothing. It was built during World War Two, specifically for amphibious flying boats, but had been lying more or less unused ever since. It leaks a bit in the rain, but no too badly, and the slipway doon to the water is still intact. So I bought it and set up my workshop here. I've had tae stop work on the plane from time tae time, tae take on temporary jobs in Edinburgh and save up more funds for materials and equipment. But at least my living costs are low — I live here in the hangar.' She pointed to a corner where a basic bed had been constructed from three wooden packing cases and a foam-rubber mattress.

'Cool,' said Ben.

'I'm no *too* far from completing her noo,' said Amy. 'She's starting tae look like a proper plane. I've just registered her with the Civil Aviation Authority — a couple o' days ago.'

Sam studied the plane some more. 'Where's the engine going to go?' he asked.

'She'll have two engines, there and there,' said Amy, pointing up at two spaces where the two struts joined the wing. 'But I dinnae have the skills tae build engines from scratch, so I'll have tae save up and buy them. Time tae find another job in a bar or restaurant.'

A thought struck Marcia. 'Professor Ampersand's been

finding it hard to interest car makers in his electric motor,' she pointed out, 'and you need engines for your plane. Why don't you team up?'

'That's a brilliant idea!' said Zara. 'We'd all help too.'

'Yeah!' agreed Sam, enthusiastically.

Amy McAirdrie looked at her aircraft through half-closed eyes. She seemed to be visualizing the new idea. 'Pollution-free flight!' she said. 'That'd be brilliant — it'd take my plane tae a whole new level.' Then she checked herself and turned to Professor Ampersand. 'But you're maybe too busy tae take on a new project,' she said.

A grin spread over Professor Ampersand's face. 'Not too busy to take on a new project like this,' he said. 'I'm sure we could build another two motors using bits and pieces from other half-finished inventions back at the house. Let's do it!'

In the dappled shade of the copse, well away from the track, a man wearing a flat cap peered through a compact pair of binoculars. A book entitled *A Field Guide to British Birds* protruded visibly from a pocket of his khaki jacket, but the subject of his gaze was not ornithological. He was studying the hangar and the motorbike-and-sidecar parked next to it.

'Just an auld guy, an auld woman and some kids,' he said, speaking quietly into a tiny microphone in his upturned collar, continuing to hold the binoculars to his eyes. 'They've been in there a few minutes.'

'Continue to monitor the situation,' ordered another man's voice, coming through the watcher's invisible earpiece. 'And take the motorcycle's number so we can ascertain who these visitors are.'

'Understood,' said the man. 'Though this is a waste o' time, if ye ask me, sir. We've very little reason tae think McAirdrie knows anything aboot the Silver Turtle project. Just because she's registered a self-built aircraft, with this hangar as the address, doesnae mean she's working on anything connected tae —'

'It is not your place to question orders,' rapped the voice. 'The Leader has decreed that any lead concerning the Silver Turtle project, no matter how slight, is to be followed up. Do I need to inform the Leader that you wish to be relieved of your duties and replaced?'

'No!' said the watcher quickly, his face turning pale. 'I wasnae questioning orders, sir.'

'You have been monitoring the hangar for nearly two days, Lerkner,' said the voice, 'and still we know virtually nothing about the aircraft this McAirdrie woman is working on.'

'I told you, sir: I havnae been able tae get intae the hangar tae take a look. McAirdrie seems tae be living in it full time — hasnae moved from the building. If we really want tae know what McAirdrie's up tae, mebbe we're going tae have tae bring her in for interrogation.'

'No!' insisted the voice. 'Not until we are sure she has anything to tell us. We must not jeopardize our secrecy for nothing. McAirdrie will leave the hangar unattended eventually. Then you can break in, make a proper inspection of her aircraft and plant an audio-surveillance bug, so that we can listen in on any future conversations that McAirdrie conducts with visitors. Then we shall know whether she has really discovered the secret of the Silver Turtle project.'

Up on the main road, the elderly woman cyclist whom Professor Ampersand and the children had passed earlier brought her bicycle to a standstill. After checking that no traffic was approaching, she reached into her handlebar basket. From beneath a folded suede jacket, she took out an old, leather-clad pair of binoculars. She scanned the copse for some moments, before finding the man in the flat cap. She brought her view of him into focus and watched him spying on the hangar, nodding her head slightly, as if confirming something in her mind. Frowning, she replaced her binoculars in the basket, taking care to conceal them once more, and cycled on.

Chapter Four

'How's that looking?' asked Professor Ampersand. He was kneeling on top of the wing, tightening a screw on the side of the newly fitted left motor.

'Looks good tae me,' said Amy McAirdrie. She stood on a ladder beneath the right motor, making an adjustment to the large two-bladed propeller. 'Could you pass me the long screwdriver, Sam?'

Two and a half weeks had passed since their first fortuitous meeting with the young aircraft designer, and the project had been going well. They had used Amy's truck to transport everything they needed from 12 Pinkerton Place to the hangar and, with the three inventors and four children working together, progress on the motors and on the rest of the plane had been speedy.

Apart from short picnic-lunch breaks and occasional cooling swims from the sandy beach, work on the plane had taken over their entire lives. Amy usually joined them for supper back at the house where discussions about the plane's progress went on all evening.

Sam was in heaven. For as far back as he could remember, he had longed to build a real aeroplane, one in which he could really fly. He remembered an afternoon when he was only four, when he'd taped two sheets of paper to the sides of an old cereal box. He'd pelted round the garden, holding his home-made aeroplane to his chest as he leapt forward, half-convincing himself that the flimsy paper wings were at least *slightly* delaying his bellyflop landings on the lawn, urgently wanting to believe that he was flying. He could still remember the fluttering, yearning excitement he'd felt that afternoon. He'd felt it throughout his childhood, whenever he'd made up an aircraft design in one of his invention notebooks. And he'd felt it more frequently than ever over the past two and a half weeks.

The plane was almost ready to leave the hangar now. All the panels of her shiny silver surface had been riveted into place, Professor Ampersand's energy-cell system had been installed inside the base of her hull, and the two stream-lined electric motors had been bolted into position.

Sam emerged from the plane's front hatch, where he and Zara were fixing on a pair of sliding covers, and passed Amy the required screwdriver. 'Do you still think we'll have her ready for a first test flight by tomorrow?' he asked her.

'Aye,' replied Amy. 'I reckon we will.'

In a small dark blue van, parked several miles along the coast, Lerkner sat eating a sandwich. In his left ear, he wore an earpiece connected to a short-range radio receiver concealed in the back of the van. In his right ear, he wore the invisible earpiece that was connected to his jacket. 'They're talking aboot conducting a first test flight tomorrow, sir,' he reported into his collar.

'Ensure that you are well positioned to observe,' instructed his superior's voice.

'I'll be there, sir,' answered Lerkner, 'though I'm still doubtful we'll see anything tae interest us. Nothing we've heard them discussing since I planted the bug two weeks ago suggests a definite link tae what we know of the Silver

Turtle project. Nor anything I could spot aboot their aircraft when I was in the hangar.'

'Yet their aircraft *is* distinctly unorthodox in design and in its power source,' said his superior. 'We cannot rule out the possibility that the technology we are looking for may be secretly concealed within it. Continue to monitor.'

'We'd better think of a name for her before her first flight,' said Zara, as she and Sam continued to work on the hatch cover.

What to name their flying boat had been the subject of much discussion over the previous fortnight, but no one had come up with a name on which everyone could agree. Amy had modestly insisted that the *McAirdrie Flying Boat* sounded too dull and anyway didn't seem right for what was now a team project. Ben had suggested *Pelican* but Zara had reckoned *Puffin* suited the little plane's round shape better. Marcia, looking at the crescent-shaped wing, had thought *Swift* would be a good name. Sam thought that all these names had been used for planes already, but he hadn't been able to think of a good name which hadn't.

'I'm sure we'll think of a name tonight,' said Amy. 'Let's get her finished first, eh? How's the wiring going, Petunia?'

'Swimmingly, m'dear,' answered Professor Hartleigh-Broadbeam from the cockpit, where she was working with Marcia and Ben. 'We've nearly connected all the dials and switches. But this reel of two-millimetre wire is about to run out. Have we any more in our stores?'

'I'm not sure,' said Professor Ampersand. 'I think that might have been our last reel.'

'I'll check,' said Ben. He clambered out of the cockpit and made his way over to the back of the hangar, where they kept their equipment, plans and materials. Their electrical supplies were kept in a big plastic toolbox that sat on a shelf that was fixed to the hangar wall. The shelf was slightly out of Ben's reach, so he climbed onto a small camping table below it. In trying to avoid treading on any of the plans and diagrams that were spread out on the table, he stood too near to the edge and the table tipped over. As sheets of paper, rulers, pencils and an Anglepoise lamp cascaded to the floor, Ben instinctively grabbed the edge of the shelf to steady himself. This was another mistake. The entire shelf came away from the wall, and crashed down on Ben as he fell to the ground, along with the toolbox and a whole load of junk that had been on the shelf too – crusted-up paint tins, oily rags, rusty springs, a shoe box full of assorted nuts and bolts, and various other odds and ends.

'Are you all right, Ben?' called Zara.

'I'm fine,' said Ben, picking himself up and rubbing his head where a paint tin had bounced off it. 'Sorry. I hope I haven't broken any of our stuff.'

'Och, dinnae worry about that,' said Amy, coming down her ladder to help him. 'There was nothing very breakable in that toolbox, and the rest of the stuff on that shelf was just old junk. It was there when I moved in.'

Something had been broken, though. A tiny black plastic disc that two weeks earlier had been secretly fixed to the edge of the Anglepoise lamp's heavy circular base now lay shattered beneath it.

In the van, Lerkner jiggled his left earpiece and checked the receiver unit. 'Sir! The bug's gone deid,' he reported into his collar microphone.

'*What?*' snapped his superior's voice. 'You mean they have discovered it and disabled it?'

'Nothing they were saying before it cut out suggested they'd foond it,' said Lerkner. 'Could just be a technical problem. Might be a fault with the relay transmitter I positioned near the hangar.'

'Go and check it,' ordered the voice. 'Report back without delay.'

'There's nae wire left in here anyway,' said Amy, looking in the toolbox.

'I don't think I've even got any back at the house,' said Professor Ampersand, 'but I'm sure our funds will just about run to a new reel. We can buy it from that hardware shop on St Leonard's Street on our way back home. It stays open till eight.'

'That'll be fine,' said Professor Hartleigh-Broadbeam. 'I'll complete the wiring first thing tomorrow. I'm sure it won't take me long, and we can get everything else finished this afternoon. Let's just give Ben a hand to clear up over there.'

'No – you lot get on with the plane,' insisted Ben. 'I'll pick this stuff up.'

'Well, if you're sure,' said Amy, returning to her work on the right propeller.

Ben stacked the shelf and their toolbox next to the wall, then started to gather up the fallen junk. As he scooped the nuts and bolts back into their shoe box, he suddenly noticed a black-and-white photograph lying close to where they had fallen. He picked it up and studied it.

The photograph was of a man and a woman, holding hands. Both wore one-piece flying-suits and leather flying-helmets, with goggles pushed up on their foreheads. The man, who looked about forty, was looking at the woman and smiling. The woman, who Ben guessed to be in her early twenties, was laughing, with her eyes creased and her head thrown back. They were standing just in front of a hangar, with an aeroplane visible inside. The aeroplane was an amphibious biplane painted in a camouflage pattern, with British roundel markings. It wasn't a type that Ben knew, but he recognized the hangar. It was the one he was standing in now.

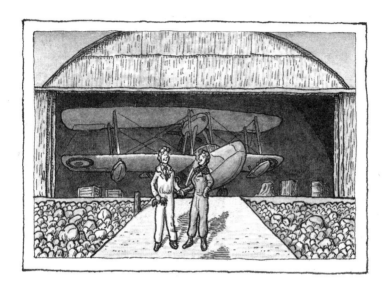

Chapter Five

'Look at this photo,' said Ben, taking it over to the others. They all came down from the plane to have a look. 'I'm sure it was taken here, by someone standing on the slipway, facing the hangar.'

'Wow!' said Zara. 'Where did you find it?'

'I think it was in this box, with these nuts and bolts,' said Ben.

'When do you think it was taken?' asked Marcia. 'That plane looks pretty old.'

'I think it's a Supermarine Walrus,' said Sam.

'It is,' said Amy. 'Well recognized. They were used during the Second World War.'

'That's when you said this hangar was built, isn't it?' said Zara.

'Aye,' said Amy, 'and, like I said, I dinnae think the place had been used much since the war, until I bought it, so all that junk that was on the shelf could well date back tae then. I never noticed this photo when I looked through the stuff, but it could have been hidden under the nuts and bolts.'

'So d'you think the man and the woman are RAF pilots?' Ben asked Amy.

'I'm no sure this was an RAF hangar,' said Amy. 'I once got chatting tae an old farmer who lives near here, and he told me that this hangar was used during the war by a Czech scientist who lived in Edinburgh. He was a Jewish refugee and he was rumoured tae be working on secret aviation projects for the British government.'

Secret aviation projects! Sam was really intrigued now. 'And do you think the scientist is the man in this photo?' he asked Amy.

Amy shrugged. 'Could be. But the farmer didnae tell me much else aboot him. Let me think . . . He said his name was Stribnik. Maskil Stribnik. Kept himself tae himself, apparently. Sometimes he was working here but mostly he worked in an office in the Royal Museum, in Chambers Street.'

'That's the big museum in the middle of Edinburgh,' Ben told Sam and Marcia. 'Not *royal*, like about kings and queens or anything. Loads of stuffed animals and dinosaur skeletons and mummies and science stuff. Everything really. It's cool.'

'I wonder who the woman in the photo is,' said Zara. 'I didn't think there were many female pilots in those days.'

'There were a lot more than most people think,' said Amy.

'See if there are any names on the back of the photo,' suggested Marcia.

Ben turned the photo over. There were no names, but something more mysterious: something that gave them each a strange, tingling feeling that they had stumbled on something more than just an old photograph. The word URGENT had been scrawled in pencil and underlined. Beneath this were two lines of handwritten letters, but they didn't seem to make any sense.

URGENT

qxhwsbiqxildblglwfhwsbvgkikqkwnliicbiixkzaknc

kdlwfcabglirbvczvcibjvkpbtchiiqxikrbdkvbrbvqg

'It's a message written using a code,' said Marcia.

'Or a cipher,' said Zara. 'We did ciphers at school. In some kinds of cipher you substitute the letters in a message for other letters.'

'But this message doesn't even have separate words,' Ben pointed out.

'Yeah, but sometimes cipher messages are written with all the words run together,' said Zara. 'If you leave the words separate, it makes it too easy for someone to spot common one-letter words like *a* or *I,* and common three-letter words like *the,* and guess which letters you've swapped for which.'

'There must be *some* way we can crack this cipher though,' said Ben. 'Have you got a notebook with you, Sam?'

Sam's current notebook of inventions was a small pad that he could carry around in one of the big zip pockets of his combat trousers. He took it out, with a pencil, and copied the message down on a blank page so they could try fiddling around with it. But he couldn't even think where to start.

'It could be a shift cipher,' said Zara. 'Where all the letters of the alphabet have been shifted along together by a fixed number of places. Lend me your notebook, Sam.'

Sam handed it to Zara, who turned to another unused page and wrote out the alphabet. She labelled it Plaintext Alphabet. 'Plaintext means non-encrypted,' she explained. Then she wrote a second alphabet below her first, starting with the A beneath the first alphabet's B, and finishing with the Z at the front, below the first alphabet's A. She labelled this one Ciphertext Alphabet.

Plaintext Alphabet   A B C D E F G H I J K L M N O P Q R S T U V W X Y Z
Ciphertext Alphabet   Z A B C D E F G H I J K L M N O P Q R S T U V W X Y

'See, that's a one-place shift,' she said. 'All the letters in this cipher alphabet are one letter on to the right. Let's try translating this message.'

The first ten letters of the ciphered message on the back of the photo – qxhwsbiqxi – translated back into plaintext as ryixtcjryj.

'That's not looking like anything,' said Ben. 'Try a two-letter shift.'

'It'd be quicker to write out the cipher alphabet on a separate strip of paper, and slide it along under the plaintext one,' said Sam. 'Then we wouldn't have to keep writing the two alphabets for each different shift.'

'Good thinking, Sam,' said Zara.

'Even so,' said Professor Hartleigh-Broadbeam, 'I can see that cracking this cipher could take a little while. Shall I get the lunch out?'

In the copse, a short distance from the hangar, Lerkner was checking a small khaki box that was hidden in a hole in a tree. 'The relay transmitter's working fine, sir,' he whispered into his collar. 'It's definitely the bug itself that's malfunctioned.'

'Malfunctioned?' said his superior's voice. 'Or been discovered and disabled? Continue to watch the hangar from a concealed position, Lerkner, while I report these developments to the Leader.'

By the time they'd finished their lunch, the children had tried out every one of the twenty-five possible letter shifts on the first ten letters of the message, but nothing looking vaguely like words had emerged.

'It doesn't have to be a shift substitution,' said Zara. 'Each letter might have been swapped directly with another letter in the alphabet.'

'That would give us way more than twenty-five possible cipher alphabets to try out,' said Ben.

'Far too many tae try oot one by one,' confirmed Amy. 'I'm as curious as you are aboot this message but, if we want tae get the plane finished, we ought tae crack on.'

They all worked hard on the plane throughout the afternoon. Sam and Zara finished fitting the covers to the nose hatch, and a little windscreen which could slide up at the front when the hatch was open. Professor Ampersand and Amy completed work on the two motors, and Marcia and Ben helped Professor Hartleigh-Broadbeam to fit the centre section of the Plexiglas canopy onto its runners so that it could slide neatly back into an open position.

At twenty past six, Amy came down her ladder to the hangar floor and stood back to admire their work. 'Just that wiring on the control panel tae finish,' she said, 'and she'll be ready for testing.'

'Och, yes, we need that wire, don't we?' said Professor Ampersand. 'We ought get a move on or the hardware shop will be closed. I'll take the children, shall I, if you take Petunia in your truck; I'm assuming you'll come for supper as usual, Amy?'

'Thank you, I will,' said Amy. 'You five get going. Petunia and I will lock up and meet you back at yours.'

'We can have another look at that secret message when we get home,' said Zara. 'I really want to know what it says.'

'Yeah, and whether it's to do with Stribnik's secret aviation work,' said Sam.

'You said Stribnik had also worked in an office at the Royal Museum, Amy,' said Professor Ampersand, as they made their way out of the hangar's back door. 'I wonder if George would remember him.'

'George is the oldest curator at the museum,' Zara told Sam, Marcia and Amy. 'He's really nice.'

'But was George really working at the museum during the war?' Ben asked Professor Ampersand. 'He's not quite *that* old, is he?'

'I think he'd have been about your age when the war ended in 1945,' said Professor Ampersand. 'But his father worked at the museum before him so George spent a lot of time there as a boy. If we showed him that photo, he might be able to tell us if the man in it is Stribnik, and tell us more about him. It might not help us with this cryptic message, but it'd be interesting to find out more about this hangar's history anyway.'

'Could we go and ask him now?' asked Zara, clambering onto the bike behind her great-uncle. 'The museum opens till eight tonight. You could drop us off on the way to the hardware shop and pick us up after you've bought the wire.'

'Good thinking, Zara,' said Professor Ampersand, starting up the electric motor. 'All aboard? Then let's go.'

Lerkner watched the motorbike-and-sidecar speed away up the track through his binoculars. He was muttering urgently into his collar microphone: 'He said Stribnik, sir. The auld guy, Ampersand, definitely said something aboot Stribnik, just before they left. Looks like you were right, sir.'

'Of course I was right,' said his superior's voice. 'The Leader was right. Now, calm down. Tell me what Ampersand said, *exactly*.'

'I dinnae ken what he said exactly. I couldnae hear properly from here. Something about a museum. I think one of the kids wanted tae go to some museum and ask somebody something.'

'A museum? Did they say the *Royal* Museum?'

'I think the auld guy might've said that. That's the big one on Chambers Street, isn't it? D'ye think it has some significance?'

'Haven't you read the file?' snapped his superior. 'Stribnik had an office there during the war. Something or someone there could be the source of McAirdrie's information on the Silver Turtle project.'

'D'ye want me tae run back tae my van and head for the museum after them, sir?' asked Lerkner.

'You would get there too far behind them,' said his superior. 'I shall arrange for Creevler to shadow them from the moment they come into Edinburgh. You stay at the hangar until the other two leave. See if you can overhear anything else.'

'If they leave the hangar unattended, I could break in again this evening,' suggested Lerkner. 'I could plant another bug and . . .'

'Pointless,' interrupted his superior. 'Now that they have found one bug, they will increase their vigilance. They will be on the lookout for any signs of further break-ins or any new audio surveillance devices. You have underestimated these people from the start, Lerkner. Let us hope that Creevler is able to find out more.'

Chapter Six

The roads into Edinburgh were busy, and it had gone half-past seven before the motorbike-and-sidecar finally whirred through the city centre. Edinburgh's annual festival was just under way and the capital buzzed with life. Extravagantly costumed jugglers, musicians and actors filled every public space, competing for the attention of bustling hoards of spectators. Posters and banners advertising shows, concerts and exhibitions adorned the walls of every building. Above it all, the hills, spires, domes and ramparts of Edinburgh's skyline glowed in the early evening sunshine.

'We should spend some time seeing all this, once the plane's finished,' said Zara as they drove across the Royal Mile, the long central street of Edinburgh's historic Old Town.

'Yeah,' said Marcia, enthusiastically. As well as taking in all the entertainment on offer, she looked forward to seeing more of the city itself. On her last visit she'd hardly had time to explore the multi-layered network of cobbled streets, bridges and passageways.

A little way on from the Royal Mile, Professor Ampersand pulled up, just before a turning on the right. 'That's Chambers Street,' said Ben. As the four children disembarked, the car behind, a black Jaguar with tinted windows, passed them and took the turning.

'I'll meet you out at the front of the museum in half an hour,' called Professor Ampersand, driving on.

The children crossed at the traffic lights and made their way up Chambers Street to the Royal Museum. 'Let's hope

George is working here this evening,' said Ben, as they ascended the front steps.

'If he isn't, we can always try his flat,' said Zara. 'George's flat is just round the corner,' she explained to the others. 'We've been there for tea a few times with Uncle Alexander.'

They headed through the museum's wooden revolving door. A few seconds later, a man wearing a grey coat and dark sunglasses followed them.

From the outside, Sam had thought the large Victorian building looked rather austere. Inside, he was surprised to find the museum's Main Hall remarkably light and spacious. In the centre, little fountains splashed into a pair of raised rectangular fish pools. All around the vast hall, lofty steel pillars supported two tiers of galleries. The hall's boat-like shape and the galleries' white latticed railings gave Sam the impression of being on an ocean liner whose decks were on the inside. High above, the whole elegant framework was topped by a beautiful glass roof, whose arching white ribs were catching the evening sunlight.

The hall was quite busy, though many visitors were already starting to leave.

Zara led the way between the fish pools to the information desk. 'Excuse me,' she asked one of the maroon-jacketed curators behind it, 'is George McTorphin working here today?'

The female curator looked slightly surprised that such young visitors should know a member of staff by name, but she checked a sheet of paper and said, 'I think he's up on the top-floor galleries this evening. But we're closing shortly.'

'We know,' said Zara. 'Thanks.'

The children hurried to the nearest set of stairs and rushed up both flights. They scanned the Main Hall's upper gallery but couldn't see any curators at all. Marcia looked down over the latticed railings. 'Wow', she said. 'We're really high up. The people down there look tiny.'

'Yeah,' said Zara. 'It's really good up here, isn't it?'

Zara and Ben had spent many hours in this museum. Professor Ampersand sometimes did bits of freelance work here, restoring some of the museum's moving models of trains and suchlike, and the two children had often explored the labyrinth of rooms behind the Main Hall by themselves. The building was packed with so many brilliant things – stuffed animals of every description, dinosaur fossils, ancient artefacts from every part of the globe – and Zara loved it all, but it was up here at the top of the Main Hall that had always been her favourite place in the museum. The bird's-eye view had often led her to imagine being able to fly, able to swoosh around the space and weave in and out of the pillars.

But there was no time for daydreams now. They had to find George.

'Here he is,' called Ben, pointing through one of the wide openings which led off from the upper gallery. The others followed Ben into a walkthrough room housing an impressive collection of East Asian antiques and art treasures. 'Hi, George,' said Ben to a white-haired curator who was straightening up a suit of Samurai armour.

'Hullo there,' said George, smiling and shaking Ben and Zara's hands. 'Are ye keeping well?'

'We're fine, thanks, George,' said Zara. 'These are our friends Marcia and Sam.'

'Pleased tae meet you,' said George, shaking their hands too.

Sam brought the photo out of his pocket and Ben handed it to George.

'Do you recognize the man in this photo, George?' asked Ben. 'We think he might be a refugee scientist who worked here during the war, called Maskil Stribnik. Do you remember him?'

George studied the photo for several seconds. None of them paid much attention to the man in the dark sun-glasses who had just wandered into the room and was examining a display of Chinese jade carvings.

'Aye,' said George at last. 'I reckon that's Mr Stribnik. I was just a lad o' course, but I remember him quite well. I think the director o' the museum had been a pal o' Mr Stribnik's before the war. Anyway, he gave him an office here, as somewhere private tae work. Spent hours locked away in there, he did, and we werenae allowed tae disturb him. But he always gave me a smile if I met him coming or going. He was a shy man, ye ken, but friendly. Must've been hard for him. He must've had friends and relatives back in Czechoslovakia who hadnae made it oot.'

The children nodded solemnly. They had all learnt about the Second World War at school, and knew how millions of European Jews, and others, had been systematically mur-dered by Germany's Nazi regime.

'The room he used as an office is just a storeroom these days,' said George. 'Come on; I'll show you.' He led them out through the room's other opening, onto a softly lit landing at the top of a grand staircase with geometric metal banisters.

This rear section of the museum had always been Ben's favourite part. Its dark walls, deep red stair-carpet and lack of daylight gave it a hushed, mysterious ambience that made a complete contrast to the bright, busy atmosphere of the Main Hall.

'This way,' said George, taking them along to a shadowy corner of the landing. He stopped at a wood-panelled door labelled STAFF ONLY.

'Ladies and gentlemen,' announced a curator's voice on the museum's public address system, 'the museum will be closing in five minutes. Please start making your way to the exit.'

'Best make it a quick look, eh?' said George, as he opened the door. 'Or they'll be locking us in for the night.'

Chapter Seven

The door led into a small, windowless room. George turned on the light. The room was full of modern, every-day stuff: boxes of glossy museum leaflets, a stack of plastic chairs, a couple of folded flip charts, and a shelving unit packed with assorted stationery. Zara felt a bit disappointed.

'Well, this was his office,' said George. 'How did ye come by that auld photo of him anyway?'

'We found it in an old aircraft hangar we're working in with Uncle Alexander,' explained Ben. 'It's by the sea near North Berwick.'

'Aye, he did go oot tae East Lothian sometimes,' recalled George. 'I dinnae recognize the lassie, though. I didnae ken he had a sweetheart.'

'We found this message on the back,' said Zara, showing him, 'but apart from the "URGENT" it seems to be written in some sort of cipher.'

'I'm no much good with secret codes,' said George, shaking his head. 'Still, if this was written as long ago as this photo was taken, I dinnae suppose it's all that urgent noo.'

Outside on the landing, near the storeroom door, the man in the sunglasses hovered beside a display case of medieval swords and helmets. The wooden door was muffling the voices inside. The man sidled nearer.

'Excuse me, sir.'

The man turned to see a young male curator enter the far end of the landing. 'The museum's just closing, sir,' said the curator, politely. The man nodded and made his way down the stairs.

Inside the storeroom, something else occurred to Marcia. 'Did Mr Stribnik stay in Edinburgh after the war?' she asked George. 'He might have had children who could still be around.'

George shook his head again. 'I'm afraid he was killed in a plane crash during the war.'

'Was he shot down?' asked Zara.

'I dinnae ken,' said George. 'I wasnae told much aboot it, but I think he was flying back up from a trip tae London when it happened. The director o' the museum was flying back with him, and was killed too.'

'That's really sad,' said Marcia.

'Aye,' sighed George. 'Though that's what it was like in the war; ye often heard that grown-ups ye'd known had been killed. As a child, I couldnae really remember any different.'

That was even sadder, thought Marcia. She wondered what had happened to the woman in the photograph.

'Do you know what Mr Stribnik was working on?' asked Sam. 'Our friend Amy said something about secret aviation projects.'

The old curator seemed lost in thought for a few moments. 'Naebody really knew what Maskil Stribnik was working on,' he said at last. 'There were rumours that he'd been working on some strange aviation research in Prague, before the war. But naebody knew much aboot that and his work here was completely secret. O' course, as a boy, I used tae imagine him working on all sorts o' weird things.' George's watery grey eyes seemed to be looking somewhere none of the children could see, somewhere far back in his memory. 'I even imagined that I *saw* one or two weird things. Things that . . .' He shook his head, snapping himself back into the present. 'Things that couldnae have been. I must have had some imagination. Anyway, we never foond oot what Mr Stribnik was working on. Ma father told me they couldnae find any sign o' work here in his office after he was killed. Nae papers or experiments or anything. Just his chair, table and typewriter. Whatever he'd been working on, he left nae trace of it here.'

 Sam was about to ask George exactly what weird things he'd imagined seeing, but then he spotted something at the back of the middle stationery shelf. Gathering dust behind a box of coloured marker pens and some rolls of paper, sat an old grey typewriter. 'Was that Mr Stribnik's typewriter?' he asked.

'Could well have been,' said George. 'It certainly looks auld enough. No much call for them noo, with today's computers.'

Sam loved old typewriters. He liked the way that, unlike computers, you could see the whole thing working, the way you could see the metal arms swinging forward to bang their little metal letters onto the ink ribbon and print their impressions onto the shifting paper behind. There was still a blank sheet of paper in the machine and Sam couldn't resist reaching past the marker pens and giving one of the keys a firm prod. *Clack.* Sam smiled. He'd pressed the *s* key but the typewriter had typed *g*. 'It's a bit broken,' he said. Maybe computers had their advantages.

'Ladies and gentlemen,' boomed the public address system once more, 'the museum is now closing. Please make your way to the exit immediately. Thank you and good evening.'

'Come on,' said George.

The four children and George hurried down the red-carpeted stairs. There were no other visitors or curators to be seen now and the museum's lighting had been dimmed still further to its after-hours level. On the ground floor, concealed in the shadows behind an antique clock, the man in the sunglasses watched them pass.

'Thanks for showing us the room, George,' said Ben.

'I'm afraid ye havnae learnt much tae help ye with that cryptic message,' said George.

'I still think it's a substitution cipher,' said Zara. 'But I don't know how we can decipher it if we don't know how the letters have been swapped round.'

Sam stopped. Zara's last sentence sparked a sudden realization that made his head tingle. A realization about the typewriter. A broken typewriter might fail to type a particular letter. But, no matter how broken, there was no way a key could operate an arm with a different letter. *Unless someone had swapped the metal letters around deliberately.*

'George,' said Sam, 'can I just nip back to the storeroom for a second? I need to check something. I'll catch you up.'

Without waiting for a reply, he tore back up the stairs, taking the photo out of his pocket as he ran. Ben, Zara and Marcia started after him but George barred their way. 'Ye dinnae all need tae go,' he protested. 'Ye'll get me intae trouble for letting ye run aroond after closing time.'

The man in the sunglasses watched impatiently as the old curator and the three children lingered around the foot of the stairs.

Sam rushed through the unlocked storeroom door and switched on the light. Panting, he cleared the pens and rolls of paper out of the way, propped up the photo so he could read the cryptic message, and tapped the typewriter's space bar a few times to get clear of the *g* he had typed before. Then he typed the first few letters of the message.

myangelm

My angel. Proper words. He'd been right! Quickly, he began to type the rest of the message.

'Come on,' called George to Zara, Ben and Marcia. He headed through the British Birds room that led back towards the Main Hall. 'We'll wait for Sam by the front doors. If we stay here much longer, my colleagues really might lock us in.' Reluctantly, the children followed. As soon as they were out of sight, the man slipped from his hiding place and padded silently up the stairs. As he neared the top floor, he removed his sunglasses, put them into his coat pocket and brought out something else.

Sam looked at what he'd finished typing.

myangelmylifeisindangersolomonwilltellyouhowt
ofindthesilverturtleprojectallmyloveforeverms

Yes! It was definitely a message. But they could look at it properly outside. He had to catch up with George and the others. He released the catch bar and quickly but carefully removed the sheet of thin old paper. Then he folded it up and started to put it in his pocket with the photograph as he left the room.

Sam gasped. At the top of the stairs, striding purposefully towards him across the dark red landing, was a man. A man with no face.

Chapter Eight

'Give me that photograph, boy,' growled the man, coming closer. 'Tell me what ye've discovered.' The man's apparent facelessness, Sam could now see, was due to a grey fabric mask that tightly covered his entire head.

Sam felt his insides churn with fear. He had to get away. No way past the man to the stairs. Or to the East Asian room. He turned round and ran the other way, fleeing from the end of the landing into a dark corridor. He heard the man breaking into a run behind him. 'HELP!' shouted Sam, as loudly as he could.

The corridor led into a murky room of old microscopes and telescopes. Sam stumbled through a shadowy maze of display cases, heading for an archway in the far corner. He looked back. The man was gaining on him.

Through the archway. A short passage. No sign of daylight. There *had* to be a way through to the upper gallery of the Main Hall. But which way? Two doorways, one each side. Sam swerved into the left-hand room and found himself rushing through a ghostly hall of dinosaur skeletons. He heard no one behind him. Had the man gone the other way? There – another doorway. Please be a way out. Please be a way out.

Sam flung himself through the doorway, then stopped. He was in a small, even darker room. Beneath a sign which read VICTORIAN CURIOS, the walls and floor were crammed with strange, dimly illuminated exhibits, including a mermaid constructed from half a monkey and half a fish, an iron cannon cast in the form of an open-mouthed dragon,

and a bloated two-headed toad floating in a jar of preserving fluid. The room had no other exit.

Could he double back? No – he could hear the man's footsteps, outside, coming into the dinosaur hall, coming closer. Trapped. Quick – *hide*. In the furthest corner of the room stood a large model of an Indian temple built entirely from the legs, claws and shells of hundreds of crabs. Sam squeezed into the space behind it. Through the framework of crab leg pillars, he saw the man enter the room.

Sam froze, his fingers gripping the photograph and folded paper tightly. Surely the man would hear his breathing. And his pounding heart. He watched the man work his way round the room, the grey, faceless head scanning the array of curios, looking behind a clockwork model of a guillotine, then behind an open sarcophagus containing a mummified crocodile. Getting closer.

The man stopped. He was looking at the temple. Now he was walking straight towards it, grey head looming down, about to peer through the windows. Closer and closer.

'Is someone still up here? The museum is closed now.' A woman's voice broke into the silence from several rooms away. The man stopped, then turned and slipped silently from the curio room. Sam heard the *clack, clack, clack* of new footsteps approaching through the dinosaur hall and a middle-aged female curator appeared in the doorway.

'Is someone in here?' she asked, sternly.

Sam emerged from behind the temple, relieved but trembling all over. 'That man!' he gabbled. 'Did you see him? He might still be here! We've got to call the police!'

'What man?' snorted the woman. 'What are you doing in here? Did you think it would be funny to get locked in?'

'It's all right, Morag; this laddie was with me,' called a familiar voice. George rushed into the room, followed by Zara, Ben and Marcia.

'We heard you yelling, Sam,' said Zara. 'Are you all right?'

'I am now,' said Sam. His heart was still racing. 'But there was a man, chasing me. His face was all covered with a sort of grey mask. He tried to get the photo off me.'

'A masked man? You're making it up!' scoffed the woman.

'I think he's telling the truth, Morag,' said George. 'He looks pretty shaken up.'

'I'll give him shaken up if I find him messing around after closing time again,' snapped Morag. 'What on *earth* were you thinking of, George, letting these kids play around up here?'

'I wasn't playing around!' protested Sam, but it was no good. George's senior colleague wouldn't hear of wasting the police's time over some silly boy's imaginary games, and in less than a minute, the four children were saying good-bye to George outside the museum's front door.

'Sorry for getting you into trouble, George,' said Sam. 'But I *was* telling the truth.'

'I ken ye were, son,' said George. 'But your masked man will have most likely slipped oot the building by noo. I'll ask the other curators if they saw anyone leaving late.'

'Why did you run back up to the storeroom anyway, Sam?' asked Ben.

'Oh, sorry about that too, but I thought of a way to decipher the message,' said Sam. 'And it worked!'

'Really?' said Zara.

'Yep,' said Sam, unfolding the sheet of paper. 'Look.'

'Och, ye'd better show me next time I see you,' said George, starting back through the revolving door. 'If I dinnae go and finish helping tae lock up, Morag wull have ma scalp.'

As they all thanked George and said goodbye, the yellow motorbike-and-sidecar came whirring along Chambers Street. They clambered aboard and Sam told the others what he'd discovered about the typewriter and everything that had happened. Professor Ampersand was very concerned about Sam's dangerous encounter with the masked man. 'I think we should report this whole thing to the police,' he said.

'We haven't seen what the message says yet,' said Ben. 'Let's have a look at that paper, Sam.'

In a shady side-lane off Chambers Street, concealed by the tinted windows of the black Jaguar, the man in the dark glasses had just finished speaking into his radio.

'So if I understand your report correctly, Creevler,' replied the voice of his superior, 'you broke your cover, but failed to discover anything useful.'

'I discovered that those kids have got a photo o' Stribnik, sir,' protested Creevler. 'And I discovered that they're trying tae crack some sort o' cryptic message. I decided it was worth breaking cover tae find oot more.'

'But you didn't find out more,' snapped his superior. 'You allowed the child to evade you and found out nothing.'

'Let me and Lerkner pay them all a home visit tonight, sir,' said Creevler. 'We'll make them tell us everything.' A trickle of saliva escaped from one corner of his mouth. 'Just give the order, sir.'

'And have all their neighbours report the incident?' rapped the voice. 'No! You've done enough to jeopardize our secrecy already. When the moment comes for these people to be brought in for interrogation, the disappearance operation will be conducted correctly and invisibly. I am making the necessary arrangements. But the Leader has decreed that we must be certain these people have discovered the secret of the Silver Turtle before we take such action. We may learn more from tomorrow's test flight. Make sure that you and Lerkner are in place near the hangar first thing in the morning.'

Chapter Nine

The four children, two professors and Amy sat around the dining table. In the kitchen, somewhere in the multi-tubed interior of Professor Ampersand's oven-boiler, their supper was bubbling and steaming away and a delicious smell of stew pervaded the house.

During the short drive home to Pinkerton Place, the three children in the sidecar had managed to work out where the word breaks fell in the deciphered message, and where to add capitals, full-stops and commas. Sam had written it out neatly in his notebook and now they all sat studying the curious message.

My angel, my life is in danger. Solomon will tell you how to find the silver turtle project. All my love forever, MS.

'MS!' said Zara, reading the initials at the end of the message. 'It *must* have been written by Maskil Stribnik.'

'He must have rebuilt his typewriter to work as an encrypting and decrypting machine,' said Sam. 'He'd be able to type anything into ciphertext really quickly. Or back again.'

'He must've had the substitute alphabet pretty fluent in his head as well though,' pointed out Ben. 'The message on the back of the photo is handwritten.'

'It must be to his girlfriend,' said Marcia. 'The woman

pilot in the photo. She must've known how to read his sub-stitution cipher too.'

'Wonderfully romantic, the way he calls her his angel,' said Professor Hartleigh-Broadbeam.

'Aye,' said Amy. 'But we'd know more aboot her if he'd used her name.'

'Well, let's go through everything we *do* know,' suggested Zara. 'We know Maskil Stribnik was a Czech Jewish scientist who had come here to escape the Nazis. We know that during the war he worked on secret projects, probably to do with aircraft. We know he worked in an office at the museum and in Amy's hangar.'

'And we know that he was killed during the war,' said Ben.

'Maybe this silver turtle project he writes about in the message is a code name for his secret work,' suggested Sam.

'That's it!' agreed Zara. 'We can see from this message that he knew his life was in danger. And we know that no work was found in his museum office after his death. I reckon that before he was killed, he hid his work and left this message for his girlfriend, telling her that someone called Solomon knew where he'd hidden it.'

'Yeah,' said Ben. 'His girlfriend must have read the message and left the photo there in that box on the shelf where I fou–'

'No,' interrupted Marcia. 'Put yourself in her shoes. If you'd found the final letter from someone you loved, written on the back of a photo of you both together, you wouldn't leave it behind. You'd keep it. You'd keep it for ever.'

'You're right,' agreed Ben. He knew he'd never mislay the photo he had of his parents.

'So I don't think she found the photo and message,' Marcia went on. 'I think the place where Ben found it was the place where Maskil Stribnik left it. Maybe that shelf was a place they'd left notes to each other before, but maybe, for some reason, she never came to the hangar. I think we're the first people to read this message since it was written.'

'But how can we find out where Stribnik hid his work,' wondered Zara, 'if we don't know who his girlfriend was or who Solomon was?'

They all thought for a few moments, but no one could think of a way forward with the mystery.

'Well,' said Professor Ampersand, standing up and walking over to the telephone. 'Whatever this is all about, my biggest concern is what happened to Sam at the museum. I'd better phone our nearest police station.'

The police officer Professor Ampersand spoke to listened sympathetically, but didn't take all the details of Sam's story very seriously. 'Tae be honest, sir, it soonds like this young lad got a bit of a fright off some drunken weirdo who'd wandered in off the street and was hassling him for money. These nutters should all be locked up, if you ask me. I've recorded the incident and I'll ask the museum staff tae keep their eyes open.'

'But I *told* you, the man was trying to take a photo from Sam!' insisted Professor Ampersand. 'A photo with an encrypted message on the back, which we think relates to secret wartime research.'

'Er, yes, sir,' said the officer, sounding doubtful. 'Are you sure these kids didnae make up this encrypted message themselves? Maybe they got a bit carried away with some school history project, eh? In any case, I cannae see how any wartime research could still be important after more than sixty years.'

'Och, I can see I'm wasting my breath,' said Professor Ampersand, wearily. 'Thank you for your help.' He hung up and reported the unsatisfactory conversation to the others.

'So he thinks I imagined half of it!' exclaimed Sam indignantly.

'And he thinks Stribnik's lost research can't be important after more than sixty years!' snorted Professor Hartleigh-Broadbeam. 'It's clearly very important to whoever was chasing Sam.'

'Do you want to phone your parents, Sam?' asked Zara.

'No, it's all right,' said Sam. 'They're away this week at one of their work conferences so they might not be easy to get hold of, and I wouldn't want to worry them for nothing. I'm fine, honestly.' The last thing he wanted was for everyone to get so bogged down in an investigation of the incident that tomorrow's test flight had to be postponed.

'What puzzles me most,' said Professor Ampersand, 'is . . . Och, it doesn't matter.' He stood up and closed the French window curtains against the darkening sky outside. 'Let's have supper.'

Professor Ampersand's oven-boiler was a more reliable machine than his auto-breakfast-preparer and the stew was delicious. Everyone tucked in, and to Sam's relief, the conversation turned away from the events at the museum and on to the last bits of work to be done on the plane.

But Zara knew what her great-uncle had been about to say before supper, and knew that he'd stopped himself saying it to avoid frightening them. What was puzzling him most was that someone had known they were in possession of the photograph within hours of them finding it. Some-one had known they were in the museum with it, and had been ready to pounce the minute Sam had been alone. Someone seemed to be keeping a very close watch on them indeed.

Chapter Ten

Just before nine the following morning, the motorbike-and-sidecar whirred down the track and arrived at the hangar. Although there were some clouds over the sea, the weather on shore remained hot and sunny.

'Good morning,' said Amy, sticking her head out of the hangar's back door as they pulled up beside her truck. 'Fine day for the test flight. Now, you know that I'll have tae carry oot many careful tests once she's ready. I'll be taxiing her across the water a good many times before I even try tae fly her, and I'll be flying her by myself until we're sure she's safe tae take anyone else up for a spin. We may no even get tae that stage today.'

'We know,' said Zara. 'We don't mind.' And they didn't. Right now, the only thing that mattered was that the day of their plane's first test flight had finally arrived.

Professor Hartleigh-Broadbeam removed Orlando the bike helmet from her head and replaced him with a jaunty tam o' shanter she'd been saving for just such a special occasion. 'Now, Rabbie,' she said to it, 'let's get that wiring finished.'

'We still haven't thought of a name,' said Ben, helping to clear away the tools they had finished with. 'She ought to have one before her maiden flight.'

'Hey, I've just thought of one!' said Marcia. 'How about calling her the *Silver Turtle*, after Maskil Stribnik's lost project?'

'I like it,' said Sam, after a couple of seconds' thought. 'It seems sort of right, when we've built her in his old hangar.'

'It would be some sort of commemoration of the poor man's work,' agreed Professor Hartleigh-Broadbeam.

'Yeah, and it kind of suits the plane,' said Ben.

'Sounds good to me,' said Professor Ampersand.

'And me,' said Zara. 'What do *you* think, Amy?'

'It's the perfect name,' declared Amy. 'The *Silver Turtle* she is.'

The last bit of wiring took Professor Hartleigh-Broadbeam a little longer to complete than she had hoped, but it gave Zara time to stylishly letter their plane's new name below each side of the cockpit in black paint.

'All done!' declared Professor Hartleigh-Broadbeam, emerging from the cockpit just as Zara completed the final *e*.

They all stood back to admire their finished flying boat and for some moments nobody spoke.

'Right,' said Amy, at last. 'Let's roll her oot of the hangar.'

Lerkner crouched down behind some rocks at the end of the wooded spit of land that separated the two beaches. From here he could just see the front of the hangar. 'I think they're bringing the plane oot now, sir,' he reported.

'Aboot time too,' came Creevler's voice on the linked-up radio system.

'Describe what you see,' ordered their superior's voice.

'Like I said before,' said Lerkner, focusing his binoculars, 'I cannae see anything aboot the plane tae confirm that it's . . . *Wait!* Sir, there's something painted on the side. It . . . it says *Silver Turtle!*'

'*What?!* You're *certain?* Why didn't you spot that before, when you broke into the hangar?'

'That writing wasnae there then, sir! I swear it wasnae!'

'No matter,' said his superior. 'Now we know for certain:

these people *have* discovered Stribnik's work. The Silver Turtle project has been resurrected. It is time for us to intervene and take possession of the secret.'

'Just give the order, sir,' said Creevler. 'Me and Lerkner are ready and armed.'

'Good. But remember, this is to be a disciplined operation,' rapped his superior. 'We are the Secret Operations Police Unit, not a Wild West show. Detective Inspector Bailey is standing by with an armed Rapid Response Squad less than three miles away. Wait for their van to reach the hangar, then move in to assist with the arrest.'

Up on the main road, the elderly female cyclist stood holding a single earphone to her ear. The earphone was connected to a complicated radio-like device in her bicycle basket. Suddenly, her frown deepened into an expression of alarmed concern. She let the earphone drop and began pedalling her ancient bike at reckless speed down the bumpy track towards the hangar.

Chapter Eleven

The *Silver Turtle* stood in front of the hangar, facing the sea, its wheel-brakes on to prevent it rolling down the slipway prematurely. The three adults had gone to get some stuff from the sidecar which they'd need for the test flight – camera, camcorder, stopwatch, logbook – and Amy had said the four children could sit in the plane as long as they didn't touch any of the controls. They sat without speaking for a moment, silently enjoying their shared sense of achievement and anticipation.

Marcia sat in the pilot's seat, looking up at the bank of white, billowing clouds that had continued to build up off shore, imagining flying through them and over them. She was sure that flying in this little plane, with its all-round view, would be almost like flying the way she sometimes could in her dreams, dreams in which she could run freely through the sky.

Ben sat next to her in the co-pilot's seat. For him, the

excitement of flying was all about exploration. He imagined flying the little plane over uncharted wildernesses, piloting her up winding jungle rivers, landing her on remote mountain lakes. An amphibious plane like this could take you anywhere in the world.

Zara sat on the back seat, looking up through the open middle of the canopy at her great-uncle's electric motors, imagining them powering the *Silver Turtle* through the sky. The optimistic working atmosphere of the past two and a half weeks had been infectious and Zara had almost allowed herself to stop worrying about their financial situation. Surely this amazing little plane would earn its inventors an improvement in their financial fortunes.

Sam sat in the open front-hatch seat, gazing out over the sloping stub of the *Silver Turtle*'s nose to the sea and the sky, then looking around at all the bits of the plane he'd worked on. He felt the familiar fluttering excitement in his chest. His lifetime's dream had finally come true. He had helped to build a real live plane and soon he would actually be able to fly in her.

Suddenly, the children's thoughts were interrupted by a noise from the other side of the hangar: the sound of a vehicle approaching at speed down the track through the copse. They turned, looking back through the hangar, but the small door at the rear of the hangar had blown shut behind the adults, preventing the children from seeing through to the yard. They heard wheels skidding to a halt in the dust, then van doors opening, men shouting.

'*Armed police!*'

'*Armed police! Stand still!*'

The children stood up in their seats and looked at each other, open-mouthed. What on earth was going on back there? They could hear Professor Hartleigh-Broadbeam's voice now: 'This is OUTRAGEOUS!'

Then a man's voice: 'Stay where you are! You're under arrest.'

Before the children could think what they should do, an elderly woman wearing a battered suede jacket came careering round the side of the hangar on a bicycle. 'Help me inta the plane!' she gasped, leaping from her bike and letting it fall onto the pebbles by the slipway. She flung herself at the *Silver Turtle*, her hands grasping the edges of the open cockpit canopy, her feet struggling to find the step-holes in the plane's side. Bewildered, but fearing the old woman might fall backwards, the three children held her arms and helped her scramble in. She tumbled down into the pilot's seat, shot out a bony hand, and released the brake lever.

'No!' shouted Zara, as the *Silver Turtle* rolled forward. Marcia and Ben both made a grab for the brake lever but, with surprising strength, the woman pushed them back and flicked the two switches labelled PORT MOTOR and STARBOARD MOTOR. The propellers whirred into life and the plane hurtled down the slipway towards the sea.

'What are you *doing?*' yelled Ben. He'd got himself back into the co-pilot's seat. Should he pull the woman away from the controls? No – going too fast. They'd swerve off the slipway and crash onto the pebbles.

Sam clung to the sides of the nose hatch, alarmed and powerless, watching the sea come nearer and nearer . . .

SPLASH! The plane ploughed into the water and a plume of sea spray cascaded down over the open cockpit and hatch. Without flinching, the woman revved the motors to full speed and zoomed the plane onward through the sea. Keeping one hand on her control column, she punched the undercarriage button and the three wheels whirred and clunked up into the hull. With the drag reduced, the *Silver Turtle* skimmed across the waves even faster. Faster and faster.

'STOP!' shouted Zara, sprawled across the back seats with Marcia.

'Stop?' cried the woman. 'Are you *mad*?'

P*TANG!* Something hard ricocheted off the plane, just behind the cockpit. Zara looked back through their tail spray and saw two armed men shooting at them from the increasingly distant shore.

Sam stared back through the cockpit windscreen. The woman was starting to pull back her control column. 'NO!' shouted Sam, realizing what she was doing. 'She hasn't been tested!'

'No time like the present,' yelled the woman, and pulled the column right back. The spray vanished, the sea fell away beneath them and they soared up into the sky. The *Silver Turtle* was airborne.

Chapter Twelve

'H-heeee!' The woman threw back her head and let out a wild cry of laughter, as she held the *Silver Turtle* in a steep climb, leaving the sea far below. 'Them plods weren't expecting that!' she crowed, in a voice cracked with age. 'We left 'em looking like a right bunch of Charlies.'

'Take us back down!' yelled Marcia, shouting above the deafening noise of the air whistling past the open cockpit canopy. The woman ignored her and held her climbing course towards the bank of clouds.

Ben stared at the woman. She was well into her eighties, her dishevelled hair white and her leathery skin deeply wrinkled. But her eyes gleamed bright from her sharp, birdlike face, and her lean frame seemed fired with energy as she sped the plane higher and higher. Who on earth was she? Ben had already recognized her as the cyclist they'd sometimes seen on the track, but he was suddenly struck by the feeling that he'd seen her face somewhere else before.

Sam sat stunned in his open front seat, his body pressed back by the g-force, his hair blasted back by the wind whooshing over the hatch's little windscreen. The cloud bank ahead seemed to grow larger and larger as the *Silver Turtle* zoomed up towards it. Then they were into it, rushing through a cold wet void of grey mist.

Sam looked back into the cockpit. The others were shouting at the woman, but with the wind and the whir of the propellers, he couldn't hear their voices. He had to know what was going on. He slithered from his seat, scrambled back through the hole beneath the instrument panel, tumbled between the two front seats of the climbing plane, and fell into the vacant back seat.

'Why are you stealing our plane?' Zara was shouting. 'Why were those plainclothes policemen shooting at you?'

'They was shooting at all of us,' yelled the woman. 'I'm not nicking yer plane; I'm saving it. Them armed coppers are under the control of one of the most ruthless organizations in the world. If they get their hands on this plane, we're all dead meat, and yer three pals back there an' all. I'll explain when we're safe, but for now you'll have ter trust me.'

The children looked at each other. What choice did they have? At least the woman was clearly an experienced pilot, thought Ben. Maybe she wasn't mad, after all.

The woman took one hand off her control column and, from one of her jacket pockets, brought out what looked like an old sardine tin, with a jumble of tiny electronic components jammed in place inside. 'Take over, co-pilot,' the woman yelled to Ben, letting go of her control column completely and sliding off her seat. 'I need ter wire in this radar-jamming device.' She started to crawl beneath the instrument panel.

'NO!' cried Ben. 'I CAN'T! COME BACK! *I* CAN'T FLY A PLANE!'

'Take over!' repeated the woman. She took out a pair of pliers and a roll of tape, wriggled onto her back and reached up to fiddle with the wiring behind the panel. She *was* mad. They were all going to die. In desperation, Ben grabbed the co-pilot's control column in front of him. The plane lurched to one side.

'Centre yer control column,' called the woman, 'and pull it back a bit ter bring yer nose up.'

Ben tried to fight down the panic inside him, tried to

remember what Amy had told them about how the controls worked, tried to understand what the woman was telling him now. He adjusted the control column and the plane came back under some sort of wobbly control, racing on upwards through the cloud. Suddenly, they emerged from the void, into a sunlit world above the billowing cloud tops.

'Level off,' shouted the woman. 'Push yer column forward. *Not that much!* What *do* they teach you in schools these days?'

'They don't teach us to fly planes!' yelled Ben, just managing to prevent the plane from plunging back into the cloud.

'I know they don't,' ranted the woman, 'but they blimming well should!'

'Take over again!' pleaded Ben, trying to stop the plane from undulating up and down as it careered along above the cloudscape. 'This isn't safe!'

'Tommyrot!' shouted the woman. She clambered back up into her seat at last and started taping the sardine tin to the bottom of the instrument panel. The tin was now connected to a wire, and in the centre of its clustered components, a tiny green light pulsed. 'Right, we're now radar-invisible,' said the woman. 'New course, co-pilot. South-south-east. Can you read a compass?'

'Yeah,' yelled Ben, his eyes finding the compass on the instrument panel, 'but how do I turn the plane?' He felt the panic rising again.

'Get both feet ready on yer rudder pedals,' shouted the woman. 'That's it. But turn by banking the plane with the wings; tilt the control column ter the right. Keep her banking at thirty degrees – use the bank-and-turn indicator there. Now add just a bit of right rudder pedal. And keep her nose up.'

Absorbed in making the manoeuvre, Ben almost forgot to be scared about crashing. The *Silver Turtle* banked round to the right. He was really piloting her!

'Good!' the woman yelled. 'Now bring her back ter straight and level . . . That's lovely! Angle her nose down just a tad and she'll go even faster.'

In spite of everything, Ben felt strangely light-headed as they hurtled along on their new course. He was piloting the plane. He was flying!

'Keep her on this course!' shouted the woman.

'But where are we going?' yelled Marcia from the back seat.

'Can't hear you!' yelled the woman. 'Somebody close the blimming canopy.'

Sam and Marcia reached up and slid the middle section of the canopy shut, while the woman found the switch to close the nose hatch too. The scream of the rushing wind stopped, leaving only the steady buzz of the electric motors.

'That's better,' said the woman. 'Now, they'll prob'ly scramble aircraft to look for us when they can't find us on their radar screens, so keep yer eyes peeled, everyone. And whatever secret power source this plane's got, now'd be the time ter activate it.'

'What do you mean?' said Ben, wishing this woman would stop talking in riddles.

'The only power source is the energy cells powering the electric motors,' said Sam.

'C'mon,' said the woman, turning in her seat to look at all of them. 'You'll have ter trust me. Our lives could depend on outpacing their planes.'

'We don't know what you're on about!' insisted Marcia, forcefully. 'We don't know what *any* of this is about! We don't know anything about a secret power source!'

The woman studied the children's confused faces for a few seconds. 'You're telling the truth!' she said. She began to grin. 'They went ter all that trouble ter try and get their hands on a pair of electric motors! *Heh heh heh! H-heeee!*'

Ben looked at the woman as she leant back in her seat cackling. Was she losing it completely? The plane veered slightly and he forced his concentration back to the controls. But then something else flashed into his mind. Something about the way the old woman threw back her head and closed her eyes when she laughed. Ben suddenly knew where he'd seen her before, and the revelation sent a tingle down his spine. '*You're the woman pilot!*' he exclaimed. '*The woman in the photo!*'

Chapter Thirteen

The woman stopped laughing and frowned at Ben, mysti-fied herself now. 'What photo?' she asked.

'The photo of Amy's hangar,' said Ben. 'With Maskil Stribnik. But I don't think we've got it with us.'

'It's OK – I've got it here,' said Sam, pulling the photo from his trouser pocket. He passed it forward to the old woman, wondering if Ben could possibly be right.

As the woman saw it, she seemed to freeze. She looked and looked at it in silence.

At last she spoke. 'That's me,' she confirmed, her croaky voice less raucous now. 'Me and Maskil. Our only photo together. I've never seen it. I always assumed Maskil was killed before he had time ter get it developed.' She paused and smiled faintly. 'I'm flattered you could recognize me after all these years. Where the hell did you get it?'

'I found it in the hangar,' said Ben. 'We think Maskil left it for you to find. There's a message on the back.'

The woman flipped the card over and hurriedly scanned the encrypted message. Ben could see her mouth moving as she silently deciphered it. 'My god,' she said, putting the photo down on her lap. 'So Solomon held the secret all the time.' She turned to the children. 'I guess if you knew it was for me, you must know what it says. But how on earth did you decipher it?'

As Ben flew them onwards over the clouds, the four children told the woman everything that had happened – how they had found the photograph, what they had learned from George at the museum, how Sam had deciphered the message and been chased by the masked man – and every-thing that they had guessed.

'I'm impressed,' said the woman, when they had finished. 'You've worked out nearly everything. I'll try ter fill in the gaps:

'Maskil Stribnik *was* working on secret aviation research – a lifetime's obsession which he called the Silver Turtle project. He fled Czechoslovakia in 1938, just as Nazi Germany began ter take over his country. Crammed as much of his equipment as he could inta a small plane and flew out, eventually making it ter Britain. Luckily, he knew some fellow scientists in Edinburgh who persuaded the authorities ter let him in.'

'Didn't Britain let *everyone* in who was escaping from the Nazis?' asked Sam.

'No!' shouted the woman, with sudden vehemence. 'That's how we'd all like ter remember it, isn't it? But the truth is, we worried about the cost and we whinged about all them Jewish foreigners taking our British jobs and we refused asylum ter thousands of people we could've saved.'

She paused, collecting her thoughts. 'But we let in some,' she conceded, 'and Maskil was lucky. Anyway, Maskil beavered away in his office at the Royal Museum in Edin-burgh and by 1941 he was able ter show some of his research ter the War Office. They gave him the use of a secluded hangar, and the occasional use of a plane – the Supermarine Walrus in this photo – and a spare pilot, ter help with his experiments. The spare pilot assigned to him was me.'

'Were you in the RAF?' asked Zara.

'The RAF didn't allow women ter fly,' said the woman, 'so I'd joined the Air Transport Auxiliary, the ATA for short. The ATA recruited civilian pilots ter ferry war planes around the country ter where they was needed, and they included women pilots from the start. I'm Gabrielle, by the way. Gabrielle Starling.'

She shook hands with Sam, Zara and Marcia, and the four children introduced themselves (Ben keeping both hands on the control column).

'I was stationed at the ATA base at Prestwick, near Glasgow,' continued Gabrielle, 'and every few weeks I'd get an order ter fly the Walrus across ter East Lothian, ter the hangar at Petticraig Bay.

Maskil needed someone ter fly the plane while he conducted aerial experiments on various bits of equipment he'd built. The tests only lasted a day or two each time, a very small part of my overall duties. But I found myself looking forward ter those days with Maskil more and more. He was a quiet man, but burning with dreams and ideas once he got talking. Spoke in a lovely Czech accent, which I found very glamorous. I'll spare you the slush – we fell in love.'

'What kind of experiments was he doing in the plane?' asked Sam.

'He wouldn't tell me,' said Gabrielle. 'He'd take all sorts of electronic devices on board, some as big as tea chests, others tiny. 'Cos I was piloting, I couldn't see what he was doing back in the cabin, but the plane's instruments often went haywire, specially the compass. Once, the whole surface of the plane flickered with blue sparks and, for no reason I could account for, we gained thousands of feet of altitude in a few seconds.

'I wanted ter know what his strange experiments were

about, of course, but he insisted it was better I knew nothing. Said if enemy agents thought I knew anything about the Silver Turtle project, I might be in danger.

'One morning in April 1942, I was due ter set off from Prestwick for another day's testing at Petticraig. I was dying to see Maskil, after three weeks apart. Then, just as I was leaving the canteen and heading out ter the Walrus, I was called back. Some news had just come through. Apparently, Maskil had just been down in London ter report ter some scientists at the Air Ministry. His friend, the director of the Royal Museum, had gone down with him and had persuaded the ministry scientists that they should fly back ter Edinburgh with them ter see Maskil's work. Their plane had crashed, somewhere near Newcastle. All five people on board – Maskil, the museum director, the two Ministry scientists, and their pilot – had been killed.' Gabrielle paused and gazed out over the clouds. 'No one could be sure why the plane had crashed, but you didn't have ter be a genius to see that Nazi agents were behind it somehow.'

'It must have been awful,' said Marcia.

'War *is* awful,' said Gabrielle bitterly. 'That was a war we had ter fight, but don't let anyone tell you that war is glamorous or fun. War is about death and misery, on all sides.

'Anyway, I got through my grief the same way many others did – threw myself inta my work. Took on as many ferrying flights as I could; flying was the only thing that seemed ter help. Soon, I got promoted and put in charge of an ATA base down near London. I moved on.'

'So we were right,' said Zara. 'You never went back to the hangar.'

'I never went back ter the hangar,' confirmed Gabrielle, shaking her head sadly. 'Maskil must've known his life was in danger. He must've driven his car ter the hangar before he went down ter London, removed any work he had there, and left this message for me, case he didn't make it back. He was trying ter make sure that, if the worst happened, someone he trusted could find his invention again. Must've decided that posting the message ter me wasn't secure enough. He knew I'd look in that shoebox of nuts and bolts, because he often used ter hide a little present there, for me to find if I arrived at the hangar before him; it had become a sort of game between us. If the news of his death had taken longer ter come through, his scheme would've worked; I'd have flown to the hangar and found this photo. If I had, Maskil's invention might have seen the light of day. And our world today would be a very different place.'

'Really?' said Sam, wondering more than ever what kind of invention Maskil Stribnik could have been working on.

Gabrielle nodded. 'I've found out a whole lot more about the Silver Turtle project than I knew back then,' she said, 'and I believe that shortly before his death, Maskil Stribnik made a scientific breakthrough of staggering importance. I believe that he discovered the secret of anti-gravity.'

Chapter Fourteen

'Anti-gravity?' echoed Sam. He was sure he'd heard of it somewhere, but couldn't remember much about it.

'Yep,' said Gabrielle. 'All the types of flying machine we use today need ter struggle against the force of gravity, whether they use propellers, rotors, jets, rockets, or lighter-than-air gases. The idea of anti-gravity is ter achieve flight by removing the force of gravity altogether.'

Sam's brain raced to think through the implications of this. 'But removing gravity would mean you could build aircraft which would fly without any engines or wings,' he said. 'Flying up would be as easy as falling down.'

'*Exactly!*' cried Gabrielle. 'Any object, however great its mass, could be made weightless, lifted up and flown wherever you wanted. Not just straight up, but in any direction, and at incredible speeds. And an aircraft that was shielded from the effects of gravity would be able ter make sudden changes of speed, height and direction without the people inside being thrown around or squashed by g-forces. You could accelerate almost instantly ter a speed that'd zip you ter the other side of the world in minutes, then come ter a stop almost instantly at the end of yer trip. Even flying up into space would be easy – no need for huge rockets ter fight the pull of earth's gravity, no crushing effect on the people inside. And think of the possibilities for cargo transport, or for constructing buildings. Anti-gravity would change *everything*. I've always reckoned that achieving flight has been humankind's most important breakthrough since we invented the wheel. But freeing ourselves from the effects of gravity altogether would be our biggest break-through since we evolved from apes. We'd be taking control of the force that holds the universe together.'

Images swirled through Sam's mind as he tried to picture the kind of world Gabrielle was describing: a world in which everything – people, vehicles, supplies, buildings – could be made to hover, float and zoom through the air, as if by magic. Was such a world really possible? 'How would anti-gravity *work*?' he asked. 'How could you remove the force of gravity on things?'

'Afraid my knowledge of science isn't advanced enough to answer that properly,' said Gabrielle. 'No one *fully* under-stands why gravity happens at all, so we're into some pretty complex physics. Some scientists say the whole idea of anti-gravity is impossible, but others disagree. If it *was* possible, can you imagine the power anti-gravity technology would give to a country at war? We now know that the Nazis had their own anti-gravity research programme, but they never made a breakthrough. Somehow, they must've discovered that Maskil had.'

'I can see why the Nazis killed Maskil before he could show his invention to the British government,' said Marcia, 'but the war ended more than sixty years ago, and the Nazi regime ended with it. Germany's a really cool place today. Who's after Maskil's work now? Who was chasing Sam in the museum? Who sent those armed police? Who are we running from?'

'We're up against one of the most evil organizations in the world,' said Gabrielle. 'An organization called Noctarma.'

The children looked at one another blankly. 'I've never heard of it,' said Zara.

'Very few people have,' said Gabrielle. 'Noctarma operates entirely in secret. Wherever there's warfare and conflict in the world, Noctarma's undercover agents seem ter be present behind the scenes: helping ter stir up hatred, helping ter start wars, assassinating peacemakers, supplying weapons, helping evil people ter seize power, and helping those evil people ter keep power. Noctarma's influence on events around the world is enormous, yet the organization itself remains almost invisible. Even those of us who know of Noctarma's activities have no idea who its leader is, who its members are, where its headquarters are or when it was founded. Whether Noctarma has long-term aims and plans, beyond making huge sums of money, is also unclear, though recently, many of its agents seem ter have been focusing their efforts on infiltrating top-secret advanced weapons programmes around the world. And it seems that, right now, Noctarma is particularly eager ter get its claws on the secret of anti-gravity.'

Zara felt cold inside. What would people like that do to her great-uncle, Amy and Professor Hartleigh-Broadbeam? Suddenly, she spotted a small dark shape a long way to the east of them, flying at a much greater height. 'Plane!' she shouted. 'Over there!'

Gabrielle grabbed her control column and Ben felt his controls being overridden as she plunged the *Silver Turtle* into the blanket of cloud. 'I'd better take her for a bit, co-pilot,' said Gabrielle, changing course as soon as they were enveloped in the mist.

'It might just have been an airliner,' said Zara. 'It was a long way off. But it didn't look like one. It looked black and kind of weird-shaped.' Somehow, her fleeting glance at the distant aircraft had left her with the impression of something strange, secret and dangerous.

'We'd best not take any chances,' said Gabrielle. 'Noctarma has its own planes.' She sped through the cloud, changing course again several times. No one spoke, sensing that she needed to concentrate. Ben sat back in his seat, relieved to relinquish responsibility, but still light-headed from the thrill of piloting the plane.

'Better not stay in this cloud for too long,' said Gabrielle, after a few minutes, 'or we'll crash inta someone.' She pulled back her control column, but as soon as their canopy emerged into sunlight she levelled out and flew through the cloud tops with their hull skimming the mist. 'Anyone see the other plane?' Everyone looked around and reported the sky clear of other aircraft.

'Good,' said Gabrielle, and returned to their previous altitude a little way above the clouds.

'How do you know all this about Noctarma?' Marcia asked Gabrielle. 'Are you some kind of secret agent?'

Gabrielle laughed. 'Me? No, dear. I'm just a pilot. After the war, some women seemed happy ter be shoved back into domestic life, but that wasn't for me. I wanted ter carry on flying and I wanted adventure, so I set off round the world picking up flying work wherever I found myself. Over the last six decades, I've flown every kind of plane in every kind of place – air ambulances across deserts, mail services between remote Pacific islands, emergency flights ter disaster areas – and always teaching other people ter fly wherever I could. Everyone should learn ter fly.

'It's a friend of mine who told me all this stuff about Noctarma. He's . . . well, let's just say he's become something of a specialist on secret stuff like that. A few weeks ago, he told me he'd found out that Noctarma agents were spying on an old hangar at Petticraig Bay, near Edinburgh, on the trail of a long-lost anti-gravity invention built by someone called Stribnik. That was how I finally came ter find out what Maskil had been working on. I decided ter fly back ter Britain ter see what Noctarma were up ter. My friend gave me a few bits of hi-tech kit – a gadget ter listen in on their radio conversations, and that radar-jamming device, in case I needed ter get ter places undetected in my plane. My plane's parked up at a little aerodrome by Edinburgh airport, but the device works just as well on yours, luckily.'

Sam looked at the sardine-tin device again and wondered how it worked. He got the feeling that Gabrielle didn't want to say too much about the friend who had given it to her.

'So, the Noctarma agents thought that Amy had rediscovered Maskil's work?' said Marcia. 'That she was building an anti-gravity plane?'

'Yep,' said Gabrielle. 'I think her registering the plane with the Civil Aviation Authority, giving her address as The Hangar, Petticraig Bay must've triggered Noctarma's inquiry. They must've been running regular automated searches of government computer systems for anything connected ter known anti-gravity research projects. *I* thought Amy might be working on anti-gravity too, especially when you lot started asking about Maskil at the museum. It was you calling yer plane the *Silver Turtle* that really clinched Noctarma's decision ter try and get hold of it. I'm sorry they got yer folks. I should've come ter warn you all sooner, but I was trying ter avoid Noctarma knowing about me. Their sudden police raid caught me by surprise, I'm afraid. Seems that Noctarma has agents in the government's Secret Operations Police Unit, and gawd knows where else. Means we can't go ter the regular police without risking Noctarma finding out where we are.'

'We should phone *someone*,' said Zara. 'Has anyone got their mobile phone on them?' They all shook their heads. No one had imagined they'd need them today.

'We shouldn't send any phone or radio messages from the plane anyhow,' said Gabrielle. 'Noctarma might detect 'em and track our position.'

'But we've got to do something!' insisted Zara.

'We *are* doing something,' said Gabrielle. 'I'm taking us ter see a friend who can help us.'

'Your friend who told you about Noctarma and lent you the radar deflector?' asked Sam.

'No,' said Gabrielle. 'I've got the means ter summon his help if we need ter, but he ... well, he operates a bit outside society, you might say, and for an emergency like this, we need someone with official clout. I'm taking us ter another old pal of mine: Lady Clarissa Mantlingham. Clarissa's what you'd call well-connected; her late husband, Sir Gerald, was once Secretary of State for Overseas Trade and these days her son, Sir Roland Mantlingham, is a senior official in the Home Office. That's the bit of the government which deals with policing and security and such, so he'll be able ter take urgent action against the Noctarma agents who've infiltrated the Secret Operations Police Unit. I'm not saying he'll be able ter close down an organization as powerful as Noctarma overnight, but he should be able ter find out where yer folks are being held and get 'em released. Always handy ter have friends in high places, and Clarissa's one of the oldest friends I've got. Known her since before she was married. Met her during the war. In fact, it was her who took this photo of Maskil and me on Maskil's camera. You can just see her shadow at the bottom of the picture, look.'

Ben looked at the photo on Gabrielle's lap and saw that the photographer's shadow was indeed visible on the slipway.

They hadn't really thought about who might have taken the photo. 'Was she in the ATA too?' he asked.

'No,' replied Gabrielle. 'Clarissa had a secretarial post with the War Office in Edinburgh. It had been her job ter find Maskil the hangar ter work from. She came over ter the hangar sometimes ter check he had everything he needed, and was always very friendly ter both of us. She knew how things were between Maskil and me, and when he was killed she was a real pal to me, a shoulder ter cry on. We've met up occasionally since the war – not very often, what with me living abroad and her being busy with all her charity work, but we've always exchanged Christmas cards. She's always said I should drop in on her whenever I was passing. And that is precisely what we're gonna do. Hold tight.'

Pushing her control column forward, Gabrielle plunged the little plane down through the clouds once more.

Chapter Fifteen

The *Silver Turtle* emerged from the bottom of the clouds. They were still over the sea, but to their right the children could see a curved coastline, fringed with pale sandy beaches, with green fields beyond.

'Bingo!' yelled Gabrielle. 'The Suffolk coast. Just where I hoped we'd be.' She banked sharply and piloted them towards the coastline, continuing to lose height all the time. There were fewer clouds over the land than the sea and, as they crossed the coast, Zara could see the *Silver Turtle*'s shadow flitting over the golden sand beneath them.

The plane's Plexiglas canopy gave them a panoramic view of fields and villages as they sped over the countryside. 'That's Mantlingham Manor dead ahead,' said Gabrielle, after a few minutes, pointing to a cluster of grey rooftops and chimneys protruding from a patch of woodland. 'Ready to take over for landing, co-pilot?'

'Me?' said Ben, half-wanting to pilot the plane again, half-scared of taking unnecessary risks. 'I'm not sure. Amy once said landing's the most dangerous bit of flying.'

'All the more reason for learning to do it,' said Gabrielle. 'Don't worry, I'll be ready to take over control the second you need me to.'

'Well, all right,' said Ben. 'As long as you promise to stay there with your hands on your controls.'

'Of course I'm gonna stay here!' cried Gabrielle. 'I'd hardly be likely to get out of my seat and leave the plane in the hands of a complete novice, would I? D'you think I'm stark, staring bonkers? Now, get the wheels down,' she continued before anyone could say anything. 'Your plane, co-pilot.'

Ben pressed the undercarriage button, then took hold of his control column once more.

'Good,' said Gabrielle. 'Now, keep her in flying position and keep reducing the speed – that's what's making her descend. Never bring a plane down for landing by diving.'

Ben pulled back the engine speed lever. The buzz of the motors dropped in pitch and they flew lower and lower. They reached the woodland, which was bordered by a high wall, and flew towards the grey stone mansion, following the path of a long narrow driveway. The treetops flashing past beneath their wing tips looked so close that Ben winced and instinctively pulled back his control column to gain height.

'Relax – you're OK,' said Gabrielle. 'Circle the house; I'm hoping there'll be enough grass to land somewhere.'

Sure enough, as Ben piloted the *Silver Turtle* in a wide, banking turn, an expanse of lawn at the rear of the house came into view, fringed by square-cut yew hedges down each side and dominated by three massive cedar trees.

'OK, circle once more and bring her down between the house and the three trees,' instructed Gabrielle. 'Wing flaps down . . . That's it . . . Come in parallel with the back of the house . . . Nose slightly up ter slow her right down.'

Ben could feel his heart thumping as they made their final approach over the flower bed at the edge of the lawn. A couple of times he felt Gabrielle overriding his controls, to adjust their angle, but apart from that he could feel the plane was in his hands. Keep her steady . . . Over the hedge . . . over a flower bed . . . over the lawn . . . *Bump!* They were down, bouncing on their wheel-strut shock-absorbers, careering towards the far hedge. Too fast!

'Cut the motors!' yelled Gabrielle. Ben complied, but was

still sure they were going to crash into the hedge. 'Right rudder pedal!' ordered Gabrielle, at the same time easing the back wheel brakes on. Ben pressed his foot on the right pedal and felt the nose wheel steer them round. The *Silver Turtle* made a neat 180-degree turn, her left wing-tip fin merely brushing the hedge, and trundled to a gentle halt.

Ben let go of his control column and realized that his hands were shaking. The thrill of flying the plane in the air had been exhilarating, but the relief of having landed safely was euphoric.

'Well done!' yelled Gabrielle, whacking him on the shoulder. 'Blimming well done!' She stood up and slid back the canopy. Everyone looked towards the house.

Two figures stood on a stone terrace beside an open French window in the centre of the house's enormous rear façade. One was a slim elderly lady wearing an elegant cream summer dress. The other was a white-haired man dressed in the kind of English butler's outfit the children had only ever seen in films. They both stared at the plane in silence. The butler was holding a shotgun, which he raised slowly.

Gabrielle clambered out of the plane. 'Hallo, Clarissa,' she called. 'Nice way ter welcome guests.'

'Gabrielle!' exclaimed the lady on the terrace. 'I should have guessed it was you. Always so unorthodox.' She spoke in a high, rather musical voice. 'And, goodness, you've brought quite a little gang with you,' she said, noticing the four children who had followed Gabrielle down onto the lawn. She turned to the butler. 'It's all right, Graves,' she said, with a tinkling laugh. 'I think you can put away the gun now.' The butler nodded and disappeared into the house.

'Come on,' said Gabrielle, grinning. The children followed her across the lawn to the terrace, taking in their new surroundings: the sun-baked stonework of the stately home, the perfectly clipped yew hedges, the ancient cedars casting their deep shadows on the flawlessly mown grass, the rhythmic coo-cooing of a woodpigeon. The sky was cloudless here, and the air hot and still. On one of the shallow stone steps leading up  to the terrace, Sam spotted a tiny lizard, which had presumably been basking there undisturbed all morning. This felt like a place where time had stood still for centuries. As they approached the steps, the lizard flickered its tongue and darted down through a crack in the masonry.

'Excuse Graves's over-vigilance,' said Lady Clarissa, smiling apologetically. 'We thought you must be some sort of intruders or terrorists. One can't be too careful these days, can one?' She kissed Gabrielle on the cheek. 'Lovely to see you, my dear. I had no idea you were back in the country.'

Gabrielle introduced the children to her friend. 'Charmed to meet you,' said Lady Clarissa, flashing them a dazzling smile and shaking their hands. She had pale, delicate features, still beautiful in her old age, and an air of grace and sophistication. 'Do come in,' she said, leading them through the French windows into a large high-ceilinged room with dark wood-panelled walls.

'We need yer help, Clarissa,' said Gabrielle. 'Or yer son's. It's a bit of a long story, but it's kind of urgent.'

'My dear, you know I'm always ready to help an old friend,' said Lady Clarissa. 'Sit down and tell me all about it.'

They all sat down around a small oval dining table and Gabrielle showed Lady Clarissa the photograph. The children gave Lady Clarissa a brief account of how they had discovered it and how they had decrypted Maskil's secret message, and of all that had occurred since. Gabrielle told her everything she'd told the children about the nature of Maskil's secret work and about Noctarma (though Sam noticed she omitted all mention of her mysterious friend and the radar-jamming device).

'Goodness, what a time you've all had,' exclaimed Lady Clarissa when Gabrielle had finished. 'You poor children must be out of your minds with worry. These Noctarma people sound simply dreadful and it's outrageous that they should be misusing sections of our police force to do their dirty work. I shall telephone my son immediately. Excuse me for just a moment.'

'See?' said Gabrielle to the children, after Lady Clarissa had swished out of the room. 'I told you old Clarissa would get this sorted out. Some place she's got here, eh?'

'Yeah,' agreed Zara, looking round. Everything about the room – its antique furniture, its huge stone fireplace, its smell of old polished wood – exuded tradition, order, and a timeless serenity that matched that of the garden. After the mad chaos of the morning's unexpected events, Zara began to feel slightly calmer. Although the leaden anxiety in the pit of her stomach remained, she began to share Gabrielle's confidence that Lady Clarissa and her son really would be able to get Uncle Alexander, Professor Hartleigh-Broadbeam and Amy released before too long.

After some time, Lady Clarissa returned. 'My son is taking immediate action to resolve this matter,' she reported, 'and he's promised to let us know the minute there's any progress. So you mustn't worry; you children will be back with your people in no time at all. Now, I've asked Graves to bring us some luncheon. I'm sure you all must be simply starving.'

'*I* certainly am,' said Gabrielle. 'Mind, I'm also bursting for a pee. Where's yer loo, Clarissa?'

'Oh, just at the end of the corridor, on the left,' said Lady Clarissa.

After Gabrielle returned, the children each went to use the toilet too, passing polished suits of armour as they made their way along the corridor, as well as ancient swords and axes mounted along the wood-panelled walls. On his way back to the room, Sam (who'd been last to go) noticed a small antique clock standing on a little shelf. The clock was intricately crafted in dark metal in the shape of a stylized castle, with turrets and pointed towers. Beneath the red and gold clock face, Sam spotted two little arched doors, and wondered if anything might appear through them when the clock struck the hour. It was less than a minute to one o'clock, so he lingered to see. As the minute hand reached the top, the doors flipped open and two miniature metal knights emerged, each armed with a sword and shield. They trundled round a semicircular platform to face each other in the middle. One knight raised his shield; the other raised his sword, then brought it down on his mechanical opponent's shield with a single *ting*. Then each knight retreated backwards through his doorway. Sam bent down and peered, catching a glimpse of the tiny cogwheels moving inside before the doors closed.

'Ahem!' A dry cough made Sam look round to see Graves approaching from the far end of the corridor, wheeling a laden serving trolley.

'That's a brilliant clock!' said Sam, walking ahead of the butler and holding the door to the room open for him.

'It's rather old and valuable, sir,' said Graves, in a tone that suggested that Sam's mere enjoyment of the antique might somehow damage it.

Sam joined the others round the table, as Graves transferred an enormous silver platter of sandwiches from the trolley, laid out six plates and glasses, and poured out some iced lemon squash from a beautiful cut-glass jug. 'Do help yourselves,' said Lady Clarissa. Graves left the room and the children tucked in ravenously. It seemed a long time since their early breakfast and the food lifted their spirits considerably.

'Thanks, Clarissa,' said Gabrielle, polishing off her third cucumber sandwich. 'You're a real pal.'

'My dear, it's the least I can do for my oldest friend,' said Lady Clarissa. She picked up the photograph and sighed. 'Poor Maskil,' she said. 'I remember that day so well. You made such a perfect couple.' She turned the photo over. 'But how extraordinary that this message from him should turn up after all these years.'

Zara realized that, with so much else to worry about, she'd almost forgotten about Maskil's message. 'Could the message still lead us to Maskil's lost invention?' she asked Gabrielle. 'It says that someone called Solomon would tell you how to find the Silver Turtle project. Do you know who Maskil meant?'

'Oh, I know who Solomon is,' said Gabrielle, 'and it's possible he can still tell us what Maskil wanted ter know. But getting hold of him's gonna be blimming tricky.'

'You mean you don't know where he is?' asked Sam.

'I know exactly where he is,' said Gabrielle. 'He's at the bottom of a lake.'

Chapter Sixteen

'At the bottom of a lake?' echoed Lady Clarissa. 'You mean he drowned? Gabrielle, dear, how can the poor man tell us anything if he's dead?'

'Solomon isn't a man,' said Gabrielle, 'and he was never alive.' She paused to take a sip of lemon squash. 'Solomon is a silver jewellery box, about seven inches long and made in the shape of a turtle, with a shell that hinges up. He'd been in Maskil's family for decades. Maskil's granddad was a silversmith and he'd made it as a wedding present for Maskil's grandma. I think Maskil's dad had given it the name Solomon when he was a kid.'

'So Maskil named his secret project after an *actual* silver turtle?' said Marcia.

'I guess so, yeah,' said Gabrielle. 'And I can see now that the actual silver turtle was the logical place for him ter have hid information about the project, but it never occurred ter me before. Solomon was one of the few possessions Maskil had in the small bedsit room in Edinburgh where he lived. It turned out he'd made a will a few months before he was killed and he'd left Solomon ter me. He had no family left.'

'But surely you'd have noticed if Maskil had left a message for you in the compartment under the shell,' said Lady Clarissa.

'I definitely would've,' agreed Gabrielle. 'And there was nothing. But maybe he left information somewhere else on Solomon; I dunno – engraved in tiny letters or something. If I'd found this photo and the message back then, I'd've examined Solomon more thoroughly.'

'But how did Solomon end up in a lake?' asked Ben.

'He crashed in,' said Gabrielle. 'Near the end of the war, in 1945, I was assigned ter fly an Avro Anson – a twin-engined plane – down ter the south of France. The fighting was all but over in Europe so it was reckoned a pretty safe mission, but exciting for me – my first trip out of Britain. I was carrying a couple of army generals ter a conference in Nice, and our route took us right down the eastern side of France. We was over halfway there, just passing the

Jura mountains, when our left engine suddenly conked out and started belching out flames and black smoke. Gawd knows what had gone wrong. Could've been sabotage, I s'pose, given how important my passengers were, but it was prob'ly just engine failure. Not uncommon in those old kites. Anyway, we didn't have time ter wonder about that. I told my two passengers ter bail out, pointed the Anson towards the mountains, hoping she'd crash away from any people, and bailed out myself. All three of us got down safely and made our way ter the nearest town, where we found some American soldiers, one of whom took us on down ter Nice in a jeep. You'll remember me telling you about all this, Clarissa, when I got back ter London.'

'Of course,' said Lady Clarissa. 'Such a narrow escape you'd had! I was always enthralled to hear about your adventures.'

'Anyway,' continued Gabrielle, 'later I found out that the Anson had actually cleared the Jura mountains, flown right over the Swiss border and come down in Lake Geneva. Sank straight ter the bottom. The Swiss weren't too happy about one of our planes entering their territory – they were strictly neutral during the war, of course – but it all got smoothed over and forgotten.'

'And Solomon was in the plane?' said Sam.

'Yep,' said Gabrielle. 'Since Maskil's death, I'd carried Solomon with me in my small kitbag wherever I went, and that had been tucked under one of the spare passenger seats. You don't stop ter collect personal belongings when yer plane's on fire, even precious ones. I was sad ter lose Solomon, of course, but I was lucky ter be alive and I knew it. I'd seen too much loss of human life ter waste tears on possessions.'

'So you never tried to recover Solomon from the crashed Anson, even after the war?' asked Marcia.

'Never even considered it,' said Gabrielle. 'You have ter understand that Lake Geneva is one of the deepest lakes in Europe – three hundred metres in the middle. Getting down ter a wreck that deep would've been dangerous, expensive and prob'ly impossible anyway, back then. I'd've been mad ter even try it just for the sake of a little jewellery box, whatever its sentimental value. But *now* . . .'

'But now we know that Solomon isn't just a jewellery box,' said Clarissa. 'He's our only chance of finding out where poor Maskil hid his work. I'm simply hopeless at understanding scientific things, but from what you say, this anti-gravity invention of his sounds terribly important.'

'Terribly important is an understatement,' said Gabrielle. 'If we really *can* rediscover Maskil's invention, and get it inta the hands of responsible scientists, it could change the world for everyone's good. But if the secret of anti-gravity falls inta the clutches of people like Noctarma, God help us all.'

'Don't worry,' said Lady Clarissa. 'My son will ensure that these dreadful Noctarma people won't be at large for much longer.'

'He might manage ter round up all the Noctarma agents behind this morning's wrongful arrest,' conceded Gabrielle, 'but like I told you, Noctarma's a big international network. They won't give up looking for Maskil's invention. This secret message gives us a chance ter find it before they do. As soon as Clarissa's son's got yer folks safely released, we should start making a plan ter retrieve Solomon. It won't be easy. But with modern diving equipment, it might just be possible.'

'But do you know where exactly on Lake Geneva the Anson crashed?' asked Lady Clarissa.

'I don't,' said Gabrielle. 'I never saw it come down, remember. And it's a blimming big lake. But I guess there'll be a record of the incident somewhere.'

'No doubt,' said Lady Clarissa. 'I'm sure we'll be able to find it. How exciting: a real treasure hunt! Now then,' she said to the children, '*do* tell me more about your marvellous aeroplane out there. You say you actually helped to build it yourselves?'

Zara wondered whether Lady Clarissa was genuinely interested in aeroplanes or was trying to take their minds off their worries while they waited to hear back from her son. Either way, she was happy to join the others in telling their kindly host all about the *Silver Turtle* and, for the next forty minutes or so, they chatted about Amy's ideas and designs and Professor Ampersand's electric motors and energy cells. Lady Clarissa said she was sure she knew people who'd be interested in investing money in such remarkable technology, and Zara began to hope that some good might come out of this whole mess after all. If only her great-uncle and Professor Hartleigh-Broadbeam and Amy could be released soon.

Shortly after two o'clock, Graves the butler entered the room. 'Excuse me for interrupting, madam,' he said, 'but your son is here. You asked me to inform you the minute he arrived.'

'Ah, splendid,' said Lady Clarissa, standing up. 'Do stay seated, everyone. I shall bring him straight through.' She followed Graves from the room.

The children looked at each other. News at last. They were all thinking the same thing: please let it be news of the adults' release. But something puzzled Zara. 'I thought Sir Roland was in London, sorting out the wrongful arrest from there,' she said. 'Lady Clarissa didn't say he was coming here.'

'It's only been an hour and a bit since she phoned him,' said Gabrielle. 'I don't think that he could've driven here from London that quick.'

'You're quite correct, Gabrielle,' said Lady Clarissa, returning with a tall grey-haired man in his mid-fifties, immaculately dressed in a dark suit and tie. 'Roland was already on his way here when I called him on his car-phone.'

'Yes indeed,' said Sir Roland. He spoke in a low, slightly whispering voice. 'When my agent reported that this morning's attempt to seize your plane had been a complete fiasco, I decided I needed to be here at our headquarters to take control of the situation personally. There's only so much I can do from London without my Home Office staff becoming suspicious.' He smiled at their bewildered expressions, and brought out a slim automatic pistol from his jacket pocket. 'I am the Supreme Leader of Noctarma,' he explained. 'You can't believe how surprised, relieved and delighted I was when my mother rang to say you'd flown straight into our hands.'

Chapter Seventeen

Zara felt her brain go numb with shock. She turned, like the others, to Lady Clarissa to see that she too was now holding a pistol in her right hand. Lady Clarissa smiled, but the warmth of her previous smiles had vanished, replaced by a steeliness in her eyes and a slight curl to the corners of her mouth. It was a smile that made Zara feel cold inside.

'*Clarissa, what are you doing?*' cried Gabrielle.

'Have you discovered anything useful from them, Mother?' hissed Sir Roland, ignoring Gabrielle.

'Oh yes,' said Lady Clarissa. 'In spite of its name, their plane is actually a worthless irrelevance, a ridiculous electric toy, but Creevler was right about them having a cryptic message.' She picked up the photo from the table and handed it to her son. 'Stribnik left this message hidden in the hangar. These brats found it and managed to decipher it,' she explained.

'Aah!' breathed Sir Roland, his eyes shining and his mouth widening into a greedy smile that showed every one of his little white teeth. 'And does the message reveal the hiding place of his invention?'

'Not directly,' said his mother. 'It tells us that Stribnik left *that* information concealed in or on a jewellery box, whose location Gabrielle here has kindly revealed. It will be complicated to retrieve the box but not impossible.'

'Excellent,' purred Sir Roland, putting the photo into his pocket.

'*Clarissa!*' cried Gabrielle again. 'I don't know what lies your son's told you about Noctarma, but these people are –'

'Oh, I know *everything* about Noctarma,' interrupted Clarissa. 'I'm proud to have been my son's greatest support in founding Noctarma more than thirty years ago, and proud to be his closest confidante in running the organization.' Her voice was different now too: deeper and more powerful.

'*NO!*' yelled Gabrielle. 'You *can't* be in with these evil people! You don't know what you're doing!'

'I've always known *exactly* what I was doing, Gabrielle,' said Lady Clarissa, calmly. 'But y*ou've* never known what I was doing at all, even back in our war days. *Especially* back in our war days. Did you really think that someone like me would befriend a common little guttersnipe like you and a Jew like Stribnik? The reason I came to see you at the hangar so often was to find out how Stribnik's work was progressing and report back to my superiors in Berlin.'

There was a stunned silence as Gabrielle and the children took in the meaning of what Lady Clarissa was saying.

'My God!' gasped Gabrielle, at last. 'You were a *spy! You were working for the Nazis!*'

'I was an agent for the side of civilization, yes,' said Lady Clarissa, 'and I'm proud of it. I carried out many secret duties, but preventing Stribnik from handing his invention over to the British government was my most important achievement of the war. When, in 1942, I learnt that Stribnik was down in London and was about to bring Air Ministry scientists up to Edinburgh, I realized he must have made some sort of breakthrough. I just had time to alert one of our agents in London, who ensured that the Air Ministry plane never reached Edinburgh. I believe the pilot and his four passengers were served some rather special coffee before they took off, to help them sleep.'

'You *MURDERER!*' screamed Gabrielle, rising to her feet.

'Stay where you are,' ordered Lady Clarissa, pointing her gun at Gabrielle's head. 'It really has been tiresome having to pretend to like you, Gabrielle: tiresome having to spend time with you during the war; tiresome having to let you cry all over me after we'd killed Stribnik, in the hope that you'd tell me something that would lead me to his hidden work. By the time it became apparent that you had nothing to tell me, you had decided that we were the best of friends. I almost succeeded in freeing myself of you in 1945. I was worried that you'd had the opportunity to see some incriminating documents in my flat, worried that even someone as stupid as you might have begun to suspect the nature of my work, so I arranged for your death. But the agent who sabotaged your plane failed to sabotage your parachute, and there you were, plucky little Gabrielle, back from France without a scratch and with another heroic escapade to go on about. Then the war was over. For me to have you murdered privately in peacetime would not have been worth the risk, especially since it had become clear that you really were completely unsuspecting of my wartime allegiances. So for sixty years I've had to pretend to appreciate your efforts to stay in contact, pretend to enjoy our occasional lunches in London, pretend to be grateful for those cheap little Christmas cards you've sent every year. Well, my tolerance has finally been rewarded. At last you have turned up with some information. At last you have been of some use, you common, vulgar, pathetic little nobody.'

Gabrielle fell back in her chair. She suddenly looked the great age she was, her wrinkled features contorted with shock and with anger. '*Traitor!*' she spat.

'*You* were the traitor,' retorted Lady Clarissa. 'A traitor to your race, taking up with that Jew. People like me were acting in Britain's true interests. Britain and Germany could have ruled the world together, partners in a thousand-year Reich of order and beauty and purity. Instead, our world is in the hands of inferior races.'

The children flashed a horrified glance at one other. They'd let this woman charm them, reassure them, feed them. Zara felt sick with disgust, contaminated by having even been in this house. And she felt frightened. Normally, she tried not to let racists get to her and dismissed them for the pathetic idiots they were. But this woman and her son had power. Power from their wealth and positions. And power over them right now. While Lady Clarissa kept her gun pointed at Gabrielle, Sir Roland kept his aimed towards the children. Zara gave Ben's hand a squeeze, feeling suddenly protective of her younger brother.

'If Maskil was from an inferior race,' croaked Gabrielle, defiantly, 'how come his work was so superior to anything yer Nazi scientists came up with? Face it, Clarissa: you're living in the past.'

'I am not living in the past,' said Lady Clarissa. 'I kept my head after the war; I accepted that the side of civilization had lost that particular battle, and I concentrated on the future. I continued to play the part of the perfect English rose who'd done her bit towards Hitler's defeat. I married an up-and-coming Member of Parliament with an impeccable war record, Sir Gerald Mantlingham, and supported his long and distinguished career. But all the time, I made secret preparations. Gerald's government posts gave me access to all sorts of information and people and, without him ever knowing, I built up an extensive network of knowledge, covering international finance, the arms industry, the police, the armed forces, and the security services. At the same time, I brought up Roland to understand the true values of this world, to understand his heritage and his destiny. I shared my secret past with him and I shared my knowledge, and we drew up our plans together. Of course Gerald knew nothing of this, and would have been frightfully in the way as our plans developed. His sudden death, just as Roland came of age, was most convenient.' A horrible smirk of complicity flashed between Lady Clarissa and her son. 'Now there was nothing to stop Roland bringing our plans to fruition,' continued Lady Clarissa. 'He founded Noctarma, a new organization to carry the ancient ideals of order and purity into a new age. As you will have realized by now, my son has always been exceptionally gifted and intelligent.'

'I've realized he's exceptionally spoilt and repulsive,' said Gabrielle, 'and as barmy as you are, inta the bargain. No one supports yer ridiculous ideas about order and purity any more. Not in Britain, not in Germany, not anywhere.'

Lady Clarissa's cheeks flushed with anger. The children held their breaths, terrified that Gabrielle had provoked their captor too far and was about to be shot there and then.

But Sir Roland looked quite unperturbed by Gabrielle's insult. 'We do not care what you think of us,' he purred, 'and we do not care who supports our ideas. Public support is unnecessary in today's world. When I planned Noctarma, I saw that the age of mass rallies, flag-waving crowds and huge armies was coming to an end. I saw that power in the twenty-first century would belong to those who held control of information, control of secrets and control of technology. My strategy throughout the last thirty years has been simple: firstly, to build up Noctarma's influence around the world. You wouldn't believe just how extensive my network is; the Secret Operations Police Unit is just one example of the many government agencies around the globe that I covertly control. Secondly, to use that influence to keep the world in a state of perpetual conflict, ignorance, weakness and paranoia. And thirdly, to infiltrate every sector of the international arms industry – every corporation, every secret government research facility – enabling Noctarma to acquire knowledge and control of the world's most advanced weapons technology.

'But the secret of anti-gravity is the secret that will enable Noctarma to bring about its ultimate goal, enable me to fulfil my destiny. Many scientists, research facilities and governments have attempted to crack the problem of anti-gravity and we have investigated all their efforts thoroughly, but no one appears to have made the breakthrough that Stribnik is believed to have achieved. Although no one had succeeded in finding his work, I never gave up hope; Noctarma's antennae were always alert for any hint that the Silver Turtle project had resurfaced. And that day has come. The moment the secret is in our hands, Noctarma's underground factories will go into production, building anti-gravity craft that will make today's most sophisticated military aircraft look like vintage biplanes. Combined with the weaponry we already possess, our anti-gravity craft will make Noctarma invincible. We shall rise above this chaotic, disunited, primitive world like gods. We shall destroy rival air forces, obliterate armies, seize control of global communications and transport systems. We shall decide which peoples will be allowed to serve us and which shall be eradicated. We shall cleanse the world and the thousand-year reign of order, beauty and purity shall at last be established.'

Graves entered the room, once more armed with his shotgun. 'The basement cells are all prepared,' he reported.

'Good,' rasped Sir Roland. 'Let's get these tiresome people

locked up. I've wasted enough breath on this rabble.'

Nobody asked you to, thought Ben, but he held his tongue.

Sir Roland pondered for a second. 'Or perhaps we should simply kill them now. Do we require any further information from them?' he asked his mother.

'I am hopeful that what Gabrielle has already told us will be sufficient to track down Stribnik's work,' said Lady Clarissa, 'but we cannot be certain. We may need to interrogate our prisoners further, persuade them to recall some additional scrap of knowledge that they have neglected to share with us. I take it the three you had arrested at the hangar are secure?'

'Quite secure,' said Sir Roland. 'My Secret Operations Police Unit are holding them at their Edinburgh HQ – a location unknown to the authorities – and I've ensured that no official record of this morning's arrest will ever exist. I shall have them kept alive too then, for the time being. But the minute Stribnik's invention is finally in our hands, all eight prisoners will be dispatched. I'm sure I can organize something that won't arouse suspicion.' He smiled at Gabrielle and the children, but continued to talk as if they weren't there. 'A tragic accident, perhaps, involving that ridiculous little aeroplane of theirs. Wreckage found at sea . . . bodies washed up on a beach. These home-built planes are notoriously unsafe.'

'I'm sure you'll arrange everything perfectly, Roland,' simpered Lady Clarissa, again exchanging a superior, complicit smirk with her son. They reminded Marcia of some girls at her old school, who had formed what they called a Secret Society and spent the whole time passing secret messages to each other saying horrible things about the girls they wouldn't let join.

'Shall I summon two of the men in from the grounds to assist us with the prisoners?' asked Graves.

'I hardly think that will be necessary,' answered Sir Roland. 'My mother and I can guard them up here while you take them down one at a time. Take her first,' he rasped, indicating Gabrielle.

Graves prodded Gabrielle with his shotgun, forcing her out through the door and into the corridor. Their footsteps receded, then within a few seconds there came a crash that sounded like a suit of armour being knocked over. Lady Clarissa and Sir Roland winced and gripped their guns more tightly. 'Watch where you're walking, you stupid old cow!' came Graves's voice, its silken civility gone. 'Do anything like that again and I'll blow your brains out!'

'Roland, perhaps you should go and help Graves to lock up Gabrielle,' suggested Lady Clarissa, frowning. 'She is not intelligent, but she is devious and she may be more dangerous than she looks. I wouldn't put it past her to try to seize an axe from the wall or something.'

Sir Roland looked at the children and at his mother. 'Maybe,' he said doubtfully, 'but are you sure you can —'

'Roland, dear, I hardly think I've become so old and decrepit that I can't manage to guard four little brats like these for five minutes,' said Lady Clarissa reproachfully.

'Of course not, Mother,' purred Sir Roland, leaving the room.

'Now,' snapped Lady Clarissa to the children. 'You will all sit still, without talking. Put your hands on the table where I can see them. Anyone trying anything will be shot.'

The children obeyed. They were sitting around one end of the small oval table where they had eaten, with the door behind them. Lady Clarissa stood at the other end, her back to the French windows.

Marcia's brain pounded. She was terrified of that gun, pointing straight at them, but she had to think clearly. They had been left alone with only one armed captor. Although any attempt to escape right now would be highly danger-ous, any attempt to escape after Sir Roland and Graves returned would be impossible. Once they were locked in the cells, nothing but certain death awaited them. They had to try something now, or never. She looked down at the table. The cut-glass squash jug, now empty, looked old and valuable, the kind of thing Lady Clarissa would care about. A desperate plan was coming together in Marcia's head. The plan relied on her being able to start speaking without being shot immediately. What could she say? She had an idea.

Sir Roland's footsteps in the corridor outside faded away after Gabrielle's and Graves's. Somewhere in the bowels of the building, a door creaked. They were on their way down to the basement, guessed Marcia. This was the moment. The plan also relied on the others being ready to react to events with lightning speed. Marcia couldn't risk even glancing at them. Something inside her told her they would be alert for any opportunity. But if she was wrong, she was about to get herself shot and possibly them as well. Heart thumping, throat dry, Marcia opened her mouth to speak.

Chapter Eighteen

'P–please, miss,' stammered Marcia, 'I'll tell you about another secret message we found if you let me go.'

'SILENCE!' ordered Lady Clarissa. 'Do you expect to fool me with such an obvious lie?' No, thought Marcia, but you haven't shot me.

'But it's true,' she persisted. 'It's in the plane out there.' She pointed towards the French window behind Lady Clarissa and, as she did so, deliberately knocked the top of the glass jug with her hand. The jug toppled over, falling towards the edge of the table.

As Marcia had hoped, Lady Clarissa instinctively stepped forward and almost reached out her left hand to save her antique jug. She stopped herself immediately and let the jug crash to the floor, her eyes flitting back to Marcia, burning with anger and suspicion, her right hand aiming the gun, squeezing the trigger. But in the second for which Lady Clarissa's attention had been distracted, Marcia had grabbed the silver sandwich platter and flung it with all her force at the gun.

P*TANG!* Lady Clarissa's shot skimmed off the platter, which struck her arm, sending her staggering back, fumbling to retain her grip on her weapon. 'Get her gun!' yelled Marcia leaping from her chair, but the others had already sprung into action, Sam and Zara charging round each side of the table, Ben diving underneath it, flying towards Lady Clarissa's legs. BANG BANG BANG! As Sam and Zara seized her wrist, wrestling her arm upwards, Lady Clarissa fired desperately, her bullets blasting into the walls and ceiling. *Wham!* Ben cannoned into her ankles in a crude rugby tackle, clinging on as she went over backwards. *Thud.* Others thrown off. Gun in his face. Roll sideways. BANG! Deafening noise. Stench of hot metal and explosives. Gun aiming again. *Whack!* Marcia's foot kicking gun from woman's hand, sending it flying out onto the terrace. Sam and Zara's hands grabbing his shirt, pulling him up, out through the French windows.

The four children tore across the stone terrace, leapt down onto the lawn and kept running. '*ROLAND!*' screamed Lady Clarissa, pursuing them onto the terrace, scrabbling for her gun. '*GRAVES!*'

'Get to the plane!' yelled Marcia, swerving towards the *Silver Turtle*.

'No!' gasped Zara. 'Ben doesn't know how to take off! This way!' She pointed past the cedars to the edge of the woodland, but at that moment two khaki-clad men emerged from the woods, looked towards the house, and came running up the lawn towards them. Both carried shotguns.

'Plane,' panted Ben. 'Only chance.' They reached the *Silver Turtle*, scrambled on board and tumbled into the seats, Ben and Marcia in front, Sam and Zara behind. Ben grabbed a control column and flicked the motors on. They whirred into life but the plane remained stationary.

BANG! BANG! Lady Clarissa had found her gun. Staggering down the terrace steps. Getting nearer. Firing again. P*TANG!* Her third shot ricocheted off the plane's nose. Ben gave the motors full power. Plane still stuck. Come on! What was wrong? Two men nearly on them, past the cedars, aiming their shotguns . . .

'Brakes!' yelled Sam. Marcia yanked the wheel-brake lever and the *Silver Turtle* shot forward like a bolt from a crossbow. BANG! BANG! The two men fired and Sam felt a shower of lead shot spatter the back of the plane. Now Sir Roland was bursting from the house, barging past his mother, racing across the lawn like a demon, trying to intercept them, face red with fury, gun held forward in both hands. *BLAMBLAMBLAMBLAMBLAM!* Ducking down, Zara heard bullets buzz through the air just above her head, passing through the open canopy.

Ben tried to ignore everything. Look ahead. Hedge looming up fast. Pull back column. He felt the plane float away from the lawn. But they weren't straight. And weren't climbing fast enough. They weren't going to clear the yew hedge . . . *Crrshhh!* Their right wheel smashed through the hedge's uppermost foliage. But they were free, flying up into empty blue sky. He had taken off.

Sam and Zara looked down through the back of the cockpit canopy at the shrinking figures, now joined by Graves, all firing after them with increasing futility. Ben banked around to the front of the house, levelled out and sped the plane low over the woods, back the way they had come. 'Did anyone get hit?' yelled Ben, anxiously, keeping his eyes ahead.

They all confirmed they were fine and, as they left the Mantlingham estate behind, gave a collective whoop, their hearts and brains racing with adrenalin and relief.

'You did it, Ben!' cried Zara, shutting the canopy so they could hear one another more easily. 'You took off!'

'I didn't know I could,' said Ben, modestly, 'but we didn't have much choice. Well done to Marcia for thinking of a way to attack that old witch.'

'I nearly got us all shot by her,' said Marcia, trembling now. 'It was you lot ploughing in so quickly that saved us.'

'We were ready,' said Sam. 'I could sense you were planning something as soon as Sir Roland and Graves left the room with Gabrielle.'

'I wish we could have saved her too,' said Marcia. 'It's horrible to think of her locked up back there.'

'Yeah,' agreed Zara, 'but she'd have wanted us to escape. She'll be laughing like a drain when she finds out we flew away.'

The *Silver Turtle* whizzed over the fields and hedges, Ben maintaining a low, level course, eastwards towards the sea. It felt very scary piloting the plane without Gabrielle on board, and the idea of trying to land without her help terrified Ben, but he forced himself to stay calm. 'What now?' he asked the others. 'I could try to land on the sea, near that beach we flew over. Might be a *bit* safer landing on water. Then we could find somewhere to ring the police from.'

Zara frowned, thinking fast. 'No,' she said. 'If we land near here and go to the police, we might end up straight back in Noctarma's hands. They'll already be planning how to recapture us. Gabrielle said that Noctarma must have agents in the Secret Operations Police Unit but it looks like she was underestimating them; from the way Sir Roland was talking, it sounds as if he controls the whole unit, like some sort of private army. And we don't know what other parts of the police force he controls.'

'We could phone Sam's parents,' suggested Marcia.

'Might not be easy, though,' said Sam. 'All the details and phone numbers for their hotel and conference centre are back at your house. Maybe we'll just *have* to phone the police and hope for the best.' They had almost reached the sea. They had to do *something*.

'But even if we don't get intercepted by police working for Noctarma, I'm not sure the real police would believe our story,' argued Zara. 'From what Gabrielle said, hardly anyone's even heard of Noctarma, but Sir Roland and Lady Clarissa are important people. They'll turn on the charm and say we're making the whole thing up. And they'll probably be moving Gabrielle to somewhere else already.'

'But we could make someone believe us eventually,' said Ben. 'They'd have to at least investigate.'

'Yeah, but it all could take ages,' said Zara. 'And we don't *have* ages. You heard Sir Roland: as soon as Noctarma finds Maskil's invention, the adults will be killed. We *have* to find someone who'll believe us and who can persuade the police to take action immediately. And we *have* to find Solomon before Noctarma does.'

'So what's *your* plan?' said Ben, sensing that his big sister had one.

Zara hesitated. Even to herself, the plan that had come into her head sounded a bit reckless. But she couldn't think of a better one. 'I think we should fly to Lake Geneva,' she said.

'Lake Geneva?' exclaimed Ben.

'Of course!' said Marcia, picking up on what Zara was thinking. 'Professor Sharpe! She lives in Geneva and works for the United Nations. She knows all sorts of people; she's bound to know someone who can take action against Noctarma and get the adults released.' She remembered how, during their recent adventure in the Arctic, Professor Sharpe had called on the help of a senior UN military officer whom she knew.

'Yeah,' said Sam, 'and I bet she could find out exactly where the Anson crashed and organize an underwater salvage.' Professor Sharpe was an extremely efficient woman and Zara's plan sounded good to him.

'And I've got Professor Sharpe's phone number and address in my diary here,' said Marcia, checking the pocket of her jeans. Marcia phoned and e-mailed Adam quite often.

'But I've only had one flying lesson!' Ben pointed out, panicking slightly. 'I should be trying to land as soon as possible, before I lose control, or crash into another plane or something. I don't think I could fly as far as Switzerland.'

'*I* didn't think you could take off back there, but I was wrong,' said Zara. 'You're really good at flying this plane. I'd trust you to get us there.'

Sam and Marcia added their agreement. Strengthened by the others' confidence in him, Ben fought his panic down. 'Well, *maybe* we could try,' he conceded. 'But do we have enough energy left in the energy cells to get that far?'

'How far is it?' asked Zara. 'You're the walking atlas.'

The walls and ceiling of Ben's bedroom at home were completely covered in maps. Ben pictured in his head the map of Europe and added up the distances he more or less knew. 'Must be about eighty or ninety miles from here to Dover,' he said, 'plus twenty more to Calais. Switzerland's about halfway down the eastern edge of France, or maybe a bit further, so say another four hundred miles . . . It can't be much more than five hundred miles to Lake Geneva from here in a straight line, maybe even a bit less.'

'The energy cells are still more than half full,' said Marcia, pointing to the gauge on the instrument panel. 'See, the dial goes up to ten units for fully charged and the needle's only down to six now. How far did we come this morning?'

Ben pictured their morning's journey out over the North Sea and down the east coast. 'About three hundred and sixty miles,' he guessed.

'So if . . . um . . . four-tenths of our energy took us three hundred and sixty miles,' said Sam, 'one-tenth equals . . . ninety miles.' The maths part of his brain was working quicker than it ever did at school. 'So *six*-tenths will take us . . . um . . . five hundred and forty miles. We can make it!'

'So how long will it take us to get there?' said Marcia, looking at the speedometer. 'We're doing about two hundred and twenty miles per hour, so . . .'

'We've still got the wheels down,' said Sam. 'They'll be causing extra drag.'

Ben raised them and the speedometer needle whizzed round to settle at the 250 mph mark.

'We could be there in just two hours, then!' said Marcia.

Ben was finally convinced. The thought of being able to place everything in the hands of the super-competent Professor Sharpe in so short a time was very appealing. 'OK,' he said. 'Let's give it a go.'

As they crossed the strip of sand and flew out over the sea, Ben banked the *Silver Turtle* round towards the south.

Chapter Nineteen

'No clouds to hide above now,' said Ben, looking at the clear blue sky ahead. 'I'd better fly fairly low to make it harder for them to spot us from inland.' He was piloting the *Silver Turtle* on a southerly course, with the Suffolk coast to their right.

'At least we're still radar invisible,' said Sam, looking at the green light pulsing in the centre of the sardine tin, 'and Gabrielle never mentioned the radar-jamming device to Lady Clarissa.'

'We'd better keep a good lookout for Noctarma planes, like the one you thought you saw earlier, Zara,' said Marcia.

'Let's hope they don't guess which way we're heading,' said Zara. 'I'm hoping they'll think we've headed back home to Edinburgh, the way we came.'

They scanned the sky anxiously and spotted three other aircraft at different distant points in the sky, but they all looked like ordinary airliners.

'We'd better keep well away from ordinary planes too,' said Sam. 'If we're spotted visually by someone who can't see us on their radar, we'll have the authorities investigating us. If we're made to land and get arrested, Noctarma will find out about it.'

'You're right,' said Zara, 'but as long as we're careful, I think we've got quite a good chance of not being noticed by the authorities. There must be dozens of little planes flying over the Channel and the North Sea every day. And over France too. We probably don't stand out as much as we think we do.'

'Yeah,' said Ben. 'I think our biggest worry is getting lost before we find Lake Geneva at all.'

'How well do you know the way?' asked Sam.

'Well, I'm fine for the first bit,' said Ben, envisaging a map of south-east England in his head and matching it with their amazing aerial view. 'We need to go south across the mouth of the Thames Estuary, past the tip of Kent, which I reckon you can just see on the horizon, then down to Calais. But going the right way across France to hit Switzerland and Lake Geneva is going to be harder. There's no coastline to follow and I don't know the positions of any towns well enough to navigate by them. I'm pretty sure we have to go sort of south-eastish, but I don't know the exact bearing. I wish we had a map.'

'Hang on,' said Marcia. She reached into her jeans pocket and brought out her slim red diary. 'I'm sure this has got a map of the world in it somewhere,' she said, flipping through the back pages. 'I should've remembered sooner . . . Yes, here . . . Oh. It's very small scale.'

The world map was squeezed onto two narrow pages and the whole of Europe was only the size of a postage stamp. The map had no room to show country names, cities, lakes or any other information, but Marcia could spot France, which was about five millimetres across, and Switzerland, which was less than two millimetres. She held it up and Ben gave it a quick, close examination.

'It's a lot better than nothing,' he said, looking ahead again. 'At least it looks pretty accurate. If we pinpoint where Calais and Geneva are and draw a line between them, we might be able to guess the right compass course.'

'Calais is right at the top of France, isn't it?' said Marcia, as Sam passed her a pencil.

'Yep,' said Ben. 'Put a dot there. And Geneva's right at

that far western point of Switzerland, where it juts into France.'

Marcia drew the straightest line she could between the two points.

'Now draw a vertical line straight through Calais,' said Ben, 'to give us a north-to-south line. Whatever the angle is between the line going north from Calais and the line going to Geneva is our compass bearing.'

'Hmm,' said Marcia. 'It'll be easier to judge the angle if I draw a horizontal east-to-west line through Calais too.' She did so.  'Right, dead east from Calais would be a 90-degree bearing. Dead south would be 180 degrees. Our line's somewhere between the two, but slightly nearer to the 180-degree line. I'd say it's about 150 degrees, but it's really hard to judge, especially with this map being so tiny.'

'That's OK,' said Ben. 'We'll fly on a 150-degree bearing from Calais and maybe that'll take us close enough to spot Lake Geneva from the air. It's a big lake.' He wasn't at all sure it would be so easy, but nothing would be achieved by worrying himself or the others. 'What's the plan when we get there? Everyone's going to see us land. We're going to be in trouble for flying without a pilot's licence, entering Switzerland illegally and all sorts of stuff. We don't even have our passports.'

'Yeah, it won't take long for the Swiss police to come and question us,' said Marcia. 'What if Noctarma has agents in the Swiss police force?'

Zara shrugged. 'We won't be telling the Swiss police anything that we haven't already told Lady Clarissa,' she said. 'The important thing is to get hold of Professor Sharpe really fast so she can take action before any Noctarma agents catch up with us. We'd better land near Geneva, get ashore quick and find a phone box. But I don't have any money on me.'

'Nor me,' said Ben. 'We'd need Swiss francs anyway.'

'It's all right,' said Marcia, taking a slim purse from her jeans pocket. 'I've got my cash card and I'm sure I can use it in cash machines all over Europe.'

'Cool,' said Zara. 'Anything useful in *your* pockets, Sam?'

Sam emptied his big trouser pockets onto the seat, reporting the contents as he did so: 'Notebook, spare pencil, biro, eraser, my clock-compass-magnifying-glass, two rubber bands, my compact binoculars, a few coins but not very many, a key ring with a small torch on it, an old lolly stick, my Swiss Army knife . . . and half a packet of sweets. Anyone want some?'

Sharing the sweets, they zoomed onwards over the blue sea, their little silver plane gleaming in the bright sunshine. Soon, they were flying past the seaside towns and chalk cliffs of Kent, the coast of France looming into view on the horizon ahead; then they were hurtling across the Strait of Dover, overtaking the car ferries below, following the ships' course to lead them to Calais.

'Well, we've made it to France, at least,' said Zara, as they flew over Calais, leaving the sea behind.

'Yep,' said Ben, banking onto a 150-degree bearing. 'So far, so good.' Ben could feel his control of the plane becoming smoother and safer all the time; Amy really had designed a plane that a beginner could learn to fly in a few hours. The thought of landing by himself still scared him though, but he told himself not to worry about that for now.

The others had worries too: worries about being intercepted by Noctarma's aircraft, worries about not being able to get hold of Professor Sharpe after all and, most of all, worries about the plight of the adults. But all four children realized that there was no point in depressing one another by fretting out loud over things that were out of their control.

They flew over the French countryside, a vast sunny patchwork of fields, vineyards and woods crossed by roads, railways and rivers, interspersed with villages and towns. Ben avoided flying directly over any large towns, to lessen the chances of their unusual aircraft being reported, but otherwise he stuck firmly to their estimated bearing. He looked at the land stretching away to the horizon in every direction. This was indeed very different from flying with a coastline to guide him, and Ben hated not really knowing where he was or where he was going. Was it completely crazy to think they could find their way without any knowledge of the landmarks and no proper map?

It had become very hot in the cabin, so they flew with the canopy slid back a little bit. For the first hour or so, the countryside below was fairly flat. Then, the landscape began to rise in rolling hills. Ben gained altitude and their view became longer and wider.

'Look,' said Zara, after a while. She was pointing to the horizon, slightly to the left of the way they were heading. 'Mountains.'

Sam had a look through his binoculars at the distant row of green-grey ridges with even more distant blue-grey and white peaks just visible beyond. 'They're pretty big,' he said. 'Some of them have got snow on the top. D'you reckon they're the Jura mountains that Gabrielle said she was flying past?'

'I reckon the really big ones must be the Alps,' said Ben. 'I think the Jura mountains are the lower ones slightly nearer to us. And I'm *almost* sure that Lake Geneva lies somewhere between the two.'

'My parents took me to the French Alps once, to go skiing,' said Marcia. 'The Alps stretch across several countries, don't they?'

'Yeah,' said Ben. 'If we've got our course vaguely right, I think at least some of the mountains we can see must be in Switzerland. I'll steer a bit towards them and see what we can see when we get closer.' He veered a few degrees eastward.

The mountains were a long way ahead, but the fact that they were reasonably sure they could now see the country they were heading for made Ben feel considerably more confident, and lifted everyone's spirits greatly.

After a while, the landscape below became a rugged terrain of rocky crags, grassy hill plains, pine forests, river gorges and waterfalls. The *Silver Turtle* zoomed over farms and little villages, flying higher and higher as the hills became more mountainous. Ben piloted them towards the very highest ridges of grey rock and scrubby vegetation, which he hoped were the top of the Jura range. The snow-capped Alps beyond looked pretty close now.

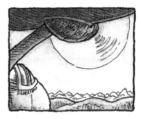

'Let's hope we're nearly there,' said Ben, anxiously. A warning light marked ENERGY LOW had been flashing on the instrument panel for a few minutes, and the needle on the energy-cell gauge was getting pretty close to zero. He wondered if they'd crossed the border into Switzerland yet. They flew over ridge after ridge, and Sam scanned the valleys to either side with his binoculars. He could see several lakes but these were relatively small. He knew they were looking for something much bigger. Ben's worries about the impossibility of finding their way returned. They might be miles off course, nowhere near their intended destination. The others began to silently worry the same thing.

Then the *Silver Turtle* cleared the broad top of a massive mountain ridge and everyone's heart leapt at what they saw beyond. The mountainside sloped steeply down to a wide strip of fields, woodland and villages, beyond which lay a huge lake, directly across their flight-path. The binoculars were completely unnecessary; the lake was several miles across, and stretched away for many more miles to either side. It had to be Lake Geneva.

Chapter Twenty

Everyone whooped, and Sam, Zara and Marcia patted Ben on the back. Ben reduced their speed, causing the *Silver Turtle* to descend towards the lake.

'Better put our seat belts on,' said Marcia, clipping Ben's on for him so he could keep his hands on the controls.

'Is that Geneva?' asked Sam, pointing left to a small city on the lake's northern shore.

'I'm not sure,' said Ben. 'I *thought* Geneva was at the western end of the lake.'

They all looked down the lake, which actually curved round to the south-west as it narrowed. At the lake's end, beyond several towns and villages that fringed the shore, they could just make out another city. Sam peered at it through his binoculars. 'I can see a tall thin white thing,' he said. 'I think it's a huge fountain, shooting straight up from the lake.'

'That's the Jet d'Eau!' said Marcia. 'Remember, it was on Adam and Professor Sharpe's postcard. It's right beside Geneva.'

'Good,' said Ben, banking the plane round. 'I'll land as near to the city as I can. The sooner we get hold of Professor Sharpe, the better.'

They flew along the lake, losing speed and altitude all the while. The Jet d'Eau was soon easily visible without binoculars, an unbelievably high column of white water, feathering out to one side near the top. It looked taller and taller as they flew lower and nearer.

There were many boats on the lake, but Ben spotted a

stretch of water that looked clear. He concentrated hard. Motors slower . . . flaps down . . . 'I'm sure Amy once talked about some special knack for landing a flying boat on water,' he said.

'Something about letting the rear end of the hull touch the water before the front, so the impact doesn't make you somersault over,' said Sam.

'Well remembered,' said Ben, quickly bringing the nose up a bit more. They were almost down and the surface of the lake seemed to rise up to meet them. Bluey-green water flashing by, very fast. Faster than their landing on the lawn, surely.

WHACK! The plane slapped onto the lake, ricocheted clear, then slammed down again and went bouncing along the surface like a skimming stone. *SLAP . . . SLAP . . . SLAP!* Ben gripped the control column, ignoring the violent thrashing of his head, ignoring the painful jolting of his body against his seat belt, ignoring the spray crashing up over the canopy. Keep control . . . keep her straight . . . 'Motors off!' he yelled and Marcia flicked the switches. The plane slowed and the bouncing stopped. The cascades of spray became a churning bow wave, then a burbling ripple as the *Silver Turtle* glided to a standstill at last.

'Sorry about that,' said Ben.

'Sorry about what?' said Sam, his white-knuckled fingers releasing their grip on the back of Ben's seat. 'You got us down in one piece.'

'Brilliant landing,' agreed Marcia.

'Yeah, well done, Ben!' said Zara.

The water ran down off the Plexiglas canopy, and they sat in silence for a few seconds, breathing in the distinctive damp smell of lake water and taking in their surroundings. The nearest shore of the lake lay just a few hundred metres to their left, fringed by yacht marinas and little beaches, with trees, a road and a big park behind. The Jet d'Eau, shooting up from the end of a long stone jetty, was less than half a mile ahead of them, with Geneva's handsome city centre just beyond.

They were all struck by the heat. Sam and Zara slid the middle of the canopy fully back, but it made little difference. There was no wind at all and the air was heavy and humid. The surface of the lake was smooth and the late afternoon sunlight had a hazy quality.

Zara glanced at her watch. 'It's only half-past four,' she said. 'It's hard to believe that it's less than six hours since we were sitting on the slipway outside Amy's hangar, isn't it?'

'Yeah,' agreed Ben. 'Mind, it's half-past five here, with the time zone change.' They all adjusted their watches.

'Right, let's get to the shore quick,' said Zara. 'I think we should taxi over to that bit where it's less busy.' She pointed to a section of lakeside past the end of the nearest beach, where there were no people.

Ben lowered the small water rudder beneath the rear of the plane, and also the wing-tip stabilizer floats. Then he switched the motors back on and taxied towards the shore at low power.

FLIGHT PATH FROM PETTICRAIG BAY TO LAKE GENEVA

Edinburgh

Mantlingham Manor

Dover

Calais

Geneva

The beach was busy with people, most of whom were now staring at the plane, and some of whom were waving. A sudden toot made the children turn round. A white river steamer was cruising up the centre of the lake and her passengers were also waving at them. Clearly, a flying boat landing on Lake Geneva was an unusual event.

'Smile and wave back,' said Marcia, starting to do so herself. 'They probably won't be able to see how young Ben is from that distance, and if we act like we've got permission to land here, maybe everyone will assume we have.'

'Everyone will see that none of us are adults if we all go ashore though,' said Zara. 'Maybe just you and Sam should go, Marcia, while Ben and I taxi back out onto the lake. Then, by the time the police get a boat out to investigate us, you might have already found a cash machine and a phone box and got hold of Professor Sharpe.'

'Good idea,' said Marcia.

'Yeah,' said Sam, 'and it means we don't have to leave the plane unattended.' Something else occurred to him and he crawled forward to the instrument panel. 'I think we should hide the radar-jamming device before the police start examining the plane,' he said, untaping and unplugging the adapted sardine tin. 'I got the impression Gabrielle would want us to keep it secret, if possible, didn't you?'

'Yeah,' agreed Zara. 'She was very secretive about everything to do with that friend of hers. We'll give it back to her if we get her rescued. I mean *when* we get her rescued.'

As Sam carefully slid the device into a trouser pocket, he wondered once again how it worked. He'd have to have a good look at it later.

They approached the shore. 'Don't run aground, Ben,' said Marcia, looking down through the clear water to the shingly bottom. 'It's almost shallow enough for us to wade from here.'

Ben cut the motors, swerved the *Silver Turtle* gently round and let her drift to a halt with her side a few metres from the water's edge. Sam and Marcia, barefoot with their jeans rolled up, clambered out and started to wade ashore through the refreshingly cool water, holding on to their trainers and socks.

'Good luck,' said Zara, as Ben began to taxi out again. A light marked EMPTY was now flashing above the energy-cell gauge, but there seemed to be just enough power left to get them back out onto the lake.

Sam and Marcia scrambled up onto the wide lakeside path and hurriedly pulled their footwear back on. A main road ran parallel to the path, behind which lay a big park with very few buildings. 'I think we'll need to head into the centre a bit to find a cash machine,' said Marcia.

As they jogged along the path, they got a few curious looks from people who must have seen them disembark, but no one questioned them. They soon passed the end of the park and crossed the main road to head away from the lake into a smart urban area. Within fifteen minutes they had found a cash machine, withdrawn twenty Swiss francs, obtained some change by buying a bottle of juice, and located a public phone box.

Marcia had three numbers for Professor Sharpe in her diary: home, work and mobile. Knowing Professor Sharpe spent a lot of time looking after Adam these days, Marcia tried the home number first.

'Professor Sharpe speaking,' said a familiar crisp voice, after two rings.

Marcia felt a surge of relief. 'Professor Sharpe, it's Marcia,' she said. 'We're in Geneva. We flew here in the flying boat.' She had mentioned the flying boat project in her last e-mail to Adam.

'Goodness, what a nice surprise,' said Professor Sharpe. 'I didn't know your plane was ready to fly. Are you at the airport?'

'No, Ben landed it on the lake,' said Marcia. 'We –'

'*Ben* landed it!?' echoed Professor Sharpe. 'Amy let *Ben* land it?'

'Amy's not with us,' said Marcia, beginning to gabble. 'All the adults got arrested by armed police who are working for a secret criminal organization and they nearly got us too and so we flew here by ourselves. We need your help.'

'Marcia, where are you now, exactly?' said Professor Sharpe, after the briefest of stunned silences.

'I'm in a phone box with Sam, near . . .' she tried to remember the name of the big road they had crossed from the lake . . . 'near the Quai Gustave something. The plane's on the lake, a little way past the Jet d'Eau.'

'Go back and wait at the edge of the lake, near the plane,' said Professor Sharpe. 'We'll be with you in five minutes.'

Soon, Marcia and Sam were crossing the main road to the lakeside path, able to see the *Silver Turtle* again, lying in her previous position a few hundred metres out on the lake. They were also able to see a motorboat approaching the plane. The word POLICE was clearly visible on the side of its hull.

'Let's hope Professor Sharpe gets here soon,' said Marcia, looking back along the road as they ran along the path, longing to see her pulling up in a car.

By the time they reached the place where they had come ashore, the police boat had stopped alongside the *Silver Turtle*, and a single police officer could be seen standing up, talking to Zara and Ben. Sam started to get his binoculars out while Marcia looked anxiously up the road again. Then they both saw another motorboat speeding into view from the direction of the city centre, past the Jet d'Eau and straight towards them. As it drew nearer, they could see a dark-haired boy waving his hand above the open boat's windscreen. 'Marcia! Sam!' he yelled.

'It's Adam!' exclaimed Marcia. 'Gosh, he's really grown!'

'And Professor Sharpe driving,' said Sam.

Professor Sharpe, a petite, grey-haired woman in her early sixties, wearing sunglasses, pulled up beside them, keeping the engine gurgling in neutral. In the back of the boat sat three men, also in their sixties: a lean, bony man wearing a wide-brimmed leather hat; a pear-shaped man in a crumpled cream suit and panama hat, sporting a polka-dotted red bow tie; and a small man with round spectacles and a rather unsuccessful beard. Sam and Marcia knew them well – Professor Eric Gauntraker, Professor Garrulous Gadling and Professor Bob Pottle.

Chapter Twenty-One

'Hop aboard, shipmates!' boomed Professor Gadling, helping Marcia and Sam into the boat. 'Terrific to see you again. As you can see, we're back from our Alpine tumbling snail expedition a little sooner than planned. Righty-ho, Ivy. Anchors away!'

Professor Sharpe sped the boat out towards the *Silver Turtle* and the police vessel.

'From what you told Ivy on the phone, Alexander and Petunia's situation sounds extremely grave,' said Professor Gauntraker. 'You'd better tell us the whole thing.'

'It would be simpler to explain everything to us and to that gendarme at the same time,' suggested Professor Sharpe to Marcia and Sam.

'Yeah,' agreed Marcia. 'Though our big worry is that the gendarme could be an agent for Noctarma, the criminal organization I told you about; you'll see why when we've told you what's been going on.'

'Hmm,' said Professor Sharpe. 'It's going to be difficult not to tell the police anything, given you've just landed a plane on the lake without any licences or any authorization, but I can see you don't want to risk giving these criminals any information.'

'Actually they already know everything we've got to tell anyway,' said Sam. 'The real danger is that he might arrest us and have us handed over to Noctarma.'

'If he goes for his gun, I'll be on him in a flash,' said Professor Gauntraker.

'We certainly won't let him take you into custody,'

promised Professor Sharpe, 'and if I get the impression we can't trust him, I'll get us away as quickly as possible, so we can contact someone we *can* trust.'

'Thanks,' said Marcia. 'Zara was dead right to say we should come to you. You were really quick getting to us. I'd forgotten you had a boat.'

'We keep it at the city marina,' said Adam. 'And our flat's near there.' He turned round to face Sam and Marcia, and smiled. 'It's great you made it all the way here. I'm sure that Mum will be able to sort everything out.'

Adam was an unusual child, with an even more disturbing background than Marcia's. His extraordinary genetic make-up gave him advanced mental powers and physical abilities, and also caused him to mature at an accelerated rate. He looked about nine. When Sam and Marcia had first met him a few months before, he had looked about seven. And they both knew he was actually very much younger than that.

His appearance had changed in other ways too, noticed Marcia. His face looked less solemn, his features softer, his smile more natural, his skin less deadly pale. Some people had been surprised when Professor Sharpe had offered to adopt Adam; she could come across as a rather stern person. But what Professor Sharpe lacked in easy charm, she made up for in total reliability, and kindness too. She knew what it was like to be an academically gifted child and had taken great care to ensure that Adam never felt as lonely as she once had. Adam was able to attend an international school in Geneva for the children of UN employees where, in the multicultural mix, he didn't feel any more of an outsider than anyone else, and where awkward questions about his background were rarely asked. And Marcia knew from Adam's e-mails that he and

Professor Sharpe had a lot of fun together. Now that Marcia looked, Professor Sharpe's features seemed somehow softer too.

They neared the *Silver Turtle* and the police boat. Ben was the first to notice Professor Sharpe's boat approaching and Sam could see him telling the gendarme and pointing.

'Remarkable plane,' said Professor Pottle approvingly. 'Reminds me a bit of that manure-powered flying machine I once built.'

'Except that yours never flew,' muttered Professor Gauntraker rather unkindly.

'Ssh, you two!' said Professor Sharpe, as she cut her engine and drifted alongside the police boat. 'Bonjour, monsieur,' she hailed the gendarme.

'Good afternoon,' he replied in English, with a slight French accent. 'I am Lieutenant Doltaine of the Gendarmerie Genève, Police Boat Division. Are you Professor Sharpe? I am trying to establish where this aircraft has come from and whether it has permission to land on the lake. These children have insisted that we wait for you to come before they explain anything.'

'Well, I'm here now,' said Professor Sharpe, showing him her passport and her UN staff pass, 'and I'm as eager to hear what they have to say as you are. You can take it from me, officer, that these are extremely trustworthy young people and that what they have to tell us will be the truth.'

Doltaine shrugged. 'OK,' he said. 'You had better tie your boat and this plane to my boat and come aboard.'

Within a few minutes they were all seated in the police boat's semi-enclosed driving cabin. As quickly as they could, Zara, Ben, Marcia and Sam recounted everything that had happened.

'I find this all very difficult to believe,' said Doltaine,

when they had finished. 'You are asking me to accept that you flew this plane all the way from England by yourselves?' He looked down at the notes he'd made while they'd been talking. 'And you are really claiming that a section of the British police force is being controlled by a criminal organization that no one has ever heard of?'

'The reason hardly anyone's heard of them is because they're secret!' said Zara. 'That's why they're so powerful and dangerous. Gabrielle said –'

'Ah, yes, this mysterious Gabrielle,' interrupted Doltaine. 'She sounds dangerously unstable. People who abduct children often tell their victims that they are protecting them. Perhaps her mind was not quite in the real world, hm? . . . Fantasizing about wartime love affairs and secret inventions . . .'

'She wasn't senile and she wasn't abducting us!' cried Ben. 'And she wasn't fantasizing. We told you – she's with Maskil Stribnik in the old photo we found. The ciphered message on the back was written to her.'

'Show me this photo,' demanded Doltaine.

'We can't,' said Zara. 'Lady Clarissa took it and gave it to her son, the leader of Noctarma.'

Doltaine rolled his eyes wearily, in a way that made it clear he doubted the photo even existed.

'Officer, I can assure you that these children should be taken seriously,' said Professor Sharpe. 'The lives of four adults are in danger. We must contact Interpol immediately.'

'And we must find that Anson wreck before Noctarma does,' added Zara.

'We can easily establish that this crashed aircraft is part of an old woman's fantasy,' said Doltaine. He turned to a computer screen built into his boat's dashboard and brought up a page headed: *Épaves*. 'This database contains details of every wreck in the lake,' he said. He typed the word 'Anson' into a search box and clicked on the button next to it.

After a few seconds, a map of Lake Geneva came up on the screen, with a red dot nearly halfway along from Geneva, near the southern shore (which, the children noticed, was actually part of France). Beside the dot was a line of text:

Avro Anson, 1945, avion militaire, 33 mètres.

'That's it!' exclaimed Sam. 'Now do you believe us?'

'Hmm. It seems the account of the Anson crash may be true,' conceded Doltaine, clearly surprised. 'But I am still not convinced by the rest of your story. I will return to my office and make further enquiries to ascertain whether this Noctarma organization actually exists.' He turned to Professor Sharpe. 'If you give me your address and phone number, you are all free to leave. I will tow the plane to my police boat station for now.'

The children started to protest, but Professor Sharpe stood up, politely but tersely thanked Doltaine for his assistance, gave him her contact details, and began to bustle everyone into her boat. Soon they were motoring towards the city marina. The children forlornly watched the police boat towing their beautiful plane towards the opposite shore.

'Don't worry,' said Professor Sharpe. 'You'll get the plane back soon enough. At least it'll be safe at his police boat station.'

'So you don't think he's working for Noctarma?' asked Sam.

'I didn't get the feeling he was,' said Professor Sharpe. 'He wouldn't have shown us the Anson wreck on his computer, nor let us go. But I *did* get the feeling he was completely useless, and we were wasting valuable time there; I need to phone someone we can trust to deal with this properly.' She put her hand into her jacket pocket, then frowned. 'Oh bother! I was in so much hurry after you called, I left my mobile behind at the flat, in my work jacket. I'll need to go back and make the call from there.'

'Who are you going to phone?' asked Ben.

'I'm going to call Chief Commissioner Grayloch, head of the Edinburgh City Police,' said Professor Sharpe. 'I've known him for years – from when I used to live in Edinburgh – and I'm certain he wouldn't be involved with any of Sir Roland Mantlingham's secret activities. I'll make sure he gets this sorted out with the utmost urgency. He's got the clout to be able to take on the Secret Operations Police Unit and locate this Edinburgh HQ of theirs where they're holding Alexander, Petunia and Amy. And I'm sure he'll know people in the Suffolk Constabulary whom he can trust to get Gabrielle released from Mantlingham Manor. And he'll be able to contact Interpol, the international police agency, to put out an arrest warrant for Sir Roland and his mother. I'm not saying it will be easy – it could take a long time to get to grips with a powerful international organization like Noctarma – but Grayloch's a good man and I'm sure he'll at least be able to get the four prisoners freed before too long.'

'Hmm, that sounds promising,' said Professor Gauntraker, 'but what if this Chief Commissioner Grayloch's not on duty and you can't get hold of him?'

'I've got his home number too,' said Professor Sharpe. 'His flat's in Duggan's Close, very close to his headquarters, so it won't take him long to get on the case. And if I can't get hold of him, there are other people I can ring.'

The children felt somewhat reassured; they had heard Professor Sharpe on the phone before, and didn't doubt her ability to make people get things sorted out with the utmost urgency. Zara's plan to come here and find Professor Sharpe was proving to be a good one. But they all knew their anxiety wouldn't really leave them until Uncle Alexander and the others had actually been released safe and well.

And Zara hadn't forgotten their other urgent priority. 'We still need to find the Anson wreck and recover Solomon before Noctarma beats us to it,' she said. 'If they get hold of Solomon, they'll discover where to find the anti-gravity invention, and we told you what Sir Roland said: once they've got Maskil's invention, they'll kill Uncle Alexander and Professor Hartleigh-Broadbeam and Amy and Gabrielle. Then anything Chief Commissioner Grayloch or Interpol can do will be too late.'

'Zara's right,' said Professor Gauntraker. 'We need to steal a march on the enemy. I wish that confounded gendarme had given us a longer look at his computer map, so I could remember the Anson wreck's exact position.'

'I can remember the exact position,' said Adam. 'I thought that map might be important, so I told my brain to keep it like a photograph in my head.'

'Wow!' said Sam. Adam was such a pleasant, unassuming boy that it was easy to forget how extraordinary his brain was.

'Well done, Adam,' said Professor Sharpe, ruffling her son's hair. 'That's going to be really useful.'

'Absolutely!' agreed Professor Gadling. 'It's a pity I don't have my scuba diving gear with me, or I could have a crack at getting down to the Anson wreck this evening.'

'Mum's environmental biology department has a boat at the marina,' said Adam, 'and I'm sure they keep diving equipment on board. Mum doesn't dive but she uses the boat for other research trips on the lake sometimes. I'm sure you've got a key, haven't you, Mum?'

'Well, yes,' said Professor Sharpe, 'but I think this needs planning properly.'

'We're planning it now,' said Professor Gadling. 'I think the map text said the Anson was only thirty-three metres down – easily diveable. The plane must have crashed quite near the lake's edge, which is lucky, considering the middle of the lake gets to three hundred metres in the deepest part – way beyond what's possible with ordinary scuba gear.'

'But it's not safe to dive alone, is it?' said Professor Sharpe, still looking doubtful at the whole idea. 'I'm sure my colleagues always dive in pairs, so they can keep an eye out for each other.'

'*I* learnt to scuba dive last summer,' said Marcia. Her parents had taken her on holiday to the Maldives and, as usual, had wanted to spend the whole time lounging around their exclusive hotel's pool, while constantly criticizing Marcia for her supposed shortcomings. So she had gone off by herself and had found a scuba-diving school running from the beach, with old, scruffy equipment and few checks on age or parental permission. The fact that her parents would have gone ballistic if they'd known about it had somehow added to the pleasure of escaping into the tranquil undersea world each afternoon.

'Now we're cooking!' exclaimed Professor Gadling, clapping his hands together. 'There's nothing stopping us. Come on, Ivy; let us take your department's boat out right now, whilst you're back at your flat phoning this Chief Commissioner Grayloch fellow. It could take you a while to get through to him and there's no point in the rest of us simply standing around when we could be doing something to save the lives of the prisoners too.'

'I agree,' said Professor Gauntraker. 'And we need to leave now anyway, if we're to have any chance of finding the wreck and putting down divers whilst it's still light. The sun will be setting around nine and it's already half-past six.'

Professor Sharpe considered the matter as she steered her boat round the base of the Jet d'Eau and into the city marina. 'Very well,' she said. She parked next to a medium-sized motor cruiser, whose bows carried the name *Bernoulli*, and detached a key from the bunch on her key ring. 'I'll give you a quick rundown of how everything on board works and you can get going straight away,' she said. 'But for goodness' sake, don't take any risks. If there are any other boats moored near the wreck site – anything to suggest that Noctarma agents are already in the vicinity – stay clear.'

Inside the enclosed cabin of a sleek black speedboat, parked on the other side of the marina, a blond-haired man looked out through its tinted windscreen with a pair of binoculars. 'She's showing them over that motor cruiser,' he muttered to a petite woman with short dark hair who sat next to him. 'Who *is* she? Who are the three men and the boy?'

'Clearly the brats know people here,' said the dark-haired woman. 'Now, ssh. Lieutenant Doltaine is radioing his head office from his boat.' She had a set of headphones on her ears, and sat frowning with concentration. 'The woman is a Professor Ivy Sharpe, apparently,' she reported after some moments. 'She lives here in Geneva, and does indeed know the children. Two of them phoned her when they landed.'

'And the children have told Doltaine everything?' asked the blond man.

'They must have done,' said the woman. 'But fortunately, it seems Doltaine was wholly unconvinced by the children's account, in spite of Professor Sharpe vouching for them, and he hasn't bothered to pass on any details to his superiors. He merely told his head office that the children had given him an unlikely-sounding story about criminal organizations and secret inventions, and relayed nothing they'd told him about the events of this morning, nothing about Noctarma and Sir Roland, and nothing about the Silver Turtle project and the Anson wreck.'

'Thank God for that,' said the blond man.

'Now Doltaine is towing their plane across to his boat station, to conduct further enquiries,' said the woman. 'He told his superiors he'll report on his findings later. That gives us some time.'

'Look – Sharpe's leaving the others,' said the blond man, pointing as Professor Sharpe stepped down from the motor cruiser, left the marina and started walking along the lake-side path. 'Looks like she's heading into the city.'

The dark-haired woman stared hard at the retreating figure of Professor Sharpe, pondering for a couple of seconds. 'Quick,' she said, taking a compact digital camera from her pocket. 'Drive along the lakeside and drop me off ahead of her. I can see a way to resolve this situation in our favour but we must act fast. Do you have your passport and pilot's licence on you?'

'Yes,' said the man, starting the speedboat engine and setting off. 'But, look, the others have started up the motor cruiser. What if they're going out to look for the Anson?'

The woman pressed a button on the camera causing its round lens section to telescope out from the front with a soft whir. 'Arrange for Ivan and his men to tail the motor cruiser at a safe distance, and to keep us informed,' she said. 'If these people have discovered the Anson wreck's location, they will save us a great deal of work.'

Chapter Twenty-Two

Professor Sharpe walked briskly along the lakeside path in her sensible flat-heeled shoes. A young dark-haired woman, who had stopped to take a photograph of the lake, stood aside to let her pass. There were many other people about, but none close enough to see the pin-sized dart fly from the camera's lens hole and land in Professor Sharpe's neck, none close enough to see Professor Sharpe's face contort for an instant with pain and surprise, then suddenly sag, dazed and expressionless. All anyone saw, if they were happening to look that way at all, was the young woman smile, clasp Professor Sharpe's arm as if she had recognized an old friend, then walk with her, arm-in-arm, to a black speedboat parked next to them, steadying her as its driver helped them aboard, down through the opened front section of the low, tinted-glass cabin.

The dark-haired woman manoeuvred Professor Sharpe onto one of the back seats as the blond man pressed a button to slide the canopy shut. He sped the boat away from the lakeside, while the woman took a small aerosol canister from her handbag and sprayed it into Professor Sharpe's nose and mouth.

Almost instantly, life returned to Professor Sharpe's face. 'Take me back at once!' she snapped angrily, struggling to rise from her seat. 'This is an outrage!'

'Take me back at once!' parroted the woman in a perfect imitation of Professor Sharpe's voice. 'This is an outrage! Thank you,' she added. 'It is so important to get the voice right.' She fired two more darts from her camera into her prisoner's neck, and Professor Sharpe flopped back on the seat, now completely unconscious.

Quickly and efficiently, the woman removed Professor Sharpe's fawn trouser suit and changed into it herself. Next, she flicked a switch which opened up a secret compartment in the other back seat, a compartment which contained sticks of make-up, racks of differently shaped spectacles, a clear plastic tub of false-nose putty, and a dozen wigs, neatly arranged by colour and style. She turned back to Professor Sharpe, taking her sunglasses and studying her captive's face and hair for several moments, before reaching into the compartment for what she needed.

The *Bernoulli* ploughed along the lake in the amber evening sunlight. Professor Gauntraker was at the wheel, with Professor Pottle, Sam and Zara standing beside him at the front of the enclosed cabin.  Adam and Ben sat behind, studying a detailed chart of the lake, which they had taken from the boat's map drawer and laid flat on a table. Professor Gadling and Marcia were down below, checking out the diving gear. The children were munching biscuits and peanuts, which Professor Sharpe had said they could take from supplies in the small galley downstairs.

'That's the position marked on the gendarme's computer map,' said Adam, pencilling a cross on the chart, 'but we don't know how precise that was.'

'Professor Sharpe said we should be able to spot the wreck with this sonar imaging device once we're in the right area,' said Sam, switching on a machine on the dashboard. Its screen flickered on, showing the lake's floor passing beneath them. The grey picture, Sam knew, was digitally generated from reflected sound waves, yet it showed every contour of rock, mud and shingle as if they were seeing it for real.

Zara had borrowed Sam's binoculars. Looking across the lake, she could just see the *Silver Turtle*, still being towed towards the furthest shore. She turned to look out of the front windscreen instead, putting her anger at that stupid gendarme out of her head. They hadn't expected the police to believe them, anyway. Things were working out as they'd hoped. They were on their way to retrieve Solomon from the Anson, and Professor Sharpe would be at her flat already, firing off instructions to Chief Commissioner Grayloch, Zara told herself. Her great-uncle and the others would soon be free.

Lieutenant Doltaine stood glaring at the small silver flying boat, which he had just tied up next to his boat. It was an odd-looking plane, and its oddness irritated him. He looked at his watch. Six fifty-five. He *had* been hoping to get home in time to watch the football. Now he would have to spend hours making complicated telephone enquiries, trying to get to the bottom of the unlikely-sounding story those British children had told him. Sweating in the hot, humid air, and feeling a headache coming on, he plodded along the wooden decking to the boat station's tiny office. Before he reached it, a sleek black speedboat zoomed into the police marina and pulled up beside him. The front section of the tinted canopy slid back and a woman with short grey hair, wearing a fawn suit and sunglasses stepped out. That annoying English woman! Back to try and tell him how to do his job again, no doubt.

'Professor, I promised I would make enquiries into the children's story,' he began. 'There is no need for you to —'

But the woman interrupted him. 'I'm most terribly sorry, officer,' she said, 'I've been a complete idiot, letting those naughty children fool me like that. This is Maximilian de Lamprey,' she added, introducing a handsome blond man in a brown leather jacket, as he stepped out of the speedboat behind her.

'Delighted to meet you,' said the blond man in French, shaking Doltaine's hand. 'I am the owner and pilot of this plane. It was I who landed her on the lake this afternoon. All authorized with air traffic control of course. Here's my ID.' He produced his passport and pilot's licence. 'The four children you met were my passengers — part of a summer project for disadvantaged kids from the UK that the de Lamprey Foundation is running near Interlaken. After I landed, I quickly went ashore to register our plane's arrival with the harbourmaster, foolishly trusting the children to stay with the plane. They thought it would be a great prank for two of them to run off and phone up Professor Sharpe, the only person they knew in Geneva, and spin her a ridiculous yarn about flying the plane here themselves from England and about criminal organizations and secret inventions and lord knows what else. I believe they even dragged in the story of a wartime aircraft wreck that I'd happened to mention to them when we flew over the lake.'

'I can't believe I fell for it!' cried the woman. 'Of course, officer, you had more sense than to believe them, and after you towed the plane away, the little hooligans broke down and confessed.'

'I really am most terribly sorry that you've been put to so much trouble, lieutenant,' said Maximilian. 'Your cool-

131

headedness has been commendable. I'll mention it to your senior officer.'

'It's been no trouble at all, sir,' said Doltaine, feeling his headache lifting. He had heard of Maximilian de Lamprey, of course – a very private man, but one of Switzerland's wealthiest bankers, highly respected for his Foundation's charitable good works. He owned several homes in Switzerland, including a small castle up at the eastern end of this lake. 'Your plane's quite in order, sir,' he said, leading him to the *Silver Turtle*.

'Thank you,' said Maximilian, giving the gendarme a warm smile and another firm handshake, before tying the plane to the back of the speedboat.

Doltaine watched Maximilian and the woman head off up the lake in the speedboat, towing the aircraft behind them. He found the pages of notes he had taken from the children earlier, tore them from his notepad and screwed them up. He would be home in time to watch the football after all.

Inside the speedboat, Maximilian turned to the woman. 'Even a gendarme as stupid as Doltaine will begin to doubt my story eventually,' he said. 'Especially when the real Professor Sharpe is reported missing.' He glanced back at the motionless rug-covered heap on the floor by the back seat. 'Then he will begin to believe what the children told him about us: the identity of our Leader, the location of our UK headquarters . . . And he will realize that *I* am connected. He will –'

'Stop fretting, Max,' said the woman, looking unconcerned. 'I have the feeling that our brave Deputy Boat Lieutenant will meet with a little accident tomorrow. Nothing suspicious, but something fatal. And I'll make sure that any records of the radio reports he made to his head office also disappear.'

'You think of everything, Lucrezia,' said Maximilian admiringly.

Chapter Twenty-Three

'How do we look?' asked Professor Gadling. He and Marcia had changed into two blue wetsuits, and were now standing in the cabin, trying on their hoods, masks and gloves. On their feet were what Marcia had been taught to call fins, but what Professor Gadling insisted on calling flippers. With his large beaky nose and double chin, Professor Gadling had always reminded Sam of a pelican, and the flippers on his feet now completed the effect. Even so, the diving gear gave him an air of earnest determination, and Marcia looked positively glamorous.

'Pretty cool,' said Sam.

Marcia felt anything but cool, in either sense of the word. She was sweltering in the wetsuit and feeling more than a little nervous about the dive. Her week of scuba training felt like a long time ago and thirty-three metres was deeper than she had dived back then. She took a step forward and found herself tripping over her own extended feet.

'Better put the flippers with the rest of the gear on the deck for now,' said Professor Gadling. 'We'll get kitted up once we've spotted the wreck.'

They had just passed the point where the lake curved sharply, putting Geneva out of sight behind.

'We're coming into the area shown on that computer map now,' said Adam. 'The Anson should be beneath us somewhere nearby.'

'Right you are, lad,' said Professor Gauntraker, slowing the *Bernoulli* down to her lowest speed. 'No other boats in the vicinity,' he observed. 'Looks like we've definitely got one ahead of Noctarma.'

The *Bernoulli* slowly criss-crossed the area, while they all peered intently at the sonar screen. When they drove within two kilometres or so of the shore, the screen showed that they were over a natural rock shelf that sloped gently down from the land to a depth of around thirty-five metres, before plummeting steeply to the deepest part of the lake. They focused their search on the rock shelf, but after forty-five minutes had seen nothing remotely plane-shaped on the screen. Zara looked at her watch. It was already quarter-past eight. The sun would set in less than an hour and then, even if they found the Anson, it would be too dark to dive safely.

Professor Pottle examined the sonar imaging device more closely. 'You know, I'm sure I could improve the efficiency of this gadget,' he said. 'If I just − erm − took the back off and adjusted the −'

'Don't you *dare* start meddling with it!' growled Professor Gauntraker. 'It's working perfectly well and we want it to stay that way.' He turned to the children. 'You should have seen what he did to my camping stove on our expedition earlier this week.'

'My concept for making it run on goat dung was perfectly sound,' protested Professor Pottle. 'Rich in methane, which is a well-known source of combustible energy.'

'So combustible it blew the tent up,' recalled Professor Gauntraker. 'And all our food supplies. We were forced to eat raw grasshoppers and caterpillars. Fortunately, I once learnt how to survive on such things whilst living with the Xafilah people of Outer Mongolia.'

'You didn't *have* to eat grasshoppers and caterpillars, Eric,' pointed out Professor Gadling. 'There was a perfectly good café half a mile down the road. But the loss of all my scientific equipment did rather cut short our search for the Alpine tumbling snail.'

'What cut short our search for the Alpine tumbling snail,' said Professor Pottle huffily, 'is the fact that it doesn't exist, like most of the creatures you claim to be an expert on.'

'The fact that certain species have yet to be officially verified by the scientific establishment,' said Professor Gadling, 'doesn't mean that they don't exist. The Alpine tumbling snail is one of the most remarkable animals in the world. Protected within its incredibly hard shell, it can roll down mountains with the speed of a stooping falcon, ricocheting from precipice to precipice with the controlled agility of an ibex, before emerging from its shell mid-bounce to stick onto a section of rock, always within centimetres of a sprig of the rare European snow fern, its only food source. How it detects specimens of this plant whilst travelling at such high speeds is one of the great mysteries of science.'

'The only great mystery, Garrulous,' said Professor Gauntraker, 'is how you persuaded us to believe such rubbish and to accompany you on such a pointless expedition.'

'*Pointless?*' cried Professor Gadling. 'You're a *fine* one to talk about pointless expeditions, Eric. You –'

'THERE!' exclaimed Adam suddenly. He was pointing to a corner of the sonar screen, where an angular shape could just be made out, near the edge of the rock shelf. Sam worked the zoom controls until the shape filled the screen. Though buckled, broken and incomplete, the shape was unmistakably that of an aeroplane.

Chapter Twenty-Four

'Well spotted, lad!' said Professor Gauntraker.

'Stand by to heave to, m'hearties!' cried Professor Gadling.

The professors' squabble was forgotten as quickly as it had flared up, as everyone worked together. Ben and Adam logged the wreck's exact position and Professor Gauntraker manoeuvred the *Bernoulli* directly over it. Professor Pottle helped Sam and Zara to lower the anchor while Professor Gadling and Marcia got themselves kitted up with the rest of their diving equipment.

Over their wetsuits, the two divers each put on a buoyancy-control jacket, with a bulky cylinder of compressed air attached to the back. Their cylinders were also connected, with narrow hoses, to their regulators (breathing mouthpieces), their emergency spare regulators, and their air pressure gauges (which showed both their cylinders were filled to 280 bar). They each had a waterproof torch hanging from a short line, a dive computer fastened to a wrist (showing depth and dive time), and a weight-belt around the waist (for counteracting the buoyancy of the wetsuit).

Professor Gadling had already been through the dive plan with Marcia, but, as they sat on a hatch and pulled on their fins, he did so one last time. 'Step entry off the side,' he said, 'swim round to the anchor rope, and go down it to the bottom. It'll be dark down there, so stay close. We'll check each other's air gauges every few minutes. If we can get into the wreck safely, we'll look for Gabrielle's kit bag.

But, after ten minutes, whether we've found it or not, we *must* return to the anchor rope and make our ascent. Remember to ascend slowly: ten metres per minute, a two-minute decompression stop at six metres and another minute to ascend from there to the surface.' They had used a special chart called a dive table to calculate a safe dive time and safe ascent rate for their dive to thirty-three metres, erring well on the side of caution. Marcia remembered being told about the dangers of ascending too quickly during her training. An overly sudden decrease in pressure on your body could, she knew, cause decompression sickness, with possible effects ranging from painful joint damage – known as the bends – to paralysis, brain damage and death.

After a final check of hand signals and of each other's equipment, and a quick spit, rub and rinse to the insides of their masks to prevent misting, they were ready. Marcia stood up and, feeling very unsteady with the heaviness of her cylinder and weight belt, followed Professor Gadling across the deck, her fins slapping down on the boards as she took big, careful steps, her breathing loud and hissy through her regulator. She hoped she didn't look as nervous as she felt.

Professor Gadling stepped up onto the low gunwale and took a big stride out over the port side. Marcia followed suit, remembering to hold her mask firmly in place as she hit the water.

SPLASH! Once she was actually in, she felt her confidence begin to return. The sensation of water seeping slowly through the neoprene fabric of her wetsuit was familiar and pleasantly cooling, like a damp flannel held to the skin. She returned Professor Gadling's OK signal and followed him round to the anchor rope. He switched on his torch, gave the thumb-down descent signal and his head disappeared from view. Marcia followed, expelling air from a valve in her buoyancy-control jacket with one hand, holding the anchor rope loosely with the other. The water rose up over her mask, giving her a brief half-and-half view of two worlds: the lake's sunlit surface, and its muted blue-green interior. Then she was under.

They descended feet first. The white anchor rope was visible a long way down before it faded into the depths. Marcia's breathing sounded louder than ever to her, accompanied by a stream of silvery bubbles emitting from her mouthpiece with every out-breath. From two metres down, her eardrums started to hurt with the increasing pressure. Remembering her training, she swallowed to equalize the pressure inside, and the pain vanished.

Down they dropped, metre after metre. This deep, dark lake was very different from the bright lagoons and reefs of the Maldives. Above them, the pale shimmering underside of the lake's surface faded into a faint, undefined turquoise glow; beneath them was darkness, equally obscure. They were descending through an eerie featureless void, seeing nothing but occasional tiny fish, glinting in their torchlight before darting away into the gloom.

Eventually, Marcia caught sight of something materializing into view almost directly beneath them, pale and angular, barely discernible at first, then taking shape as the tail fin of a plane. Her heart raced. Professor Gadling had seen it too and aimed his torch downwards, picking out the rest of the tail. And now, beyond the pool of torchlight, the whole aircraft wreck was visible, lying where it had lain undisturbed for sixty years, ghostly beneath a coating of pale grey silt.

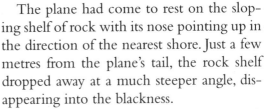

The plane had come to rest on the sloping shelf of rock with its nose pointing up in the direction of the nearest shore. Just a few metres from the plane's tail, the rock shelf dropped away at a much steeper angle, disappearing into the blackness.

Professor Gadling and Marcia paused, made a quick check of each other's gauges, put just enough air in their jackets to give them neutral buoyancy, then swooped from the anchor rope into a slow glide along one side of the plane. The Anson was in a bad state, completely missing its left wing and left engine (the side where the fire had been, remembered Marcia). Much of the fuselage had been reduced to a skeletal metal framework, thickly encrusted with rust, with its original fabric covering reduced to rotting fragments. As the divers swept the wreck with their torch beams, the complex framework cast eerie, moving shadows across the plane's interior. The seats, although dilapidated and strewn with debris, looked more or less in place. Was it really possible, wondered Marcia, that Solomon the silver turtle jewellery box still lay beneath one of them? Was it really possible that Gabrielle's kitbag could have stayed in place when the plane crashed? They had to get in and find out.

Professor Gadling found the plane's door, a plywood panel in the right-hand side of the fuselage, just behind the wing.

He grasped the door handle, sending a flurry of silt pluming up through the water, but his attempts to open the door proved fruitless. Brushing away the silt layer from the metal door frame, Marcia could see that it was rusted shut for ever. They finned towards the front of the plane. The Anson's large side windows were blocked by their Plexiglas panes, opaque and green with algae now, but the elaborate greenhouse canopy around the front of the cabin had very few panes left in place. Most must have been knocked inwards on impact with the water, Marcia realized. Many of the spaces in this front canopy were as narrow as those in the fuselage frame-work, but one of the gaps above the pilots' seats looked just big enough to swim through. That was their way in.

Professor Gadling signalled that he would go through and that Marcia should wait outside. With his arms stretched out in front of him, he started to swim down through the gap. CLUNK. Halfway through, his cylinder jammed against the edge. He reversed, twisted slightly, and tried again. CLUNK. It was no good. With his bulky equipment and rather rotund figure, there was no way he was going to get through.

Once Professor Gadling had backed right out, Marcia pointed to herself, then to the gap. She was considerably slimmer than him and was sure she could get through. The professor pondered for a few seconds, then gave the OK signal. But before Marcia made the attempt, he pointed to the blue illuminated screen of his wrist computer and held up five fingers. Marcia checked hers and saw that he was right: in only five minutes they would have to begin their ascent. They also checked their air gauges again. Professor Gadling had 200 bar left; Marcia was down to 170. Reminding herself to breathe more slowly and calmly, she began to swim down through the frame.

Head and shoulders through. Cylinder scraping. Breathe in . . . twist sideways . . . keep going . . . Through! She gripped the top of a seat to steady herself and sent a cloud of silt swirling round the cabin, obliterating her view. Cursing her own clumsiness, she descended down to the floor of the cabin to get below the silt cloud, trying to keep her movements small as she hovered just above the carpet of debris.

Marcia reckoned she could ignore the two front seats; Gabrielle had said she'd stuffed her kitbag under one of the spare passenger seats, which surely meant one of the four in the cabin behind. She searched beneath the nearest one, reaching her gloved hand between the rusted metal legs, picking carefully through bits of Plexiglas and smashed flight instruments. Inevitably, more silt got disturbed and, by the time she had moved onto the second seat, visibility was down to a few inches.

A beam of light flashed on and off beside her. Marcia looked up to see Professor Gadling flickering his torch through a section of exposed framework next to her, to get her attention. He pointed to his wrist and held up two fingers. Only two minutes left. As Marcia gave him an OK signal, she thought she glimpsed something in the dark water far behind him: a fleeting impression of a black shape moving. She tried to focus on it, but the shape faded back into the gloomy void as quickly as it had appeared. Must have been just a shoal of fish, she told herself.

Marcia hurried back to her search, rummaging beneath the third seat. Nothing. And almost no time left.

She *had* to check the last seat, however briefly. She scrambled frantically, ignoring the silt, relying on her fingers as much as her eyes. There! She felt something jammed under the back of the seat. Letting her torch hang from its line, she tugged the object with both hands and it came free. Felt like it *could* be a bag. She finned quickly back to the front end of the cabin, where the silt had settled enough to restore visibility. It *was* a bag – a small canvas kit-bag. Feeling the canvas disintegrating in her hands, she quickly put the bag down on a seat. Gripping her torch in her left hand once more, trying to stop it trembling, she pulled out the bag's contents. Wooden toothbrush, comb, lipstick, spare underwear – and, yes! Something heavy, at the bottom. She brought it out and held it in the centre of her torch's pool of light. There it was, darkly tarnished but intact: a small silver jewellery box in the shape of a turtle. She had found Solomon.

Elated, Marcia held her find up for Professor Gadling to see, expecting him to be just outside the plane's canopy. But he wasn't there. The other side? No one. No torchlight. No bubbles from his regulator. Just dark, empty water. She felt suddenly anxious, suddenly alone in this alien world. Maybe he hadn't seen her come forward. She looked back down the cabin, looking for his torch beam shining through the fuselage framework. Nothing. Darkness.

She should have kept better contact, should have signalled to him before examining the bag. What if he'd got snagged in something, needed her help? What if – Stop! Stop panicking. Breathe slower. Can't be far away. Probably back at the anchor rope, waiting. Leave the plane. Be able to see him then.

Marcia finned up to the gap in the canopy by which she'd entered. Then, from nowhere, another diver appeared at the canopy – a black-clad diver, blocking her way out, his face concealed behind a black-tinted mask and a mouthpiece that emitted no bubbles. His gloved right hand held a short, three-tipped spear-gun, which he was pointing straight at her.

Chapter Twenty-Five

Marcia froze, too shocked to move for a second. Several metres behind the diver, she could see a black shark-shaped underwater vehicle gliding into view. Two more black-clad divers sat astride it, one driving with handlebars, the other holding a struggling blue-wetsuited diver – Professor Gadling – between their two seats.

Marcia backed away, looking for another way out through the canopy. Too late! The faceless diver was already swimming in, left hand reaching for the silver turtle box. Marcia attempted to turn, instinctively trying to get away from the man, even though she knew there was no way out at the back of the plane. *PHZZ!* A short spear from the gun hissed past her head. No room to move. Cylinder crashing into seats, fins snagging. Clouds of silt swirling everywhere again, obscuring everything. Could she slip under the diver? Return to the front canopy unseen? *Argh!* A gloved hand burst in through the fuselage framework and gripped Marcia's forearm. A fourth diver. The hand dragged her wrist to the edge of the plane. His other hand appeared and began prising Solomon from her fingers. As her unseen adversary gained a hold on the jewellery box, she saw the first diver looming through the silt cloud. He pointed his spear-gun straight at her and pulled the trigger.

PHTT! The black-clad diver watched the barbed spear fly from his gun and thwack through the girl's buoyancy-control jacket. He saw her body jerk, then go limp. His colleague's hand grabbed the silver turtle box from the girl's trailing fingers and dragged it out through the fuselage framework. The diver watched the girl's mouthpiece fall from her mouth, watched a last stream of bubbles escape from her lips, and watched her eyes freeze into a lifeless stare. Then he turned, sleek in his streamlined hi-tech diving equipment, and swam effortlessly from the plane.

'They should be up soon, shouldn't they?' said Sam. He and Professor Gauntraker were at the back of the motor cruiser, hooking a specially built ladder over the *Bernoulli*'s low stern, all ready for Marcia and Professor Gadling to climb up after they surfaced.

'Can't see them yet,' said Ben, who was leaning over the port bow, peering down the anchor rope as far as he could. They *had* hoped to be able to follow the divers' progress on the sonar imaging device, but Professor Pottle had been unable to resist trying to improve the picture. He was still trying to bring the blank screen back to life, with a series of clinks, clunks and tuts emanating from the cabin doorway.

Apart from these noises, all was quiet in the sultry stillness  of the evening. In the distance, long, white steamer ferries completed their final runs of the day. From time to time, slightly scraggy dark birds, which Adam told them were black kites, flew overhead. The sun was very low now, and the hazy light that it cast on the Alps to the south-east was turning from amber to pink.

Big towering clouds had been rising in the mountains for some time, Ben noticed, and the air continued to feel oppressively hot, heavy and humid. He wondered if a thunderstorm was brewing.

'What was their total planned dive time?' said Zara, after another minute. She was not yet anxious that they were overdue but was impatient to find out if the divers' search for Solomon had been successful.

'Well, say it takes them two minutes to get down,' said Ben, 'then ten minutes on the bottom, then coming up at ten metres a minute for twenty-seven metres, a two-minute stop, then another minute for the last six metres. That would all add up to . . .' He paused, trying to do the tricky bit in his head.

'Seventeen minutes, forty-two seconds,' said Adam, almost instantly.

'Easy one for you,' said Zara, smiling, remembering the amazing powers of mental arithmetic they'd seen Adam display before.

Adam shrugged. 'Actually, I can't do the kind of *really* big sums I could do when you met me a few months ago,' he said. 'At least, not so fast, and not in my head.'

'Oh,' said Zara, concerned. 'You mean your brain's . . .' She stopped herself.

'Deteriorating?' said Adam. 'No. It's growing. Before, when I could instantly spit out the answer to any sum, I didn't know *how* I was doing it. It felt as if my brain was just a machine, not part of *me*. Now, when I do maths, it takes longer and I often need paper, but I understand what I'm doing, and I can actually do much more complex maths. More interesting. Mum reckons the effects of my genetic make-up were being enhanced by drugs and hormones before. My accelerated ageing rate is becoming less extreme now, as well. I'm developing more naturally.' He grinned. 'Mum won't even let me eat anything with E-numbers in it.'

'Hey!' yelled Sam. 'Someone's towing the *Silver Turtle* towards us!'

Everyone looked, and saw the unmistakable form of

their little flying boat, being pulled behind a speedboat. The vessels were approaching from the west, with the hazy orange sunlight behind them, and they had to squint to see properly.

'It's not that gendarme's boat,' said Zara, seeing that the speedboat was black.

Sam took his compact binoculars from his trouser pocket. As he did so the sardine tin radar-jamming device got accidentally dragged out too and fell on the floor. It emitted a single quiet beep and, although the green light remained off, an even tinier red light, which Sam hadn't noticed before, began to pulse. Had he damaged it? he wondered. Well, he'd have to look at it later. Carefully, he slid it back into his pocket and concentrated on focusing his binoculars on the speedboat, making sure not to look at the low sun. He spotted a woman's head and shoulders emerging from the top of the speedboat's tinted canopy, her arm waving to them. 'It's Professor Sharpe,' he said.

As soon as Marcia's apparently lifeless eyes saw the diver disappear through the Anson's front canopy, she lunged for her mouthpiece, shoved it to her mouth and gulped in a huge lungful of air. She couldn't have held her breath out for another second. She breathed hard for several more breaths without trying to move, trembling with delayed shock. She knew that if she hadn't instinctively shifted sideways as the diver pulled the trigger, she really would be dead. She had felt the spear burst through her buoyancy-control jacket, then slash the side of her wet-suit, cutting her skin, before passing out through the back of the jacket, to one side of her air cylinder. She had made a split-second decision to play dead, relying on the poor visibility to prevent the diver from seeing where his shot had actually gone. A slim chance, but her only chance to put him off firing his third spear. And it had worked. She was alive.

Now what? Wait till they've definitely gone. Then leave the plane. Get to the surface. Back to the boat. Or would Noctarma have sent men to attack the boat as well? Probably.

The cut in her side didn't hurt too badly. Was that because it was minor, or because the cold water was numbing the pain? No way of examining it with her buoyancy-control jacket and her gloves on. Just a scratch, she told herself. Check air. Almost down to one hundred bar. Calm down. Breathe slower. Have to get going. See if divers have gone.

Marcia cautiously started to make her way back to the front of the plane. Her buoyancy control jacket was useless now, with air able to bubble out through the spear holes, and she felt very heavy. She had to half-clamber, half-fin between the seats.

BUMP! Something struck the front of the Anson, and Marcia felt the whole plane shift backwards. BUMP! The second jolt sent the plane into a slow backwards slide, the wrecked fuselage scraping loudly over the sloping rock shelf. Through the framework above her, Marcia glimpsed the underside of the divers' shark-sub – no, two shark-subs – swerving away and upwards, out of sight. They had rammed the Anson – sent it sliding tail first towards the edge of the rock shelf.

Frantically, Marcia scrambled and kicked up to the front canopy and pulled herself up through the window frame. CLUNK. Cylinder jammed. Stuck. Can't move. Suddenly the plane lurched into a much faster scraping slide down an almost vertical rock face. They had gone over the edge.

Marcia twisted and jerked. Still stuck. She was being dragged down to the bottom of the lake, where she would die and never be found.

Chapter Twenty-Six

With desperate violence, Marcia twisted, kicked and pulled, until, at last, she felt her cylinder scrape through. The Anson's long nose slid past her, plummeting on down, and then she could just make out the rock face. She lunged at it, clinging on with her fingertips. Looking down, she watched the Anson continue its slide, until – THUD! – its tail hit an outcrop of rock. The jolt caused the plane to peel, nose first, away from the rock face, looping on downwards in a series of slow-motion backwards somersaults. Marcia watched the pale, one-winged plane tumbling down and down, becoming smaller and fainter, until it was swallowed up in the blackness of the abyss.

Shuddering, she checked her wrist computer and her air gauge. Depth: forty-two metres. Air: seventy bar. She was way too deep, she had used up too much air, and she had been down too long. But she was alive.

'You're right, Sam,' said Zara, as the speedboat and plane drew near. 'It is Professor Sharpe. And I think she's smiling. But that's not her boat.'

'Maybe it's another police boat,' suggested Ben. 'Chief Commissioner Grayloch must have got Interpol or the Swiss police to send someone senior here to talk to us, picking up Professor Sharpe and our plane on the way.' This seemed the most likely explanation and everyone felt their spirits lifting.

'That's impressively quick progress,' said Professor Gauntraker.

'Ivy *is* rather good at chivvying people up,' said Professor Pottle, who had joined them on the deck.

'They'll be in danger of colliding with Garrulous and Marcia as they surface,' observed Professor Gauntraker. 'Hoy, Ivy!' he called. 'Keep clear till the divers are up.'

The woman in the speedboat gave no indication that she'd heard and the speedboat began to draw alongside the *Bernoulli*'s port side, still towing the *Silver Turtle* behind.

'Keep clear, Ivy!' repeated Professor Gauntraker.

'*That's not Mum!*' said Adam suddenly.

But it was too late: the woman had produced a compact submachine-gun, fitted with a silencer. 'Sorry to disappoint you,' she said, in a sneering voice quite unlike Professor Sharpe's. 'You will have to make do with my company instead.' Keeping the gun pointing at them, with one hand, she removed her grey wig, revealing her own short black hair.

The children stared at the woman in bewilderment and shock. Where was the real Professor Sharpe? How had this woman got hold of their plane? Had the gendarme been working for Noctarma after all?

The woman leapt aboard, while the speedboat's blond driver backed her up with another submachine-gun. 'Hands on heads,' she ordered. 'If you try anything, we will shoot you. You will find we run Noctarma's Swiss operations with precision and efficiency. We had agents watching out for you the moment our Leader put out his international alert call. Your arrival was reported within seconds of your plane landing. And, of course, we were already making the necessary arrangements to find the Anson wreck, following the helpful chat you had with Lady Clarissa earlier today. The further assistance you have just given in leading us straight to the wreck site is much appreciated. Ah, some news of that operation now, I think.'

A soft splashing noise made everyone look round to see a narrow, streamlined vehicle breaking through the lake's surface near the *Bernoulli*'s stern, ridden by two black-clad divers. The vehicle rose up until it sat high in the water like a jet-ski, then purred closer, the rear diver wielding a spear-gun. A second vehicle surfaced, with Professor Gadling manacled between its two divers.

Already stunned and scared, the children felt a cold dread growing in their stomachs, as they all wondered the same thing: where was Marcia?

Professor Gadling spat his regulator mouthpiece from his lips. 'MURDERERS!' he roared, straining against his chains. 'YOU FILTHY, COWARDLY MURDERERS!'

'Shut it!' ordered the diver behind him, holding a jagged-edged knife to his throat.

Zara looked at the others, her sense of dread deepening. Murderers. He'd said murderers. He couldn't mean . . .

The diver with the spear-gun vaulted nimbly up onto the *Bernoulli*'s deck, his fins retracting with a whir into the soles of his rubber boots as he landed. He removed his mask and mouthpiece, revealing a handsome sun-tanned face. Keeping his spear-gun on the children and the two professors, he reached his left hand into a pouch at the front of his diving suit and brought something out. There, on the palm of his hand, sat a small, tarnished silver, turtle-shaped box: Solomon.

'Good work, Ivan,' said the woman, taking the box from him and putting it in her pocket.

'The girl had just found it when we reached them', said the diver. 'I had to shoot her to ensure Leon could take it from her.' He smirked slightly, with the corners of his mouth curling down.

Zara gasped. 'NO!' she screamed. '*NO!*'

Sam felt sick and dizzy, unable to speak at all.

'*You evil little* —' began Professor Gauntraker, stepping towards the diver.

'SILENCE!' barked the woman, and everyone fell still. She turned to Ivan, frowning. 'The Leader's orders were to take these people alive. They may possess information we require.'

Ivan shrugged. 'We don't need them now,' he said. 'We've got the jewellery box.'

'Its information may be encrypted, or even lost after so many years in the lake,' snapped the woman. 'All prisoners are to be kept alive for possible interrogation until Stribnik's invention is actually in the Leader's hands. And when the time comes to dispose of the prisoners, their deaths shall be arranged properly; the last thing we need is this girl's body washing up at the side of the lake.'

'The body will never be found,' said Ivan. 'We sent it down to the deepest part of the lake, inside the plane.'

Adam started to cry quietly. Ben, fighting back tears himself, started to put an arm round Adam's shoulders.

'Hands on heads!' snapped the woman. Seeing her finger tighten on her trigger, Ben reluctantly obeyed.

'Moor your shark-subs to this boat and help take these prisoners down below,' the woman ordered Ivan and the other three divers.

'One of you transfer the Sharpe woman from the back of our speedboat,' instructed the blond man. 'She's rolled in the rug on the floor by the back seat, still unconscious.'

Zara's last faint hope – the hope that the real Professor Sharpe might be at her flat, phoning Interpol – died inside her. Everything had gone completely and irrevocably wrong. Noctarma had captured them all and gained possession of Solomon. And Marcia was dead.

★

Marcia clambered with her hands up the steep underwater rock face, while finning hard with her legs. With her buoyancy-control jacket punctured and airless, upward progress was difficult and slow.

The dark water was swirling with silt, disturbed from the rock by the sliding Anson, and visibility was down to almost zero. Her torch merely illuminated the cloud of particles without penetrating beyond, making the problem worse. Exhausted, alone and disorientated in the dark featureless void, panic began to overwhelm her. Her desperate, instinctive urge to get back to the surface made her long to tear off her weight-belt, but she knew she mustn't. Without the weight-belt, she'd end up in an unstoppable accelerating ascent that could result in a severe case of decompression sickness. Also, she had to surface quietly and carefully. If Noctarma agents had captured the *Bernoulli* too, she mustn't let them see her. Forcing herself to stay calm, she continued her struggle up the rock face.

As she eventually hauled herself back onto the rock shelf, she heard a distant, muffled crash from the depths behind her. The Anson had finally reached its new resting place. Marcia shuddered again, imagining herself still trapped in the plane down there.

Now what? Still thirty-three metres to go. No buoyancy.  No rock face to climb. The silt had begun to resettle and, through the murk, something materialized into view a few metres ahead. A vertical pale line – the anchor rope! A link to the world above, and one she could use to get there safely. She wished she knew what was going on at the top of it.

Air check. Fifty-five bar, almost onto the red part of the dial that marked the recommended safety margin. Trying to slow her breathing again, and finning steadily once more with her aching legs, Marcia began to haul herself hand over hand up the anchor rope.

Chapter Twenty-Seven

Sam, Zara, Ben, Adam and Professor Pottle stood on the *Bernoulli*'s deck, hands on their heads, watching Professor Gauntraker being led into the cabin and down the stairway to join Professor Gadling and the still unconscious Professor Sharpe.

Sam tried to make his brain think of a way to escape, but it was hopeless. The Noctarma agents were being extremely thorough. Ivan had fully reloaded his three-tipped speargun and the other three divers were now armed with submachine-guns, taken from the speedboat. One of the divers was helping the woman take the prisoners below deck, one at a time. The blond man and another of the divers were down there, guarding the prisoners as they arrived. Ivan and the fourth diver remained on deck to guard the prisoners yet to be taken down.

Sam had no doubt that they would be searched downstairs before being locked up, and that all potential aids to escape, such as his Swiss Army knife would be removed. Noctarma would get its hands on the radar-jamming device too, he realized gloomily. He wished he'd had a chance to drop it over the side.

The sun would soon set behind the Jura mountains. None of the remaining boats on the lake was anywhere near them, and the shore, though less than two kilometres away, was devoid of houses or people along this stretch. The chances of anyone spotting what was going on aboard the *Bernoulli* seemed non-existent.

For one mad moment, Sam thought about leaping over

the stern and trying to escape on one of the divers' shark-subs. He'd watched the vehicles carefully as they'd motored over to the *Bernoulli* and was pretty sure they were built to drive over as well as under the water. But he knew that if he so much as started to move, Ivan and Leon would shoot him. He wouldn't even make it to the end of the deck. It was hopeless. Everything seemed hopeless now that Marcia had been killed.

At twenty metres, Marcia's wrist computer began beeping, and flashing text on the screen told her to make an extra decompression stop here of two minutes. This, she realized, was necessitated by her unplanned slide down to forty-two metres, which had increased the risks of decompression sickness. Holding onto the rope, she hung stationary in the water. Though her limbs appreciated the rest, her brain was anxious as she read her air gauge: less than forty bar. Would it last out? She made herself take the full two minutes' stop then continued upwards. She was feeling cold now, and the cut in her side was beginning to sting badly.

The greenish glow above her gradually became paler and brighter until at last she could make out the milky underside of the surface. There was the silhouetted hull of the *Bernoulli,* and four smaller hulls, featureless silhouettes at first, then visible in more detail as she rose closer to them: two narrow black vehicles moored at the back end of the *Bernoulli* – the shark-subs. This didn't look good. A speedboat hull, also black, moored along the *Bernoulli's* port side. And a silver hull, a little further off, with a distinctive stepped and ridged shape and a wheel neatly retracted into the centre of its bows – the *Silver Turtle*. How had their plane got here? And what should she do when she surfaced?

She felt her body growing more buoyant as the pressure on it decreased, and she hardly needed to haul on the rope now to keep ascending. At six metres, her computer reminded her to take her second decompression stop. She checked her air. Almost at zero. But not quite. Enough to do the stop, Marcia thought.

Halting, she tried to form a plan. She had to assume the four Noctarma divers, and possibly other Noctarma agents, *had* taken over the *Bernoulli*. She had to surface unseen and unheard, and spy out how things were. Too risky to surface at the anchor rope − anyone at the front of the motor cruiser would see her. She hoped no one had already seen her air bubbles breaking the surface there. Marcia looked up at the shark-subs, near the *Bernoulli*'s stern. She could see that they were unoccupied. They might give her some cover if she came up just behind them. Could she make the final part of her ascent without the aid of the rope? Yes, she decided; if she finned hard enough.

Marcia felt her air becoming thinner and much harder to draw into her lungs − a horrible feeling. She had to get to the surface now, had to risk cutting the stop short. Go!

Marcia powered herself up through a steady diagonal ascent beneath the motor cruiser's hull. Nearly there. Under the boat's propeller. Breaths feeling even thinner. Keep going. Almost under shark-subs. Uhk. Out of air!

Marcia kicked and clawed her way through the last two metres, experiencing a sudden rush of light as her head broke through the surface. She ripped the dead regulator from her mouth and gasped in lungful after lungful of air. She had made it.

But she couldn't afford to relax now. She had come up where she intended, hidden from the *Bernoulli* behind one of the shark-subs. She'd have to risk peeking round to see what was going on. But first she unclipped and peeled off her punctured buoyancy-control jacket and empty cylinder; they were bulky and dragging her down for nothing now. She took off her weight-belt too and refastened it through the arm hole of the jacket, so that it dragged the whole lot down to the bottom, out of sight. She could see her injury now beneath the gash in her wetsuit: a bright red line over her ribs. Not very deep and not pouring blood. Just a big scratch, she told herself, ignoring the stinging pain. Keeping low in the water, she peered round the edge of the craft.

Two divers. Both standing near the *Bernoulli*'s low stern, both with their backs to her. One armed with a submachine-gun. The other with a spear-gun. Marcia shuddered. She could also see Sam and Professor Pottle, standing on the deck, hands on head, also looking away from her. They were all facing the cabin, and Marcia could just see Ben being marched inside by a dark-haired woman and another armed diver. She guessed Ben was being taken down the stairway, guessed that was where the others were already. Apparently no one had heard her break surface.

She got back out of sight, thinking hard. Could she swim to the shore and get help? It wasn't all that far, but she was already shattered and cold. Even if she made it, it might take her a while to find anyone; she could see no houses along the nearest bit of land. And it would be dark soon. The Noctarma agents could slip away with their prisoners in the *Bernoulli* and she'd have no idea where they'd gone.

She heard a woman's voice from the cabin: 'Bring these last two down after us, Ivan. We need to get going.'

Were they all about to go below? wondered Marcia. Should she take off her fins, climb up that ladder hanging down from the stern, and try to hide somewhere on the deck? But she didn't think there *was* anywhere to hide, and anyway there might be more Noctarma agents in the cabin whom she hadn't spotted. Maybe she should stay here behind the shark-sub, and hope to get towed along when the *Bernoulli* moved off. She decided she'd have to wait and see what the Noctarma agents were going to do.

Up on the deck, Ivan kept his spear-gun pointed at Sam, while the other diver, whom Ivan had addressed as Leon, prodded Professor Pottle towards the cabin with his sub-machine-gun.

Since Noctarma's surprise attack, and especially since learning of Marcia's murder, Professor Pottle had been silent. Already a generally shy man, shock and distress seemed to have sent him into a withdrawn state. He dawdled through the open cabin doorway with his small frame hunched, his head bowed low, and his bespectacled eyes staring vacantly down at the floor.

'Move it,' Leon snarled, staying close behind. 'We have not got all day.'

Suddenly, Professor Pottle exploded into a fit of rage. 'YOU PATHETIC BULLIES!' he screamed, spinning round, flinging himself at Leon, and wrenching the submachine-gun upwards by its silencer. Leon tripped backwards over the raised bottom edge of the cabin doorway, taking Professor Pottle down with him. *TRRRRRRRRR!* The muted gun fired wildly up over the cabin as Leon hit the deck. 'YOU STINKING MURDERERS! YOU ODIOUS COWARDS!' screeched the professor, red-faced, spectacles lost, still clinging to the end of the gun as Leon tried to roll him off.

Ivan aimed his spear-gun, trying to get a clear shot. '*GO, SAM!*' yelled Professor Pottle, and in a split second, Sam realized that the professor's whole extraordinary outburst had been a deliberate diversion to give him a chance to escape. But he couldn't flee now – Professor Pottle would be killed. Leon had got on top, kneeling on the professor's chest, twisting the gun from his grip. And Ivan had his spear-gun aimed at the professor's head.

Sam charged at Ivan, pushing the weapon up as it fired. *PHZZZ!* The short spear went between Professor Pottle and Leon, and hit the submachine-gun square on, knocking it from both their grasps and sending it clattering into the cabin. Leaving Professor Pottle sprawled on the deck, Leon ran into the cabin to retrieve the gun. Ivan kicked Sam hard in the chest, sending him crashing down on his back next to Professor Pottle. Winded, Sam helplessly watched Ivan take aim at his chest, the diver's mouth spreading into a leer as his finger began to squeeze the trigger . . .

Wham! A blue-clad figure, which had appeared from nowhere at the *Bernoulli's* stern, cannoned into the back of Ivan's knees. *PHZZZ! PHZZZ!* As Ivan fell, his gun's two spears flashed over Sam and Professor Pottle, and through the cabin doorway. Sam heard Leon emit a scream of pain, he saw Ivan crash to the deck, and he saw the blue-clad figure's face. MARCIA!

Now Sam could hear rushing footsteps below deck. 'Get to one of the shark-subs!' he yelled, picking himself up. He pulled Marcia to her feet (now finless) and they ran towards the stern. Ivan sprang up, his face twisted with anger and disbelief as he lunged for Marcia, but then he was down once more. Marcia and Sam looked back to see Professor Pottle clinging to Ivan's ankles, doggedly resisting the diver's attempts to kick him off. 'YOU TWO GO!' he yelled. 'I'LL BE ALL RIGHT!'

Hearing footsteps coming up the stairs, Sam and Marcia leapt for the nearest shark-sub and just managed to land on the seats, Sam in front, Marcia behind. Marcia's numb, gloved fingers struggled to unhitch the mooring rope as Sam hit what he hoped was the starter button. Yes! The engine purred into life. Checking Marcia had got the rope free, Sam tried twisting the handlebar grip. With its engine noise rising to a roar, the vehicle shot forward, accelerating rapidly as it sped away from the boat.

Chapter Twenty-Eight

Sam clung to the handlebars, trying to keep the shark-sub under control as it careered across the lake's surface, its nose high out of the water, its stern ploughing up a huge tail spray. He felt Marcia grip the back of his T-shirt to steady herself.

'You're wounded!' yelled Sam, still taking in the fact that she was alive. He'd seen the cut on her side as he'd helped her up off the deck.

'I'm all right. Only a scratch,' shouted Marcia, just about truthfully. 'Keep going!'

TRRRRRRRR-TRRRRRRRRRRRRR! Bursts of sub-machine-gun fire ripped up the water around them. Marcia looked back through the spray to see people shooting at them from the deck.

TRRRRRRRRRRRR! Sam zigzagged slightly to spoil the gunners' aim, while trying to hold their course for the nearest bit of shore. They'd be out of range soon. They could make it. Now that Marcia was alive after all, Sam felt they could do anything.

TRRRRRRRRRRRR! More gunfire. Sounded closer. Marcia looked behind again, horrified at what she saw. 'The other shark-sub!' she yelled to Sam.

It was true. Two of the Noctarma divers were in hot pursuit, the driver crouching low over the vehicle's handle-bars, his colleague behind firing his submachine-gun. Were they catching up? Marcia couldn't be sure. She didn't think so, and she could see that the gunner was struggling to keep a steady aim from the moving craft. Maybe she and Sam could reach the shore first, without being hit. What then? They'd have to run for that line of trees. Maybe they could find a house, or a road where they could stop a car.

TRRRRRRR-PKANG-PKANG-PKANG! Marcia felt bullets blasting into the back of their shark-sub and ripping through the machine beneath their seats. The gunner had got lucky after all. The vehicle kept going, but its engine was rattling and their speed had dropped a little.

The divers' shark-sub was only a few hundred metres behind them now and closing the gap fast. It would catch them well before they got to the shore. They'd had it.

Suddenly, with a clatter of engine noise, something swooped down on them as if from nowhere, a wide wing overshadowing them, wheels almost clipping their heads. Marcia flinched, assuming this was an attack from a Noctarma plane. But rather than attacking, the aircraft manoeuvred alongside them, flying just a couple of metres above the water, matching their speed exactly.

The plane was a slightly ramshackle-looking microlight – little more than a three-wheeled go-cart with an open pilot's seat, a propeller engine at the back and a pale blue fabric hang-glider wing above. Bullets from the diver's sub-machine-gun pinged off the microlight's metal framework; clearly this was no Noctarma plane. The pilot was an old man wearing a leather flying jacket, who controlled the microlight with a horizontal bar attached to the wing above him. Apart from his hooked nose, his features were obscured by a pair of modern flying goggles and a mass of long white hair and beard, which blew back wildly in the wind. 'WHEN I FLY CLOSE ENOUGH, GIT ON BOARD!'

he roared to Sam and Marcia. In front of his seat was an empty passenger seat, supported by two long spars that converged to the microlight's small streamlined nose section. The mysterious pilot manoeuvred the microlight directly over the speeding shark-sub and, with incredible control, held the aircraft in a position that put the front seat barely a metre above Marcia's head.

'You go first while I keep driving!' Sam yelled to Marcia, keeping his eyes ahead. Trying to ignore the continuing gunfire behind, Marcia sprang and grabbed one of the spars. Sam leapt up after her and, as soon as his hands gripped the spar, he felt the plane soaring upwards and saw the lake falling away beneath their feet. Sam swung his legs up and somehow managed to clamber onto the spars. But Marcia's spring had finally exhausted the very last of her strength. She flailed her legs weakly. Couldn't get her feet up onto the spars. Could hardly move them. Couldn't hold on much longer with her hands.

Then Sam was pulling her by the arms, hauling her up and helping her scramble onto the seat. 'Thanks,' she gasped, as he helped her to fasten the seat-belt around her waist. The seat was narrow, like that of a motorbike, so that her legs hung over the sides with her feet supported on little footrest bars. It also had a reclined back, against which she collapsed, too tired to argue that Sam should have the seat. Sam sat just in front of the seat, wedging himself between the narrow spars the best he could.

The microlight hurtled over the lake's shoreline, still climbing. Sam risked turning his head to look back over Marcia at their pilot. 'THANK YOU!' he yelled above the deafening engine noise. 'WHO ARE YOU?'

'WHERE'S GABRIELLE?' the old man yelled back, frowning. His voice sounded American.

'GABRIELLE GOT CAPTURED BY NOCTARMA,' Sam shouted, wondering how the pilot knew Gabrielle and if he would know who Noctarma were. 'BACK IN ENGLAND,' he added.

'THOSE YELLA RATTLESNAKES!' yelled the pilot, seeming to understand, and frowning even more deeply.

'AND THEY'VE JUST CAPTURED MORE PEOPLE!' Sam added. 'OUR FRIENDS – ON THAT BOAT.'

'WE'LL HELP YOUR FRIENDS, SON,' shouted the pilot. 'DON'T YA WORRY. BUT WE GOTTA GIT HIDDEN FIRST.'

The pilot banked sharply to the left and Sam clung tightly to the spars with both hands, turning to face forwards again. He decided that further attempts to talk to the pilot would have to wait until they had landed at wherever it was they were going.

Apart from the nose section and small windscreen in front of them, Sam and Marcia were surrounded by nothing but air, with a vertiginous open view of the ground below – exhilarating, if a bit scary.

The inside of the nose section was rusty and the windscreen slightly scratched. Both components looked as if they had been salvaged from an old motor-scooter, thought Sam. In fact, everything about the microlight had a recycled-from-junk look, with bicycle wheels, deck chairs, hose-pipes and bits of a plastic canoe among the many things incorporated into its structure. Even the wing, he'd noticed, seemed to be patched together from several different pieces of fabric.

Then Sam noticed something fitted just below the inside of the windscreen that looked very familiar: an old sardine tin, stuffed full of electronics with a pulsing green light on the front – another radar-jamming device! Was their pilot Gabrielle's mysterious friend? That would explain why he was concerned about Gabrielle and how he knew about Noctarma, but it didn't explain how he had known that he and Marcia needed rescuing.

Well, whoever this pilot was, his rescue mission had saved their lives. Sam just wished that Professor Pottle had got away with them. Please let him be OK back there, he thought – alive with the others, not shot dead in vengeance. Sam's mind replayed the images of the small professor heroically attacking Leon, selflessly holding back Ivan, recklessly risking his own life to allow him and Marcia to escape. Sam knew that he had always underestimated Professor Pottle, and felt sorry.

Marcia sat back in her seat, also grateful to be alive and also resigned to waiting for any explanations. She was feeling terribly cold though and the scar on her side stung bitterly. She hoped they were going to land soon but that wasn't looking likely. Their mysterious pilot was holding the microlight on a climbing south-easterly course, speeding away from the flat grassland near the lake and up into the Alps.

Chapter Twenty-Nine

'Someone's coming down,' whispered Zara to Ben and Adam.

The three of them were locked below deck in the pitch-black of the *Bernoulli*'s tiny galley kitchen, manacled by their wrists to various cupboard handles and fittings, all still in shock from hearing of Marcia's death. Professors Sharpe, Gadling and Gauntraker, whom they'd seen taken down before them, were, they guessed, locked up in another room.

Just after Ben had been brought down, the children had heard noises of frenzied activity above deck – muffled shouting, bumping, clunking, gunfire, engines starting – with no clue as to what was happening. For the last couple of minutes, things had quietened down. Now they heard footsteps clumping down the stairway and into the corridor outside.

The woman was speaking quickly and crossly: 'No, Ivan, just lock the prisoner up. I'd like to shoot him as much as you would, but I told you: all prisoners are to be kept alive for possible questioning. I will not tolerate any more of your trigger-happy recklessness – that damn spear-gun could have killed Leon.'

'It was Leon's fault in the first place, for losing control of his prisoner,' protested Ivan's voice.

'Silence!' snapped the woman's voice. 'Lock the prisoner in there and guard the corridor. We need to get going without delay now.'

As her quick footsteps receded back up the stairs, the

children heard a door being opened right next to theirs. Ben thought he remembered noticing a broom cupboard beside the galley, when they'd explored the motor cruiser earlier. They heard a thud and a clatter, as if someone was being pushed violently in amongst the mops and buckets. 'Must be Sam or Professor Pottle,' whispered Ben, remembering they had been the only two left on deck after him. What on earth had happened up there?

They heard a rattle of handcuffs being fastened, then Ivan's voice, addressing his prisoner in a low growl: 'Listen, you little worm; the minute they've finished interrogating you and we're given the order to finish you all off, I am going to make it my personal business to give you the worst death I can think of.'

The children heard the broom cupboard door thud shut. No one spoke, knowing that Ivan was standing just outside, keeping guard. Then they heard the deep chug-chug-chug of the *Bernoulli*'s engine starting, building to a growl as they felt the motor cruiser begin to move.

After a few moments, the children heard a soft clunking from the broom cupboard next door. It sounded like someone – Professor Pottle or Sam – tapping a metal pail with his foot, not randomly, but in what sounded like a deliberate arrangement, with some taps short and clipped, and others more accented with longer spaces after them.

Ben immediately recognized it as a series of dots and dashes: Morse code! But he didn't know the Morse alphabet by heart, and was pretty sure that Zara didn't either. They had always meant to learn it, but never had. Was there any chance that Adam knew Morse? The tapping continued for about thirty seconds:

-- .- .-. -.-. .. .- / .- .-.. .. .. / .-.-.- / ... . /

.- -. -.. / ... .- -- / . ... -.-. .- .-.. . -.. / .-.-.-

Then, after a pause, it started again – possibly a repeat of the same message, Ben guessed.

'STOP THAT!' barked Ivan, still standing close outside. The clunking stopped abruptly.

The *Bernoulli's* engine noise was vibrating loudly through the walls and Ben reckoned they could risk whispering very quietly without Ivan hearing them. 'Do you know Morse, Adam?' he breathed.

'Yes!' whispered Adam, his breath trembling with excitement. 'Mum showed me it in a book. It must be Professor Pottle next door, because the message said: "Marcia alive. She and Sam escaped."'

They all felt a great warm wave of relief and joy rising up through their chests, felt all the grief and horror of believing her dead evaporating like a bad nightmare after waking. Marcia was alive! And out there somewhere with Sam, getting help. They were still chained up in the pitch black, but Zara felt as if a light had been switched on. Professor Pottle's tapped message had made all the difference. Marcia was alive, and they were not beaten yet.

Chapter Thirty

For fifteen minutes, the old man zoomed the microlight on a twisting course up through the mountains, swerving round crags and hurtling past rock faces at reckless speed. The setting sun was at their backs and, although the valleys beneath them had already been swallowed up in the blue shadows of dusk, the lofty peaks towering all around still glowed in the last of the rosy light. The clouds rising above the mountains formed a dramatic mélange of fiery pinks and brooding greys.

Marcia noticed a particularly distinctive cumulous cloud, floating directly ahead, clear of the others and nearer. Its pink-tinged billows were so crisply defined, it looked almost as solid as a mountain itself. It was the kind of cloud on which Marcia had always liked to imagine herself clambering.

Their pilot pulled the microlight into an even steeper climb, and Marcia feared his course would take them straight into the cloud, something she knew would make her even colder and wetter. Then she saw that they would just clear its uppermost plumes. She felt relieved, but wondered why the man hadn't simply flown around it.

The top of the cloud was relatively flat and more-or-less circular. They were halfway across it when their pilot veered the microlight into a tight banking swerve to the right, and began to make a clockwise circuit a few metres above the cloud top, holding the aircraft at a sharply tilted angle as they whizzed round.

Sam instinctively clung on even more tightly, though

actually, he realized, the centrifugal force created by their circular flight was preventing him from falling. But why was the pilot circling? wondered Sam. Was he looking for some landmark on the ground? But if so, why make the circle directly above a cloud?

Then Sam and Marcia noticed something unusual: the centre of the cloud top seemed to be disappearing, at first creating a narrow, deeply shaded pit in the water vapour, then a hole through which they could look down to the twilit valley below. The hole was almost perfectly circular and was expanding fast, transforming the cloud into the shape of an enormous horizontal doughnut. By the time the microlight completed its circuit, the hole was about fifty metres across, a diameter which matched that of their circular flight path. Sam looked down in awe as they flew round for a second time. Could this extraordinary cloud formation have been caused by some unusual effect of the wind? No – the hole had appeared too suddenly and grown too quickly for this to be a natural phenomenon. He looked back at their pilot. The man had his left hand on his control bar, but his right hand was holding something and pointing it down towards the cloud. It was hard to make out in the fading light, but the object looked about the same size and shape as a TV remote control and Sam was pretty sure the man was using his thumb to press buttons on it. But how could he be controlling the shape of a cloud with such a device? And why?

Marcia stared down, equally bewildered. Suddenly, behind the shadowy wall of cloud that made up the inside of the hole, she glimpsed something even more impossible: some sort of angular man-made structure. Then the wall of cloud began to dissipate, thinning to a veil of fine mist, and she and Sam could see more and more structures, all crammed onto a circular metal gantry that ran around the inside of the hole. They could see long radio aerials, twirling radar antennae, clusters of satellite dishes, rows of metal gas cylinders, enormous storage tanks, and all sorts of strange electronic and mechanical devices, linked together with yards of heavy-duty cables and tubing. Everything, even the most hi-tech components, shared the microlight's appearance of having been home-built from recycled junk and salvaged vehicle parts.

The whole cluttered gantry was unlit, ghostly in the shadowed dusk, wreathed by the remaining swirls of mist. Sam stared and stared. How on earth could all this be here inside a cloud? wondered Sam. What was holding it all up?

For a moment, Sam wondered if whoever had created this had already cracked the secret of anti-gravity. But if this man was Gabrielle's friend, that didn't make sense. The whole point of what Gabrielle had told them was that no one had yet discovered or reinvented Maskil Stribnik's invention.

Then, behind the gantry, Sam spotted a smooth grey surface that seemed to be made from some sort of hi-tech fabric stretched over a framework. An airship! The whole circular gantry was built into the inside of a huge doughnut-shaped airship, which was hidden by an artificial cloud. More mist cleared away, exposing the doughnut shape's circular top, as well as its inner surface, and Sam was now certain that his deduction was correct.

Marcia too had realized what they were looking at. She could see billowing plumes encircling the outer edge of the airship and she guessed that, from the outside and from the ground, the whole thing still looked like a cloud.

Their pilot was allowing the microlight to lose height, but Sam could see no part of the airship that was long and straight enough to land on, and in any case, the man was still holding them in their tight, banking circle flight. Then Sam realized what the man was doing: he was aiming to drop down on the curved rim of the hole, where the angle of the curve would match the tilt of their aircraft. The pilot was going to use the rim as a banked circular runway.

Bump! Their three wheels touched down together and rumbled loudly on the drum-tight skin of the airship as the microlight hurtled round the rim like a racing bike on a banked cycle track. After a full circuit, Sam could feel their speed reducing. What would happen once they stopped? Tilted at this angle, they would surely tumble down the side of the hole and crash onto the gantry below. However, before they had completely slowed down, the pilot steered the microlight's nose wheel slightly to the left, taking them gradually up towards the top of the airship as they continued to go round. Just as they edged onto the top, he cut the engine, allowing their remaining momentum to propel them gently into a three-sided pen of low railings, where they bumped to a standstill.

Immediately, the old man held out his controller device and pressed a button. As jets of mist began to hiss out from small vents all over the airship's surface, he pushed his goggles up onto his forehead, leapt down from the microlight and pulled two levers at the side of the railings. The first made the railings close inwards, clamping the microlight's chassis firmly in place. The second caused a series of steps to protrude from the airship's surface. They formed a ladder which curved down over the rim of the doughnut-shaped airship's hole. Sam guessed it led down to the gantry below, though this was out of sight from their position up on the airship's top.

'C'mon,' hollered the man, setting off down the ladder at breakneck speed. 'There's no time to lose!'

Sam scrambled down and helped Marcia from her seat. 'Come on,' he said. 'We'd better follow him quick, while we can still see the ladder.' The mist gushing out of the vents was covering everything fast and by the time they had got onto the top of the ladder, the microlight was barely visible.

Sam and Marcia descended to the bottom of the ladder, where it did indeed connect with the upper bars of the great circular gantry. The gantry had no walkways or ladders, but this didn't seem to slow the old man down; he was clambering round the cluttered metal framework with the agility of a spider monkey, heading downwards at the same time.

In the thickening mist and the darkening dusk, the children had difficulty seeing the man as they tried to follow his route. His wispy hair and beard seemed to merge with the cloud, and often only his brown flying jacket was visible.

Sam stayed close to Marcia as they clambered, ready to grab her if she slipped. The man reached the bottom of the gantry, and then disappeared from view. Sam made a mental note of the place they were aiming for and they somehow made it there without mishap. By now, the artificial cloud had been restored so thickly that visibility had been reduced to a few metres and the metalwork was wet with condensation. They clung to the gantry bars, looking for the man in vain through the swirling fog.

'There!' said Sam, suddenly. He hadn't spotted the man, but he had seen a thin metal staircase, that kinked like a fire escape, down into the mist. They rushed down it and found themselves on a narrow catwalk suspended from the bottom of the airship. It presumably formed a complete circle, though they could only see a few metres of it ahead and behind before it faded into the mist. They hurried along, the airship's underside above their heads, spindly safety rails to each side, and the grey void of the artificial cloud below them. They tried not to think about the long drop beneath that.

A bulky dark shape emerged through the mist ahead. As Sam and Marcia drew near, they could see it was a cabin, fixed, like the catwalk, beneath the underside of the airship. It was quite long, silvery grey, and looked as if it had once been some sort of caravan. Its windows were shuttered over and they couldn't see inside. They reached the cabin's door, opened it, and went in.

Chapter Thirty-One

As Sam and Marcia expected, they found the man in the cabin. He was its sole occupant. He was dashing this way and that along a lengthy control console that made up one wall of the cabin's softly lit interior. Although the windows were shuttered, three big monitor screens gave views of the outside world, two of the cloudscape around them, one of the Alpine landscape below. The man moved with a manic energy, his hands flitting from levers to switches, making quick, deliberate adjustments, his head jerking this way and that as he checked screens and dials, his long hair and beard in a state of constant motion, like sea spray in a storm. And all the while, his gravelly voice kept up a commentary to himself, running through what sounded like a checklist: 'Cloud cover: restored and lookin' good . . . Radar jammer: running fine . . . Visible enemy aircraft: negative . . . Course: set . . . Autopilot: activated . . . Engines: go!'

Pulling a final lever, he turned to glance at the children, acknowledging their presence in the cabin for the first time. 'Pardon me for rushin' on ahead like that,' he said, 'but I wanted to git underway quick as possi– Jeepers, girl!' he exclaimed, suddenly looking at Marcia properly. 'You're injured! That a bullet wound?'

'Spear-gun,' said Marcia weakly. Sam was helping her stand now.

The man rushed across the untidy cabin, rummaged in a cupboard and dragged out a first-aid box. 'C'mon,' he barked, taking Marcia's other arm. 'Git through here where you can lie down.' He ushered her and Sam through to a partitioned area at one end of the cabin where there was a camp bed.

''S just a cut,' said Marcia. 'We've got to do something quickly to help our friends being held prisoner on that boat – before the Noctarma agents disappear with them!'

'Now don't ya worry,' said the man. 'We ain't about to turn tail and leave your friends to be spirited away. The airship's autopilot's takin' us back to the lake now. I know where Noctarma will be headin' for with that boat, and we're gonna git there too. Should take us about forty minutes. I reckon we'll arrive not long after 'em.'

'Arrive where?' asked Sam.

'The Château de Lamprey,' said the man. 'A small castle near the eastern end of Lake Geneva, over on the Swiss side. I'm pretty darn certain it's Noctarma's local head-quarters round here. Now let's have a look at that cut . . . Hmm . . . It don't look too bad.'

Five minutes later, they had cleaned and disinfected the scratch, and covered it with a big strip of sticking plaster. The man and Sam returned to the main part of the cabin, leaving Marcia to get changed into an old fleece-lined flying suit the man had found for her. There was a sink, stove and kettle at the other end of the cabin and the man quickly rustled up some coffee. Sam stood by the monitor screens, watching their progress over the now dark landscape and past the surrounding clouds. Sam guessed there must be video cameras on the outside of the airship, protruding slightly through the artificial cloud cover, and sending these images back to the screens.

The airship seemed to be making reasonable speed, though Sam could hear no engine noise at all. The sun had completely set now, and the clouds were all blue-grey. The clouds also looked bigger than before, rising up in great dark towering formations.

'Are you Gabrielle's friend who told her about Noctarma?' Sam asked the man. 'The friend who gave her the radar-jamming device?'

'That's me,' said the man. 'Name's Hank. Hank Zootlin.'

'I'm Sam,' said Sam.

'And I'm Marcia,' said Marcia, coming back through into the main part of the cabin. The flying suit was fleece-lined and warm, and she was already beginning to feel better.

'You take the seat, Marcia,' said Hank, handing them each a mug of sweet, milky coffee. He then brought out a packet of chocolate chip cookies and some bananas. 'Help yourselves,' he said.

'Thank you,' said Marcia, accepting the cabin's only seat, a rather battered swivel chair, and tucking in. She was starving. 'And thanks for rescuing us like that.'

'You're welcome,' said Hank. 'Lucky I was in the vicinity. I've been down in northern Italy for the past coupla days, investigating a telecommunications company in Milan that I suspected of having Noctarma connections. I managed to git hold of some information on Noctarma's radio frequency scrambling codes – something I've been after for a long time, so I can listen in on Noctarma radio messages. I spent the whole of yesterday reprogramming the airship's listenin' equipment, and tried it out this mornin'. After some hours of picking up nothin', I intercepted messages between somewhere in the UK and somewhere in Switzerland. They were faint, crackly and mostly in French, but a few words stood out: *Maskil Stribnik, Silver Turtle Project* and *Gabrielle Starling*. The only other darn thing I could make out was something about getting a team of divers sent to somewhere called the Château de Lamprey. From the way they were talking, it sounded like this château was one of their bases, so I looked it up on the web and found its location. I hadn't heard from Gabrielle since she set off for Scotland three weeks ago, and I figured that if Noctarma knew her name, things didn't look good. So I decided to head up to Lake Geneva and make a reconnaissance flight over the castle in my airship, and I was well on the way when your signal came through. That's why I was able to git to ya so quick in the microlight.'

'Er . . . how do you mean, our signal?' said Sam, perplexed.

'The emergency signal transmitter on Gabrielle's radar-jamming device,' said Hank, seeming surprised that he should need to remind Sam of this. 'You activated it about ten minutes before I homed in on ya.' He unclipped something from his belt that looked like it had once been a mobile phone and held it towards Sam. Its blue screen showed a pulsing red arrow, pointing at Sam, with the words TARGET 0.4 METERS flashing below, and a detailed set of co-ordinates beneath that.

Sam dragged the sardine tin radar-jamming device from his trouser pocket. The red light was still pulsing. Next to the light was a black button. 'I accidentally dropped the device,' he told Hank. 'The transmitter's button must have got knocked then. We never even knew it *had* an emergency signal transmitter. But, as you saw, we did need rescuing when you reached us. Thanks again.'

'Any time,' said Hank. 'I was expectin' to find Gabrielle, of course, but I guessed she must've given you the device. Now, ya'd better tell me your whole story, so I've got all the facts. Tell me how you got to be mixed up in this whole darn business with Gabrielle, and where she's bein' held, and who these other prisoners of Noctarma are, and anything else ya know.'

Sam and Marcia told Hank everything that had happened, from Ben finding the old photo in Amy's hangar to them escaping from the *Bernoulli* on the shark-sub.

'Jeepers!' exclaimed Hank when they'd finished. 'You've been through one tough day. But you've also discovered a lot about Noctarma. Now we know who their leader is, where their UK headquarters is, and what their long-term goal is. This information is gold dust. But now they've got this turtle jewellery box, we're gonna have to act fast.'

'Have you been on the trail of Noctarma for a long time?' said Marcia. 'I still don't quite understand what this airship *is*. Or exactly what you do or who you work for.'

'Hey, what *is* this?' said Hank, frowning and looking suddenly edgy. 'Some kind of interrogation?'

'I'm sorry,' said Marcia, taken aback by Hank's sudden defensiveness. 'I wasn't meaning to pry. It's just that Gabrielle didn't really tell us anything about you. Sorry.'

There was a pause. Hank took a sip of his coffee, and looked at the floor, still frowning, for some moments. 'No, *I'm* sorry,' he said, sighing. 'I was being paranoid and tetchy. Comes of livin' alone and in secret. It's completely reasonable ya want to know what I do and how I came to be livin' here, and if you're friends of Gabrielle, I'm sure I can trust ya. I'll tell ya the whole thing.

'Up till about twenty years ago, I worked for a big aviation corporation in the States. We built lots of stuff for the military: aircraft electronics, computer navigation, guided missile systems, radar equipment, that sorta thing. I enjoyed my work, and I never questioned the morality of war and weapons. I was proud to be buildin' stuff I believed was necessary for the defence of my country. I had a son who was a jet pilot in the air force and I was mighty proud of him too. Then he got killed in action. Killed in some under-reported minor conflict on the other side of the world that I didn't even understand.

'At first, I was just plain grief-struck. My wife had died some years before and he'd been our only child. But eventually I started questioning everything – like why I'd raised a son to go and drop missiles on other people's children before getting killed himself at twenty-five. Or why I was makin' my living building such planes and missiles.

'Then I started digging into all the stuff about war that I'd never given enough thought to. Not just the war my son was killed in, but many other conflicts. My research opened my eyes to the murky politics, the shady dealing, the barbaric ways people get maimed and killed. I woke up to the fact that most of the work I'd been doing all those years had got nothin' to do with defending my country. Most of my work had been about making money out of death.

'So one night, I let myself into the factory and smashed up electronic components, design models, computers; I wrecked as much of our military work as I could without alertin' night security. I was pretty senior in the corporation and had a lot of access to a lot of offices and production areas. Then, I went to the part of the factory where we'd just finished buildin' this airship. It was designed as an unmanned battlefield surveillance platform for the army. It was outside, ready for testing. I told the security guards I needed to check something, climbed aboard, cast off the moorin' cables, activated the cloud cover and radar jammer, switched on the engines, and floated away.

'For the last twenty years, I've lived up here in the clouds. I built myself the microlight, for getting to and from the ground. And as ya can see, I've added one or two bits 'n' pieces of my own to the airship, such as the cabins, to make it habitable. There's another cabin round the other side that I use as a workshop. I travel the globe, doin' what I can to put a spoke in the wheels of the warmongers of this world: finding out about secret deals between dictators and weapons manufacturers, messing up the plans of arms dealers, sabotagin' bombs and landmines before they can be used to kill people. And investigatin' secret organizations like Noctarma; I've been picking up traces of their malign influence for all the years I've been doing this work.

'Guess ya could call me an outlaw. Most of what I do ain't exactly legal and I'm wanted by several governments and by dozens of corporations – includin' my old employer, for the damage I caused and for taking the airship. So now you understand why I need to be so secretive. Gabrielle's one of the few people who even know I'm here. I've known her since way back, since she taught me to fly, years ago. To most of the world, I don't exist at all.'

There was another pause when Hank had finished his story. Both Sam and Marcia found the idea of someone living in the clouds in his airship for twenty years quite exciting, but they both felt there was something sad and lonely about Hank's secret existence as well.

'Look, we're back over the lake,' said Marcia, pointing to the monitor screen. The lake looked very dark now in the rapidly fading twilight.

'We'll be at the Château de Lamprey pretty soon now,' said Hank, checking his navigation instruments. 'It's just over on the far side and along to the east a bit.'

'What's the plan when we get there?' asked Sam, wondering how the three of them could possibly take on a guarded Noctarma headquarters.

'I'll get the airship right over the castle roofs,' said Hank. 'Then, if I can spot a skylight window somewhere, I'll winch myself down to it from the airship and break in. That's my usual way of gettin' into buildings – straight down from above, while all the guards are around the doors at ground level. Once I'm in, I'll make a reconnaissance. I'll try to find and rescue the prisoners, git the jewellery box back if I can – if they haven't already learnt its secret information – and then git everyone out of there somehow. I dunno how – by takin' Noctorama's speedboat or your motor cruiser or something. If I can't rescue anybody, I'll at least try and mess up Noctarma's plans – sabotage their radio or phone lines or somethin' – *anything* to buy us a little time, to git hold of this police chief your pal was going to call, or to contact Interpol, or even the Swiss authorities again. Heck, I'll find someone who ain't workin' for Noctarma and make 'em believe us if it takes me all night. Look, I know it ain't the most well-prepared plan in the word, but we don't have *time* to sit back and do nothing. I've been pussyfootin' around with my secret investigations of these people for too long. From what you've told me, if Noctarma git hold of this anti-gravity machine, all their prisoners are dead and they become invincible. So, I'm gonna git in that castle and do what I can to stop 'em.'

'But what if you run into armed guards once you're in there?' said Marcia. Hank's plan seemed terribly vague and over-optimistic to her.

'I'll be takin' this little gadget with me, in case I run into any guards,' said Hank. From a locker in the corner he brought out something that looked as if it had been built from parts of a hairdryer and parts of a plant sprayer.

'What is it?' asked Sam.

'Is it a gun?' asked Marcia.

'Heck, no,' said Hank. 'Least, not of the lethal variety. I vowed twenty years ago I'd never build another weapon capable of killin' anyone. This is what I call my snooze-ray. Little thing I put together in my workshop a few years back. It fires a concentrated jet of sleepin' gas. Gives a very strong blast, but only where you direct it. If ya aim it straight at someone's nose and mouth, it'll send 'em to sleep in a split second, but it'll leave you and anyone else in the vicinity completely unaffected. And the gas is a concoction of my own too – doesn't have any of the unpleasant side-effects ya get from some of the knock-out gases the military use. Mine just puts ya into a peaceful sleep for half an hour. It isn't the strongest weapon in the world, but it's got me out of a few tight spots.'

'Hey, we're approaching a castle,' said Marcia, looking back to the central monitoring screen. 'Is that the Château de Lamprey?'

Chapter Thirty-Two

'Reckon that's it,' said Hank, checking the navigation system on his console. 'The co-ordinates are right and it matches the description I found on the web, too. I also discovered it's the private home of a Swiss banker, Maximilian de Lamprey and his wife Lucrezia. I'm guessin' they're the head Noctarma agents round here.'

The Château de Lamprey was a tall castle with pointed towers to either side of its main roof. Its base was actually a small island, connected to the nearby shore by a covered wooden footbridge. On the shore side of the footbridge lay a walled area of grass, trees and a few outbuildings, that looked like part of the castle's private grounds.

'It's unlucky that the Anson wreck happened to be so near one of Noctarma's headquarters,' said Sam, as Hank brought the airship closer. 'No wonder they were onto us so quick.'

Hank shrugged. 'Whichever corner of the world the Anson wreck had been located, there'd have been a Noctarma HQ pretty nearby,' he said. 'They've got agents and buildings everywhere, darn 'em.'

'There's the *Bernoulli*!' cried Marcia. 'See? On the water between the castle and the shore. And the black speedboat too. And there's the *Silver Turtle*, past the footbridge.' They were approaching the castle from the side, and, from their high vantage point, could see that the edge of the island nearest the shore had been built up to form a stone quay, with the footbridge joining it halfway along. An outer castle wall ran around the other three sides of the island, shielding the private quayside area from the lake.

Hank brought the airship directly over the castle so that the monitor screen gave them a clear view of the whole quayside. They could see several darkly clad figures bustling around the *Bernoulli*, but there was no sign of Zara, Ben, Adam or the four professors.

'Look, someone's in the cockpit of the *Silver Turtle*,' said Sam. Their view of the canopy was obscured by the plane's high wing, but he could see torchlight moving about. And he could see they had the nose hatch open, with some sort of rope or cable running in. What were they doing? he wondered. He hated the thought of these Noctarma agents poking around in their little plane.

'There's another plane there, look,' said Marcia. 'On the shore.'

She was right. In the centre of the walled wooded grounds, a streamlined plane, smaller than a normal jet fighter, and less orthodox in design, was being wheeled out from a low wooden barn-like building. Its matt black surface was almost invisible against the dark grass.

'A StratoSting stealth plane,' said Hank. 'Two-seater fighter-bomber. Vertical take-off and landing capability, virtually silent, radar invisible. Top secret aviation project for the US military. Officially shelved in development with no planes built, but somehow, Noctarma owns at least two of 'em. Looks like they keep one here and looks like they're planning to go somewhere.' Sam and Marcia had encountered stealth planes during their previous adventure, but this plane looked even more advanced: sleeker and curvier.

'Well, time for me to make my reconnaissance,' said Hank. 'No point in hangin' about. Reckon there's a thunderstorm about to break over the lake, and it might be hard to hold the airship in place if a wind blows up with it.' The towering black clouds were certainly closing in fast, obscuring the silhouettes of the mountains.

However, the first part of Hank's plan – spotting a skylight window to winch himself down to – proved harder than he'd thought. They all scanned the rooftops for several minutes, but could see no kind of opening.

'Darn these pointy roofs they've got here,' cussed Hank. 'Ain't a skylight or a trapdoor to be seen. Even their chimneys have got little tiled roofs, curse 'em.'

Then Sam spotted something. Now that they were able to see the side of the castle facing the shore, he could see that what he had thought was simply a squat little turret in the centre of the roof was in fact a clock tower. And something about the clock tower made his neck tingle. The red and gold clock face, floodlit from below and facing the shore, was the same as the one on the little clock he'd been looking at in the corridor at Mantlingham Manor - much bigger of course, but identical in design. Lady Clarissa's clock must have been a present from the de Lampreys, he guessed. And below this clock face too was a pair of little arched doors, over a semicircular platform. He was certain they would open on the hour, certain that two automaton knights would trundle out to strike each other's shields. For a few seconds at least, there would be a way into the top of the castle. Excitedly, Sam explained his theory to the others. 'There's bound to be a way through at the back of the inside,' he said. 'The knights'd have to be oiled and maintained.'

'But even if you're right that these doors are gonna open on the hour,' said Hank, 'the doorways are less than two feet high and not much more than a foot wide. I could never git myself through there.'

'No,' said Sam, 'but *I* could.'

'*No!*' said Hank. 'There is no way I'm sendin' a child in there to face that buncha ruthless killers.'

'I'd be careful,' insisted Sam. 'I could just try and find out where the prisoners are, or try and find a window or door that I could let you in by. Come on – it's five minutes to ten now. If I'm going to catch the doors opening, we've no time to spare. You said yourself we have to do *something*.'

'Well, I don't like it,' said Hank, 'but it might be our only way to git someone in there.' He handed Sam something that had once been a ballpoint pen. 'If ya find a window that ya can open from the inside and that I can winch down to, press the top of this,' he instructed. 'I'll be able to home in on ya. But if ya git into danger, press that emergency signal transmitter on Gabrielle's radar jammer and run like heck for that quayside. I'll come tearin' down there in my microlight quicker than a squirrel out of a skunk hole. And ya'd better take my snooze-ray too, just in case ya find yerself in a jam ya can't run from.'

Four minutes later, Sam was being lowered down through the bottom of the artificial cloud, dangling in a harness at the end of a rope, the other end of which was wound round a winch on the airship's gantry. The winch was being carefully controlled by Hank and Marcia from the cabin.

Sam emerged from the bottom of the grey mist, feeling scared and conspicuous, and looked down to the shadowy semi-floodlit castle, about thirty metres below. He was descending quite fast, as Hank had warned him he would be; it was best to minimize the time in which he might be spotted in the air.

Sam had his torch switched off but ready in his hand and, slung across his shoulder, he carried a small canvas bag that Hank had given him, containing the snooze-ray.

Hank's positioning had been good: Sam was dropping on a course that would land him on the steep-sloping roof just next to the square clock tower's left side, in one of the shadows cast by the floodlighting. He felt Hank slowing the descent rate for the last few metres, so that his trainers touched down gently on the roof tiles.

He detached the harness, and crept along the shadowed side of the clock tower to its front. What time was it? He could suddenly hear the whirring of machinery coming from inside the tower. The mechanism was starting. He hurriedly scrambled round the front corner of the tower and clambered onto the semicircular platform. *Clack*. The left-hand door opened sharply, nearly knocking him from the platform. He edged round it, just as the fifty centimetre-high figure of a knight came trundling out on its track, its silvery metal armour glinting in the floodlights. Without waiting to see the knight meet its partner, Sam crouched down and tried to squeeze through its doorway.

Too tight. Turn sideways. *TANG!* Noise of sword striking shield. Head through, shoulders through. *TANG!* Second strike. Now crawl through. Mind the bag. *TANG!* Torch on. Get legs in. Feet in. Get right in to the back. *TANG!* Square wooden hatch. No handle. Push it. Locked. *TANG!* No way through. Have to go back. Wait. Small rusty hinges. Might be able to prise them. Swiss Army knife, quick.

Crouching, hardly able to move his arms in the cramped space, holding his torch in his teeth, Sam wrestled frantically to get his Swiss Army knife from his trouser pocket, to unfold the tin-opener blade, and to prise the two hinges from the frame of the wooden hatch. All the time he could hear the knights continuing to strike the hour. Just as he had levered the first hinge off, the noise of striking stopped. Then he heard the mechanism whirring, and the noise of the two heavy, solid knights trundling along their ratcheted tracks. They were back through their doorways, blocking him in, moving inexorably closer to reclaim the space where he was crouching. He was going to be crushed.

Chapter Thirty-Three

Sam wrestled with the hinge. Half off. Push hatch. Thump it. There!

The hatch gave way and Sam dragged himself through, just getting clear as the knights clunked into their back-to-back resting position.

Sam found himself sliding head first down a sloping wooden ladder. He landed with a bump in a small room, whose shelves were stacked with tools, oil cans and paint tins. The room was gloomy but a little light spilled up from some wooden stairs leading down in the corner. Sam picked up his Swiss Army knife and torch, put them away in his pocket, and took the snooze-ray from the bag. Holding it in his hand, he cautiously descended the stairs.

They brought him through a little arch onto the middle of a dimly lit stone passageway. Sam turned left and made his way along it, pretty sure it would lead him to the tower on the eastern side of the castle. If he could get up into the tower, he might be able to find an unoccupied room, with a window that Hank could use to get in. He could hear no noises of human activity and hoped that the people they had seen milling around the *Bernoulli* and helping with the StratoSting accounted for most of the castle's staff. Even so, he was terrified that at any moment he would be spotted and stopped or even shot without warning. He clutched the snooze-ray tightly, keeping a finger on the trigger.

The passageway took him onto a square landing that he guessed might well be part of the tower. In one corner he could see a spiral staircase disappearing upwards, and in another corner, one going downwards. The landing's walls were lined with hunting trophies, beneath which were several wooden doors, all closed.

Sam had just started to cross the landing's wooden floor, and was wondering if he should risk going up the staircase, when the door nearest to him opened and a man in a black uniform walked briskly out, almost colliding with him. Quick! The snooze-ray! As the man reached for the gun at his belt, Sam pulled the trigger. With a short, sharp hiss, a blast of green gas shot straight into the man's mouth and nostrils. He collapsed instantly, before his fingers had even touched his gun, falling sideways with a surprisingly serene expression on his face. Sam held the snooze-ray up to the doorway, half expecting more people to come out. No one. The room, a small office, was unoccupied. He span round. Had anyone heard the man falling? Was anyone else coming onto the landing? No. It was clear. Calm down.

Sam's hands were trembling, his heart racing. He couldn't believe how fast he'd reacted, nor how fast the ray had worked. He hurriedly dragged the man into the office room, turned off its light, and started to come back out. Then he heard footsteps coming up one of the spiral staircases. He got back into the office and pushed the door almost shut, leaving just a slender crack to peek through.

Sam saw the blond man who had helped take them prisoner on the boat emerge onto the landing. 'The plane's all ready, Lucrezia,' he called.

A door on the far side of the landing opened and the dark-haired woman from the boat came out. She had changed out of Professor Sharpe's clothes, into a black suit. Sam guessed she must be Lucrezia de Lamprey. 'Good,' she said. 'I'd feared it would take longer.'

'The plane's energy cells proved to be as simple to

194

recharge as we suspected,' reported the blond man. 'And they charged up remarkably quickly. The gauge went from empty to full in just ten minutes.'

Sam realized they must be talking about the *Silver Turtle*. That explained what the men they'd seen had been doing with the cable.

'It's a pity the energy cells were empty before,' said the woman, 'or you could have pursued that blasted microlight. Now, I have just contacted the Leader and made arrangements. You must fly the plane, with the three child prisoners. They are being brought down from the tower cell now. Handcuff them to the back seats and take an armed guard, of course, to shoot any brat who steps out of line. You are to fly to Petticraig Bay, near Edinburgh. Officers of the Leader's Secret Operations Police Unit will be waiting there to drive you and the child prisoners to their headquarters at Salamander Wharf. I shall already have rendezvoused there with the Leader. Xavier will fly me in StratoSting One. The Leader needs to see the jewellery box as soon as possible.' She patted a bulky shape in her jacket pocket.

'Have you examined it?' asked the blond man.

'No,' said Lucrezia. 'The Leader issued strict orders that no one is to examine it before him.'

'And what about the four adult prisoners?' said the blond man.

'They can be kept in the dungeons here, for the time being,' said Lucrezia. 'It was the children who found and deciphered Stribnik's last message. It is they who are most likely to possess further information if any is needed. Also, the Leader wishes to punish the children for their violent assault against his mother. The adults can be taken to Edinburgh later if necessary.'

'I don't like having their motor cruiser moored up here,' said the man. 'It might be seen in the morning.'

'I shall order someone to scuttle her in the middle of the lake while it is still dark,' said Lucrezia. 'Everything is in hand, Max. Ah, here are the three brats.'

Sam shifted his position behind the door so he could see the spiral staircase that descended from higher up in the tower. Coming down it onto the landing he could see two armed guards between whom were Zara, Ben and Adam. The three children were manacled together in a line.

'I'll come down with you to show you the position of Petticraig Bay on the map,' said Lucrezia to the blond man, who Sam guessed must be Maximilian de Lamprey, and the whole group headed for the top of the other spiral staircase.

Sam thought furiously. In a second they would all be passing right by his hiding place. He'd never get another chance like this. Lucrezia and Max were not holding their guns, and neither they nor the two guards would be expecting an attack here. Had he not already witnessed the effectiveness of Hank's snooze-ray, Sam would never have dared to do what he did next. But he trusted the weapon and, without giving himself time to think any more, he burst from the doorway and sprayed four blasts in rapid succession into the astonished faces of the guards and the de Lampreys.

The rear guard almost managed to raise his gun and Lucrezia almost managed to grab Sam's arm. But in less than two seconds, all four adults were out cold. Zara, Ben and Adam gaped at Sam, but managed to restrain themselves from making any noise.

'Our plane's been charged up,' Sam whispered, unclipping a set of keys from one of the sleeping guards, then fumbling to unlock Ben, Zara and Adam's manacles. 'It's down by the quayside, past the bridge from the *Bernoulli*. Should we head straight for it or try to rescue the adults too?'

'We should get straight to the plane, if we can,' breathed Zara, as they quickly dragged the four unconscious adults to the office to join the first man Sam had sent to sleep. 'The professors wouldn't want us to get caught again. If we escape, we can get help for them.'

'OK,' whispered Sam. He extracted Solomon from Lucrezia's pocket and put it in the canvas bag that Hank had given him. 'You three lead – I don't know the way down to the quayside. I came in through the roof.'

They half-ran, half-tiptoed to the spiral staircase and hurried down it, keeping their footsteps as quiet as they could while still moving quickly. Suddenly there was an urgent, alarmed yell from somewhere above them. It sounded as if someone had discovered the sleeping people in the office, and the children broke into an all-out run, taking the steps three at a time. Knowing they would almost certainly need any back-up that Hank could provide, Sam reached into his pocket and pressed the button to activate the emergency signal transmitter.

They raced along passageways, through doorways and down staircases, trusting Ben's sense of direction and Adam's memory to retrace the route they had been taken up earlier. They encountered no one, though distant shouts and running footsteps were now echoing round the castle above them.

'The staircase at the end of here will bring us out near the castle door,' panted Adam to Sam, as they ran along a short corridor, 'but there were quite a few guards.'

Sam seriously doubted that he could take on several armed and prepared sentries with the snooze-ray.

'Wait,' puffed Zara, stopping by a narrow window and looking out. 'I think we can get down here.'

The window overlooked the quayside. To their left they could see the castle footbridge, to their right, the *Silver Turtle*. The stone quay was quite a long way down, but the window was directly over the sloping roof of some sort of shed that had been built onto the side of the castle. The window was fixed securely on the inside with sliding bolts, but not locked, and they quickly had it open.

'Come on!' hissed Zara, squeezing through and lowering herself onto the roof. The running footsteps and shouts from behind them were getting louder, and they all scrambled through the window after her. They half-slid down the roof and dropped onto the quay.

Keeping to the dark shadows of the castle wall, they ran on tiptoes towards where the *Silver Turtle* floated, facing the quay. Their plane was guarded by just one man, who was holding the mooring rope with one hand and a sub-machine-gun in the other. He was recognizable in the quayside lamplight as Ivan. Sam had the snooze-ray ready, hoping they'd be able to surprise him.

But Ivan saw them when they were still thirty metres away. He let go of the mooring rope and opened fire. The children swerved for cover behind a buttress in the castle wall, just avoiding his stream of bullets. But now they heard shots behind them too, and a bullet blasted the snooze-ray from Sam's hand. Looking back, they saw more men running along the quayside, from the castle door and from the *Bernoulli*. They were trapped.

Then Hank's microlight came clattering around the edge of the castle ahead of them, zooming down to fly extremely low along the quayside. Ivan turned to fire at the aircraft, but Hank held his course and, before he could shoot, Ivan was forced to dive sideways off the edge of the quay, into the harbour water. As the microlight tore past the children to scatter the guards who had been pursuing them, Sam saw that Marcia was in the front seat.

'Let's go!' yelled Ben, and they ran onwards. Hank came back the other way, flying just over their heads before touching down near the *Silver Turtle*. As soon as Marcia had jumped from her seat, he started to take off again. 'Git goin'!' yelled Hank to all of them. 'I'll hold these sons of so-and-sos back, then I'll try to git the Swiss police to come here and rescue the adults. You go find that cop in Edinburgh. Good luck!' And he was airborne, swerving round to harangue the armed men once more.

The five children rushed to the edge of the quay and leapt for the *Silver Turtle,* which had now floated a little way out. They all landed on or beside the hull and started scrambling in through the open canopy and nose hatch. Ben was in first. 'Is everyone on board?' he yelled, starting up the motors. The gunfire had increased and the odd bullet was hitting the plane.

'Just about,' answered Adam, helping Zara in through the left side of the canopy.

'Yep!' called Marcia, whose leap had landed her half-in-half-out of the nose hatch.

'Go, Ben, go!' yelled Sam, hauling himself in through the right-hand side.

Just as Ben opened up the motors and began taxiing out of the castle harbour, Sam felt something grab his left leg. He looked down to see Ivan, clinging on, dragging him back down. Sam's fingers lost their grip on the cockpit edge and he slipped down into the foaming water around the speeding plane. Desperately he clawed at the smooth hull and his left hand found the edge of the hole which housed the retracted right wheel. He clung on, wanting to yell for help, but finding his mouth too full of spray as the plane sped faster and faster, dragging him along. Ivan's other hand was gripping his T-shirt. And the hand that had been holding his leg was now wielding a lethal-looking diver's knife. Ivan's face contorted in a wild, malevolent grin. He raised the weapon and prepared to plunge it into Sam's chest.

Then Ivan's expression snapped to a look of startled pain, as a stream of bullets from the guards on the quayside blasted into the back of his shoulder. He cried out, dropped the knife, let go of Sam and was left behind in the dark churned-up water.

Sam struggled desperately to get out of the water and back into the moving plane. Somehow he managed to get one foot onto the tyre of the retracted right wheel and one of his hands onto the streamlined right wing-strut. He yelled for Ben to stop, but it was too late: the *Silver Turtle* had reached the open lake and, unaware of Sam's situation, Ben increased the motors' speed, pulled back his control column, and took off.

Adam had hauled Zara in from the other side of the cockpit just before take-off. He looked for Sam, heard his cries, rushed across, leant out and grabbed him. A torrent of machine-gunfire from the castle blasted apart the tyre beneath Sam's foot and, for a second, Sam was trailing from the side of the plane held only by a wrist. Then Adam and Zara were dragging him aboard and he was safe.

'Sorry!' yelled Ben. 'I thought you were in.'

'Ivan!' puffed Sam, collapsing on a back seat. 'Grabbed me, dragged me down. Tried to stab me. But he got shot by his own people. They wouldn't have known he was there in the dark.'

Ben circled tightly over the lake as he gained height, not

wanting to fly low near the surrounding mountains, which were now being completely swallowed up in rolling black clouds and sheets of rain. The storm was finally breaking. Thunder and lightning crashed and flickered all around the mountains and the air was suddenly turbulent.

Sam looked back, down at the castle, still visible through the rain. What was that? He could see a black shape rising slowly in vertical take-off from the shore, looming over the castle, silhouetted against the floodlit roofs – StratoSting One! It had already been preparing to take off, he remembered. The StratoSting hovered for a few seconds, turning this way and that. It was looking for them, Sam was sure. The pilot would spot them visually or on his radar any second.

But then another aircraft zoomed across the hovering StratoSting's nose. Hank's microlight! The StratoSting turned. Sam could see the little microlight escaping up into a cloud . . . the StratoSting starting to pursue it . . . the microlight flying out through the top of the cloud . . . the StratoSting accelerating, aiming to cut through the cloud on a diagonal course . . . and crashing into the solid outer wall of the hidden airship.

The airship cloud tipped at an angle and fell slowly down towards the lake, the crumpled black stealth fighter sticking out from its side. Sam caught a glimpse of the pilot ejecting from the plane, his parachute opening, then a last glimpse of the microlight flying away. Then he could see no more, as Ben piloted them up through the sheets of rain and the thundering clouds.

Chapter Thirty-Four

Ben held the *Silver Turtle* in a steady climb, up through the clouds, thunder and light-ning crashing and flashing all around them, terrifyingly near.

Marcia got herself down through the nose hatch, and tumbled into the cockpit and onto one of the back seats. Adam and Zara got the canopy shut, and flopped into their seats too, Zara in the co-pilot's seat, Adam behind, next to Sam and Marcia.

But then Sam was out of his seat, crawling forward. 'Got to make ourselves radar invisible again,' he yelled, scram-bling beneath the instrument panel and taking the sardine tin radar-jamming device from his pocket. 'Noctarma have got at least one more stealth plane somewhere to send out looking for us.' He passed his keyring torch to Zara, who held it as steadily as she could while he used the pliers on his Swiss Army knife to twist together the wires trailing from the device and the wires hanging down from the back of the instrument panel. He'd made a mental note of how the wires connected when he'd removed the device. Was he remembering it correctly? Would it still work after his dip in the lake? Yes! The green light began to pulse.

'Well done,' said Ben. 'I'll keep our navigation lights switched off. Everyone keep a look-out for planes, ordinary ones too; we don't want to crash into an airliner. Now, where should I head for?'

'Edinburgh,' said Zara decisively. 'Professor Sharpe mentioned Chief Commissioner Grayloch's home address: Duggan's Close. We can put everything in his hands like Professor Sharpe was going to before she was kidnapped. Duggan's Close is off the Royal Mile, isn't it?'

'Yeah,' said Ben. 'Near St Mary's Street.'

Where Marcia lived, in London, the word Close in an address usually denoted a residential cul-de-sac. But she now recalled that, in Edinburgh, closes were the little arched passageways running between the buildings that lined each side of the Royal Mile. 'Professor Sharpe didn't say what number in Duggan's Close, though,' she said.

'No, but most of the closes are very short,' said Zara. 'Some have only one or two doors, and people usually have their surnames next to the buzzers for the different flats. I bet we can find him somehow if we get there. I don't know where else we could fly to, anyway.'

'I think you're right, Zara,' said Adam. 'I don't like leaving Mum and the others back there, but she'd agree with your plan.'

'Yeah,' said Sam. 'Hank's going to contact the Swiss police, to try and help the adults in the castle, but I'm not sure they'll believe him any more than that gendarme believed us. Our best hope of getting everyone rescued is to go to Edinburgh, where we know the name of someone we can trust.'

'Is Hank that man on the microlight?' asked Zara. 'Who *is* he?'

'Gabrielle's friend,' said Sam. 'We'll tell you about him properly in a minute, when we're on the right course. Can you navigate our way back there in the dark, Ben?'

'We don't even have my diary map now,' said Marcia. 'It's still in my jeans that I had on before I went diving. Probably still on the *Bernoulli*.'

'I think we can work out our course from what we did coming here,' said Ben, who had already banked the *Silver Turtle* round to head roughly in the right direction while they thought it through. 'To get from Calais to the middle of Lake Geneva we flew for about an hour and a quarter on a bearing of 150 degrees, then the last twenty minutes on 130,' he recalled. 'So, to go back we just need to reverse the times and . . . er . . . add 180 to the angles, I think. So that's . . .'

'Twenty minutes on 310 degrees, then an hour and a quarter on 330 degrees,' said Adam.

'Thanks, Adam,' said Ben, swinging the *Silver Turtle* onto a 310-degree bearing. 'I'll drop down below the clouds once I'm sure we're clear of the Jura mountains, so that we'll be able to see when we've got to the Channel. And after that, we'll head back across to Dover and follow the east coast up to Edinburgh. I suppose that bit'll take about another two hours.'

They finally emerged above the top of the clouds. Looking down through the rear of the cockpit canopy, Marcia, Sam and Adam could still see lightning flickering around the clouds and they could all still hear the thunder's rumble above the quiet whir of their plane's electric motors. Ben levelled out, just managing to keep the *Silver Turtle* on course as she lurched and bucked in the turbulent air.

Fortunately the wind was blowing from the south-east, helping rather than hindering their progress, and soon they had escaped the storm altogether and were flying through calmer air.

Zara and Sam's clothes were soaked from being in the lake, and Adam and Marcia's were almost as wet with rain-water, but the cockpit heater was beginning to dry everyone out.

'Now tell us how you escaped, you two,' said Zara to Sam and Marcia, 'and how you found us and got into the castle, and about Gabrielle's friend Hank.'

Marcia told them all what had happened underwater, and they told her what had happened on deck. Then Sam and Marcia told the others about their escape from the *Bernoulli*, and the extraordinary things that had happened to them since. 'I saw Hank get away back there,' Sam said, 'but it looks like his airship's had it. He lured that Noctarma plane into it, to stop it pursuing us.'

Ben dropped down below the layer of cloud, veering onto the second bearing of 330 degrees as they flew over a black landscape spattered with the lights of villages and towns.

'Right, let's plan what we're going to do when we reach Edinburgh,' said Zara. 'Where do you think we should land?'

'With our right wheel shot to bits, we're going to have to land on water,' pointed out Sam. 'How far is it from the sea to the middle of Edinburgh, where this Duggan's Close is?'

'Not that far,' said Ben, 'but we can land a lot nearer than the sea. There are a few small lochs in Holyrood Park, round the base of Arthur's Seat. St Margaret's Loch is the nearest one to the city centre, and I reckon it's just long enough to land on.' Uncle Alexander had taken him and Zara there sometimes when they were little, to feed the ducks and swans.

'Arthur's Seat is that huge hill near the bottom of the Royal Mile, isn't it?' said Marcia, remembering Ben and Zara pointing it out before. 'The extinct volcano?'

'Yep,' said Zara. 'And St Margaret's Loch must be less than a mile from Duggan's Close. It's a good plan – as long as we can find the loch in the dark.'

'Hey,' said Sam, 'I've remembered something I overheard Lucrezia de Lamprey telling Max at the castle: the address of the Secret Operations Police Unit's Edinburgh HQ. It's in Salamander Wharf.'

'Well done, Sam,' said Zara. 'That could make rescuing the adults a lot easier.'

'I don't know Salamander Wharf,' said Ben, 'but Salamander Street is in Leith, the docks area.'

'I just hope this Chief Commissioner Grayloch is at home,' said Marcia, 'and that we can make him believe us. We're going to have to wake him up; assuming the journey takes us about four hours, it'll be half-past two in the morning before we get there.'

'Only half-past one, with the time-zone change,' said Ben. 'And we'll *have* to make him believe us. It's our only chance of getting the adults released before Noctarma starts moving them somewhere else or –'

'Sir Roland said he was going to keep all the prisoners alive until he'd got hold of Stribnik's invention,' said Zara, quickly, 'and without Solomon, he can't find out where the invention's hidden. So I reckon the adults will be all right.' She said this with a great deal more confidence than she felt, knowing that she mustn't let herself or the others dwell on the possibility that Sir Roland would change his plans and start disposing of his prisoners anyway.

'Hey, we should have a proper look at Solomon, now that we've finally got him,' said Sam. 'I've got my little torch. Or do you think the light would show from outside the plane? Noctarma might have another plane out there searching for us.'

'I think it'll be all right if we're careful,' said Zara. 'I think we'd better find out what Solomon's secret information is, in case we lose him again.'

Sam, Marcia and Adam sat forward on their back seats, huddled tightly together so that their bodies would prevent most of the torchlight from spilling out. Zara knelt up in the co-pilot's seat so that she could see too and tell Ben what was happening. Sam took Solomon from the canvas bag, held him between them, and switched on his torch.

Chapter Thirty-Five

Marcia looked at the little silver turtle jewellery box, the search for which had nearly cost her her life. Its surface was intricately crafted, though badly tarnished, with just a few edges of unblackened silver glinting in the torchlight.

Sam tried lifting one side of Solomon's shell. Though stiff, the shell hinged open, revealing the shallow oval box within. But as they expected from what Gabrielle had told them, there was nothing inside.

'I reckon there must be some sort of message engraved on him somewhere,' said Sam. They turned the turtle over to check its underside, but could see nothing engraved.

For several minutes they examined every centimetre of Solomon's surface – the inside and outside of his shell, his scaly neck and head, his long front flippers and short back ones. But there was no sign of any kind of engraved message. Sam even checked inside the box for signs of a false bottom, but the base seemed entirely solid.

'There's nothing,' said Marcia. 'Maybe Maskil simply left a note or something in the box and it fell out before Gabrielle ever got Solomon.'

'I'm not sure he'd have risked leaving a note somewhere so easy to find,' said Sam. 'Anyone going through his things might have looked in a jewellery box.'

'Did the message on the photo say nothing at all about where to look on Solomon?' asked Adam.

'No,' said Zara. 'The actual wording went: *Solomon will tell you how to find the Silver Turtle project.*'

'It's a funny way to word it, isn't it?' said Ben. '*Solomon will tell you* . . . I mean, it's not as if he can speak.'

'No,' said Adam. 'Though he does have a tongue.'

Solomon had been crafted with an open mouth, complete with a tiny pointed tongue between his upper and lower jaws. They'd noticed this already, of course; Solomon's rather fierce open-mouthed expression was one of the details that Sam liked about the object. But now, he examined the tongue more carefully, peering  into the turtle's mouth and holding his torch as close as he could. 'There's something odd about the way the tongue's fixed into the back of the mouth,' he said. 'It's fixed into a sort of tiny vertical slot. Here, hold the torch, Marcia, while I try something.' His stomach tingling slightly, Sam poked an index finger into the turtle's mouth, above its tongue, put his thumb under its lower jaw, and squeezed. The tongue shifted down like a little lever and, with a quiet *clack*, the top of Solomon's head flipped up, hinging at the back.

'Wow,' said Zara.

The little lid's edge was zigzagged, following the edges of the geometric scales on top of the turtle's head, so that the join had been completely undetectable when the lid was shut. Something white was visible inside the compartment. Sam pulled it and brought out a little roll of white cotton, wet with lake water. The compartment, they could now see, went right down inside Solomon's neck, and the roll of cloth was about six centimetres long. Sam could feel something hard inside the cloth, and he hurriedly unrolled it.

'A key!' exclaimed Marcia. The key was also about six centimetres long, made of brass and quite ordinary looking.

'There's something written on the cloth,' said Adam. The

scrap of cotton, which looked as if it might have been cut from a handkerchief, had a line of letters written on it in black ink, faded but still legible:

zgblwglfbqxkddltb

'It must be in his typewriter cipher,' said Sam.

'Pity we don't have his typewriter,' said Marcia.

'We might not need it,' said Zara. 'We've got the ciphertext and plaintext versions of Maskil's last message written out in Sam's notebook, remember. They might give us enough of the letter substitutions to translate this.'

'It's lucky Maskil used cloth to write on,' said Sam, as he got out his rather soggy notebook. 'I don't think paper would have survived sixty years underwater – not so you could still unroll it and read it. My notebook's only just readable after being in the lake for less than a minute.'

'You're right,' said Zara. 'Though Maskil wouldn't have been thinking this message *needed* to survive underwater when he wrote it.'

'Maybe he used cloth to act as a sort of layer of padding,' said Marcia, 'to make sure the key didn't rattle around in the neck and get discovered by the wrong person. It's certainly lucky that the pen he used had waterproof ink.'

Sam found the right pages of his notebook and they got to work on the new message. They found that all of the letters written on the scrap of cloth appeared somewhere in either the ciphertext or the plaintext versions of the message from the back of the photo, which meant they could work out all the letters' correct pairings. Adam was particularly speedy at this, and Sam soon had the translation written out:

useinsidemyoffice

'Use inside my office,' read Marcia, easily seeing where the word breaks were. 'He must have meant his office at the museum. There must have been a cupboard or drawer or something there that this key fitted. Do you think it'll still be there?'

'I don't remember seeing any furniture in there that dated from that long ago,' said Zara. 'Maybe it got moved.'

'George said they only found a chair, table and type-writer in there after he was killed,' recalled Sam. 'Maybe this key fits some sort of secret cupboard, in the wall or something, that everyone missed.'

'Well, once everything else has been sorted, we'll go and have a look,' said Zara. 'The first thing is to get the adults released.'

Sam carefully put the key into his zip pocket with his notebook and torch. 'I'll get rid of it quick if we're inter-cepted by Noctarma agents again,' he said. 'But someone else look after the cloth, so that the two things won't be connected if they do get hold of them.'

Zara took the cloth and turned to face the front again, anxiously scanning the night sky for any sign of Noctarma planes as they flew onwards over France.

Chapter Thirty-Six

Nearly four hours after leaving Lake Geneva, the *Silver Turtle* was speeding low over the eastern fringes of Edinburgh. Ahead, lay the hulking shape of Arthur's Seat and its surrounding unlit parkland, a massive island of darkness in the sea of yellow street lights.

There had been one or two points in the journey when they'd been unsure exactly where they were. Ben and Adam's compass bearings had got them to the Channel, but it had been hard to be sure in the dark that the lights they were passing over were those of Calais or that the lights they were heading for were definitely those of Dover. However, Ben's geographical knowledge had got them up the east coast of the UK on a reasonably direct route to Edinburgh. The sky had been cloudless for this part of the journey, and the moon, though not quite full, had been bright enough to cast a grey sheen over the sea, distinguishing it from the land, which had helped Ben's navigation greatly. And now they were almost there. They were tired, starving hungry, and the energy-cell gauge was almost down to zero again. But they had made it to Edinburgh. All they had to do now was land.

Ben banked onto a curving course to bring them round Arthur's Seat on its northern side, where he knew St Margaret's Loch lay. Just beyond the hill, they could see the floodlit buildings of Edinburgh's city centre.

Lower and lower they flew, rooftops slipping beneath them. They would be over Holyrood Park any minute now. Ben tried to remember everything he needed to do to bring their speed down further. Nose up slightly . . . flaps down . . . reduce motor speed more. He had been worried about landing at night for the whole flight. Now he was terrified. The whole park looked inky black and featureless. No sign of the loch. This was madness. They should have landed on the sea.

Then he could see the lights of a car making its way along the road that he knew passed through the park. He was sure St Margaret's Loch was near the road. 'There's the loch!' yelled Zara, just as Ben spotted it himself: an almost rectangular patch of moonlit water. It looked tiny. And there were trees close to the nearest end, blocking the low approach he needed to make if he was to use the whole length of the loch. Should he fly round and approach from the other end?

No. The EMPTY light was flashing over the energy-cell gauge. He had to land now. Had to try. Nose up a bit more, in over the treetops, motor speed even slower, down, down, down . . . SMACK! Ploughing through the water . . . motors off . . . speeding towards the bank . . . loch too short . . . going to crash . . . going to be killed. BUMP! The plane rode up the sloping muddy bank at the end of the loch and went skidding across the grass for about twenty metres before dragging to a stop.

Everyone was jolted and shaken but basically fine. 'Cool landing, Ben,' said Zara, patting her brother's shoulder. 'Trust you to remember that the bank sloped like that. *I* thought we were going to crash! Come on – let's get going.'

She slid back the canopy and jumped down onto the grass. The others followed her, looking around as they scrambled out, half expecting to see people running to investigate. But there was no one about and although there were a few cars passing along the road through the park, none stopped. It seemed they had got down without being seen.

'Do you think the plane will be noticed from the road?' asked Sam.

'I don't think so,' said Zara. 'Not through those trees and not in this darkness. Anyway, it doesn't matter – as long as we can get hold of Chief Commissioner Grayloch before we're stopped by anyone.'

Sam paused to give their little plane a pat on the nose before following the others. With Marcia carrying Solomon, they ran across the dark expanse of grass, with the road to their right, and the black silhouette of Arthur's Seat to their left.

They soon reached the western end of the park, where it met the eastern edge of the city centre. Here they had to join the road and they started walking instead of running, trying not to draw attention to themselves. They passed the lofty front gates of the ancient Holyrood Palace on one side, then the imposing front entrance of the modern Scottish Parliament on the other. Both buildings had long closed for the night, with no signs of life from inside their darkened windows. The wide, softly lit area between the two buildings was deserted and had a rather eerie, intimidating atmosphere. There were bound to be CCTV cameras round here, realized Ben, beginning to worry that every corner of the city might be being monitored by the Secret Operations Police Unit.

They rounded the corner of the Parliament building and

Zara and Ben led the way up the steep hill of the Royal Mile, past narrow stone buildings that were jammed together like books on a bookshelf. They began to see other people: couples and groups making their way between the city's

late-night pubs, clubs and Festival venues. The children strode purposefully on and no one paid any attention to them. After a few minutes, Zara and Ben stopped at the entrance to a narrow covered passageway that led off from the pavement between two of the buildings to their left. The black and gold sign above the entrance read DUGGAN'S CLOSE.

There were just two doors in the walls of the short close, one on each side. Each with a column of intercom buttons built into the stonework. 'Here!' said Marcia, pointing to a buzzer labelled Grayloch in the row next to the left-hand door. 'Better make sure we wake him up,' she said, pressing the buzzer button down for several seconds.

They waited anxiously for almost a minute, but there was no answer. 'Better buzz again,' said Ben, doing so. This time, after another half-minute, a gruff, sleepy voice came through: 'Who's there?'

'We're friends of Professor Ivy Sharpe,' Zara called into the intercom grille. 'Her son Adam's with us. Is that Chief Commissioner Grayloch?'

'Aye, it is,' said the voice. 'But what are ye doing buzzing my buzzer at this time of night?'

'Sorry for waking you, but it's really urgent,' said Zara. 'Professor Sharpe's been kidnapped! Please help us.'

'Ivy Sharpe? Kidnapped? Look, stay there. I'll come down.'

In less than a minute, the children heard the clatter of

feet coming down stone stairs. The door opened and a tall, grey-haired man wearing an old brown dressing-gown over his pyjamas stood facing them. 'Are there no adults with you?' he asked, his fierce bulgy eyes staring at them from beneath a pair of even fiercer hairy eyebrows. 'What's all this about?'

They all started to speak, but the Chief Commissioner held up his hand. 'Ye'd better come up to the flat before we wake the whole stair.'

They followed him up the stone stairway and into his small third-floor flat. 'Now don't all talk at once,' he said. 'One of you tell me.'

Marcia, Adam, Sam and Ben looked at Zara, who quickly told Chief Commissioner Grayloch everything that had happened and everything they knew about Noctarma's activities and members, and everything they knew about where Noctarma's prisoners were being held.

When she had finished, the Chief Commissioner stared at her for a few seconds in silence. 'Let me get this straight,' he said at last. 'Ye've woken me up at half-past one in the morning to tell me that the senior Home Office official, Sir Roland Mantlingham, is the leader of a secret international criminal organization involved in war crimes and murder, which is holding four people prisoner in Switzerland and another in Suffolk, and that the government's Secret Operations Police Unit is actually controlled by this criminal organization, and that they're holding three more people prisoner here in Edinburgh, and that Sir Roland is planning to kill all these prisoners once he's got his hands on a secret invention, and that you five children have escaped by flying a plane here from Switzerland which you've landed on St Margaret's Loch?'

Zara's heart sank. He thought they were making it all up,

just like that gendarme had. But they had no one else to go to. 'Yes,' she said, meeting the Chief Commissioner's gaze. 'We can't make you believe us, but it's the truth.'

'Oh, I believe ye,' he said, seeming surprised that she'd thought he didn't. 'I've been a policeman long enough to be able to tell when someone's telling the truth. I just wanted to make sure I had the facts straight. And actually, what you've told me tallies with some disturbing rumours I've been picking up for years about the behaviour of the Secret Operations Police Unit. But I never had any hard facts. I didn't even know they had an HQ here in Edinburgh. Salamander Wharf, ye say? There are only a couple of buildings there. Won't take us long to find the right one. Just let me get some clothes on and we'll get cracking.' He disappeared into his bedroom, but was back in a remarkably short time, dressed, and already rapping orders into his hand-held police radio. 'It's taking a bit of time to mobilize enough officers at this time of night,' he told the children, between calls, 'but we're getting there.'

Finally, after a long twenty minutes of issuing instructions on his radio, he said, 'Let's go,' and led them back downstairs. A large police car screeched to a halt at the entrance to Duggan's Close and Chief Commissioner Grayloch bustled the children into the back before getting in the front. As they sped down towards Leith, he kept up a series of forceful phone and radio calls to trusted subordinates in Edinburgh, colleagues in England and contacts at Interpol.

Then they were at Salamander Wharf, where several police vans, blue lights flashing, had already surrounded a dilapidated warehouse building. Uniformed policemen were pouring into the building, some wearing body armour. For a while, nothing much seemed to be happening. Then policemen started coming out, escorting handcuffed men from the building.

Chief Commissioner Grayloch got out of the car as an officer hurried over from the warehouse.

'All rounded up, sir,' said the officer, saluting. 'One or two of them thought aboot using their guns, but we managed tae disarm them withoot any casualties. Their senior officer, Detective Superintendent Dunnistone, tried to pull rank, but we did as ye ordered and arrested him anyway. Ye did say ye'd be taking full responsibility for this, didn't ye sir?' he added, slightly nervously.

'I certainly did!' barked the Chief Commissioner. 'I won't have sly, underhand schemers like Sir Roland Mantlingham running private armies of secret so-called policemen on my patch. I've never approved of the government setting up these kinds of secret police units in the first place. If ye let organizations operate in secret, ye don't know *what* they're getting up to. Now, what about the people they were holding prisoner?'

The children held their breaths.

'Haven't found anyone yet, sir,' said the officer. The children felt their hopes evaporating. Had the adults been moved to some other secret location? Or been got rid of some other way?

'Hang on, sir!' said the officer. 'I think they're bringing some people out the side of the building now.'

And there they were – Professor Ampersand, Professor Hartleigh-Broadbeam and Amy, emerging from a side door with some more policemen. And there was Gabrielle too!

The five children burst out of the car and sprinted across to the adults. After several minutes of hugs, kisses and joyous tears, explanations began to be exchanged.

The adults had little to tell. In the fourteen and a half hours since their arrest at the hangar, Professor Ampersand, Professor Hartleigh-Broadbeam and Amy had been locked in a windowless cell in the basement of the warehouse. They had suffered from fear, total bewilderment and, most of all, anxiety for the plight of the children, but they were otherwise unharmed. Gabrielle had been moved up to Edinburgh by van after the children's escape from Lady Clarissa's, presumably for fear that they'd send the police to search Mantlingham Manor. The children's explanation of everything that had happened to them and to the other professors took a good bit longer. Amy was amazed to hear how far the *Silver Turtle* had flown. The Chief Commissioner promised to send a policeman to Holyrood Park to guard the plane, though there were more urgent concerns to be dealt with.

'We must get the prisoners released from this dreadful castle in Switzerland at once,' insisted Professor Hartleigh-Broadbeam.

'I'm sure Interpol and the Swiss authorities are doing all they can, ma'am,' Chief Commissioner Grayloch assured her. 'We'll go to my HQ so ye can all have something to eat and drink whilst we wait for news.'

Soon they were all sitting in a comfortable room in the Edinburgh City Police's central headquarters, not far from the Royal Mile. The Chief Commissioner bustled in and out but had little to report for a long time. The children were able to fill in the details of their story for the adults, and Gabrielle gave the two professors and Amy the full history of Maskil and his work. The children returned Solomon to Gabrielle and showed her the secret compartment in his head and neck.

'Strange ter see him again after all these years,' she said, the odd tear in her eyes as she sat holding Solomon, turning him round in her hands. 'Wonder if I'd ever have noticed this secret compartment if I hadn't lost him. I reckon Maskil's grandfather must've built it inta Solomon when he originally made him, as a place for the family ter hide extra valuable things.'

Everyone hungrily devoured the hot food and drink that was quickly rustled up from the canteen, though of course no one could feel truly rested and recovered while the predicament of the four professors being held in Switzerland remained unresolved.

Half an hour went by. Everyone tried to reassure each other – and especially tried to reassure Adam – that Professor Sharpe and the others would be released safe and well. But another half-hour passed with no news.

Then, at last, Chief Commissioner Grayloch came into the room, his craggy face smiling for the first time since the children had met him. 'Great news from Interpol,' he reported. 'The Swiss police have rescued all four prisoners unharmed from the Château de Lamprey. Maximilian and Lucrezia de Lamprey have been arrested, along with several Noctarma agents. The Swiss police *had* taken your friend Hank Zootlin for a crank when he tried to contact them a few hours ago, but now he's being taken very seriously indeed and is apparently bombarding Interpol officers with invaluable information about Noctarma's other international activities.'

Everyone looked at each other, so relieved and happy they could hardly speak. All the adults were finally safe and well. Everyone hugged each other again and thanked the Chief Commissioner profusely for all that he'd done. Professor Hartleigh-Broadbeam even gave him a kiss on his cheek.

Then the Chief Commissioner looked more serious

again. 'Not *quite* such good news from England,' he said. 'Although several members of staff at Mantlingham Manor have been arrested, Sir Roland and Lady Clarissa have given us the slip. I'm hoping we'll catch them eventually, but they'll have plenty of agents around the world to help them. It could take years for Interpol to really get to grips with an organization like Noctarma.'

'Hmm,' said Gabrielle. 'If Sir Roland finds out we've got hold of that key and message from Solomon, we could be in great danger again. He's obsessed with getting his hands on Maskil's anti-gravity invention. And if he ever succeeded, the whole world would be in danger.'

'I agree,' said Chief Commissioner Grayloch. 'For your safety and everyone else's, we should try to find this invention ourselves and move it somewhere secure. Of course, I realize ye'll all be wanting to get to your homes to get some sleep right now, so I'll put a guard on the museum tonight, and tomorrow afternoon we'll go and –'

'*Tomorrow afternoon?!*' shrieked Gabrielle. 'Are you *mad?* You think after everything we've been through, after everything these kids have been through, we're all going ter toddle home ter *bed?* Let's go to the museum *right bang now* and get to the bottom of this whole blimming thing!'

'We wouldn't be able to sleep anyway,' added Zara.

'It might be a good idea to find this invention now, if we can,' said Professor Ampersand to the Chief Commissioner, 'especially bearing in mind your concerns about Sir Roland still being at large.'

'Verra well,' said Chief Commissioner Grayloch. 'Give me fifteen minutes, and I'll get a police van to take us all to the museum, with some armed officers to guard the museum whilst we're in there. I hate using armed policemen but we mustn't take any chances with these Noctarma people.'

High above England, the sleek black form of StratoSting Two sped through the air, heading north. Sir Roland Mantlingham was piloting the aircraft, with a slightly dishevelled Lady Clarissa in the seat behind him.

Sir Roland was speaking into the radio. *'How has this happened, Creevler?'* he hissed. 'Those brats should have been intercepted. We *knew* they might head for Edinburgh. I gave orders that the airport, the hangar, the docks and all police stations were to be watched.'

'The orders were carried oot, Leader,' came the voice of Creevler. 'We dinnae ken how the kids got intae the city, or how they got straight to Grayloch. But they did. Grayloch's men have arrested everyone at Salamander Wharf. Dunnistone just had time tae get a warning oot tae me and Lerkner, so we stayed away. We're heading oot of toon in my Jag.'

'Then turn round and head back in!' rasped Sir Roland. 'By now that rabble must have examined the jewellery box. By now they must know where Stribnik's invention is hidden. Find out where they are now and what they are doing and stick to them like glue. Report back as soon as you know anything. I want full information before I reach Edinburgh.'

Chapter Thirty-Seven

At 4.05 a.m. two police vans pulled up at the front of the Royal Museum. Chief Commissioner Grayloch posted two armed officers on each of the museum's front, back and side doors, including those of the Museum of Scotland, a modern building that adjoined the western end of the Royal Museum, forming a single, linked complex. The Chief Commissioner, the five children, the two professors, Amy and Gabrielle ascended the Royal Museum's front steps where they were greeted by George McTorphin.

They'd needed to find someone from the museum staff to let them into the building and deal with the alarms, and Ben and Zara had thought of phoning George from the police van. They'd hoped he wouldn't mind being woken up too much and George didn't mind at all; he'd rushed round from his nearby flat and was now enjoying the excitement of it all, pleased to help get to the bottom of something that had been a mystery since his childhood.

The museum's interior was dimly lit and shadowy, the lights being set at their after-hours level. George led the way across the Main Hall and through the British Birds rooms to the red-carpeted rear stairway.

Soon they were on the top-floor landing, approaching the wood-panelled door of the storeroom. Was it really possible that they were about to rediscover an invention that had lain hidden for more than sixty years? wondered Sam. Were they about to rediscover a secret that, according to Gabrielle, would change the world for ever?

'Can you think of anything in there which the key could

open?' Zara asked George, as Sam took the key from his pocket.

'I cannae think of anything in the room that even has a keyhole,' said George. 'Only the door tae the room itself. Ye're sure the message said the key was for something *inside* his office, no just for unlocking the office itself? We dinnae keep the room locked noo, but there is a keyhole, see.'

'*Use inside my office*' is what the message said,' recalled Sam. 'But we can check.' He tried the key in the door's keyhole. But it was too small and rattled around uselessly in the lock, unable to turn. 'It *must* be for something inside,' he said. 'There *must* be a secret cupboard in there, or something.' He opened the door and they all went in.

George switched on the light. In the harsh glare from its bare light bulb, the small room looked just as modern and ordinary as Zara remembered it.

For the next ten minutes, everyone shifted the folded flip charts, the stacks of plastic chairs and the shelving unit, and checked every inch of the room's walls and floorboards. But they found no sign of any concealed lockers or cupboards and nothing that could be a keyhole. Sam even examined the typewriter – the only thing in the room that dated from the time when Maskil Stribnik had been here – but he found no keyhole in that either.

'Well, I hate to be the one to admit defeat,' said Chief Commissioner Grayloch, 'but . . .'

'You're right,' said Gabrielle, wearily. 'There just isn't anything that key could open in here, is there?'

'Och, well, never mind,' said Amy. 'Everyone's come oot o' this business safe and well and that's all that really matters.'

'Well, safe as long as we put a police guard on your homes until Sir Roland is arrested,' added Chief Commissioner Grayloch.

In spite of the ongoing concerns about Sir Roland, Amy was right, and the children were still glowing inside with relief and happiness. Even so, they also felt a bit disappointed that the trail of messages that Maskil Stribnik had left for Gabrielle had led to a complete dead end.

Everyone left the room and started down the stairs. The children lingered on the upper flight of stairs, for a last look back at the closed door, while the adults continued down.

'He wouldn't have left Gabrielle the key for nothing,' said Marcia. 'There must have been something in there that got moved.'

'Yeah,' said Ben, as they started walking down again after the adults. 'George was right: the only keyhole in that room now is the one in the door.'

It was as they were walking back through the British Birds room on the ground floor, still a little way behind the adults, that Adam stopped and said, 'Wait a minute.' The children all stopped too. 'What Ben just said made me realize something,' Adam said, frowning. 'When I picture the inside of the room's door, and then the outside, the keyholes are in two different positions. The keyhole on the inside is higher. It must be a different lock.'

'Come on!' said Sam, rushing back to the stairs. 'We've got to check this out.' The others followed him.

'Where are you going?' called Professor Hartleigh-Broadbeam.

'Checking something,' Ben called back. 'Two minutes.'

'Och, they shouldnae run off like that,' said George. 'Not after what happened tae Sam last time he went back up there on his own.'

'I shouldn't worry, sir,' said Chief Commissioner Grayloch. 'They're safe enough anywhere in the building with my armed officers guarding all the doors.' So the adults waited in the Main Hall, discussing possible arrangements for putting a police guard on 12 Pinkerton Place.

Slowly and silently, the slender black shape of StratoSting Two dropped down towards the flat roof terrace of the Museum of Scotland. Sunrise was still more than an hour away, and the sky above was dark; none of the policemen on the pavement below noticed the aircraft's arrival as they conscientiously guarded the museum complex's various street-level doors.

The children reached the top-floor landing again and ran to the door. Sam opened it and they saw that Adam was right: the keyhole on the inside of the door was several inches higher than the one on the outside. There were two different bolt ends visible in the edge of the door too, and two different corresponding slots in the door frame.

'*Use inside my office*,' quoted Sam. He shut the door again and tried the key in the inside keyhole. The key fitted well and, as he turned it, the door locked with a click.

'So that's what the key's for,' said Marcia. 'But I don't understand why you'd have a door with different keys and locks for the outside and inside.'

'And why would Maskil have gone to so much trouble to leave Gabrielle a key just so she could lock herself in his office?' said Zara. 'How would that help her find his invention?'

'Er, if you look round, you'll find out,' said Ben.

They had all been looking at the door. Now they turned to face into the room. And gasped with astonishment. The entire wall opposite the door was slowly and silently sliding to one side, revealing another room beyond, the same size as the one they were standing in, and also windowless. 'A secret room!' exclaimed Zara.

The partition wall slid away completely, effectively making the two small rooms into a single longer room. At the far end of the new space stood a workbench, stacked with tools, spools of wire and old electronic components.

'This must have been Maskil's secret laboratory,' said Sam, leading the way through. 'When he locked himself in his office, it opened up automatically, but if anyone else came into his office when he wasn't here, it would stay hidden.'

'Yeah,' said Marcia. 'Maybe his friend, the museum's director, helped him to install it.'

'Hey,' said Sam. 'Look round here.' They all joined him behind the workbench.

On the floor, propped up against the back of the bench, was something quite large and bulky, covered by a dust sheet. The children looked at one another. Had they at last found Maskil Stribnik's long-lost invention?

The StratoSting's wheels touched down noiselessly on the roof terrace's decking. The black-tinted cockpit canopy opened and Sir Roland stepped down from the aircraft. Two men emerged from the shadowy buildings at one end of the terrace and padded across to meet him. One wore a grey coat, the other a khaki one. Both wore faceless grey masks covering their heads.

'So,' breathed Sir Roland, 'they believe Stribnik hid his invention somewhere in the museum, after all? In spite of all the searches after he died that turned up nothing.'

'It looks that way, Leader,' whispered Lerkner. 'They all arrived here fifteen minutes ago, with a substantial police guard.'

'You are certain you were not seen getting up here?' hissed Sir Roland.

'Certain,' replied Creevler. 'We climbed up the University buildings at the other end o' the street, and came along the rooftops. I've dealt with the CCTV cameras, Leader, so nae one will have seen your arrival either. The cameras are relaying footage from an hoor ago tae the monitors. And Lerkner has cracked the locks and alarms on the door tae the stairs doon from here.'

'Good,' purred Sir Roland. 'Now, what are you armed with?'

'Just oor automatics, Leader,' said Creevler.

Sir Roland produced three compact submachine-guns from the cockpit. 'Let us be certain of getting what we have come for,' he rasped. 'I shall not be long, Mother,' he promised.

'I shall be fine,' said Lady Clarissa. 'Shoot those children for me, if you get the chance.'

Quietly, the three men made their way to the roof terrace door and started to descend the staircase.

Chapter Thirty-Eight

The children removed the dust sheet. The part of the object facing them consisted of a flat circle of padded leather, a bit less than a metre in diameter. Various canvas straps with buckles hung down over the leather and two bars of metal tubing protruded forwards and upwards, one from each side of the circle. The back of the circle, the part of the object leaning against the bench, was a shallow dome made from a pale silvery metal that looked like aluminium.

'This *must* be the invention,' said Marcia, as they lifted the object onto the bench to get a better look. 'I wonder how it works.'

'I reckon these straps form a sort of harness,' said Sam, 'so you could wear it on your back, like a rucksack.'

'But it wouldn't look like a rucksack!' said Ben. 'It would look like the shell of a turtle. Maskil Stribnik didn't just name his invention after his family jewellery box – he called it the Silver Turtle project because that's what the machine looks like.'

Sam had a closer look at the ends of the two bars of metal tubing. Each one ended in a bent-up section, with a rubber hand grip attached. They looked as if they had been made from the ends of bicycle handlebars, complete with what looked like little metal brake levers. 'Looks like you'd hold these to control it,' said Sam. 'Do you think it can really fly?' He squeezed one of the levers.

'Don't!' said Zara. 'It might be dangerous.' But nothing happened.

'We can look at it later,' said Marcia. 'Let's get it down-stairs and show the adults. They're going to be amazed.'

'Hey, let's put it on someone's back with the harness, for the full effect,' suggested Ben. 'It'd be easier to carry that way anyway.'

The harness was built to fit an adult. Marcia was the biggest among them, but the harness straps would have made the cut on her side hurt, so they put Zara, the next biggest, into it. By tightening the straps fully they made it fit her pretty well. Zara found it odd walking round the room with the big silver shell on her back, but quite fun too. Sam noticed a little switch on the chunky metal clip that held the harness together at Zara's chest, but Zara insisted that they shouldn't meddle with anything. 'Come on,' she said, heading for the door. They were all elated now, and couldn't wait to show the adults.

'Hang on,' said Sam. 'I've just found this on the floor behind the bench.' He held up a little book with a battered red cover. Inside were pages of diagrams hand-drawn in black ink, interspersed with complex mathematical equations. 'I think it's Stribnik's notebook for the Silver Turtle project,' he said. 'Some of the diagrams look like this machine.'

'Trust you to find his notebook, Sam,' said Zara grin-ning. 'It could be useful for finding out how the machine works. You'd better put it in your pocket with yours.'

Ben unlocked the door and they watched the partition slide quickly back into place, before opening the door and leaving the room. They were halfway across the land-ing to the top of the stairs, when Marcia caught sight of a movement in a dark passageway at the far side of the room of old telescopes and microscopes. She screamed. Three men were rushing across the shadowy room towards the landing: two grey, faceless men and the tall figure of Sir Roland Mantlingham, all brandishing guns.

'*Run!*' yelled Ben.

'*Get them!*' came Sir Roland's voice, followed by a burst of submachine-gunfire.

The five children fled through the East Asian room, weaving round exhibits, heading for the opening on its other side, Marcia and Sam holding Zara's arms, helping her run with the heavy weight of the machine on her back, Ben just in front, making sure Adam was beside him.

Ben's brain raced, planning their route. Had to get to an outside door, where there'd be armed policemen. Had to keep out of the gunmen's line of fire. The opening ahead would bring them onto the Main Hall's upper gallery. Then they should turn left, get to the end, avoid the exposed main stairs, go through the archway there instead, then – *TRRRRRRRR! PANG-PANG-PANG!* Before they had reached the opening, they heard a burst of gunfire from behind, heard bullets ricocheting off the samurai armour display they'd just dodged round. The three men were in the room, catching them up. Had to get through the opening. Almost there . . . *TRRRRRRRR-CRASH!* Another stream of bullets blasted apart a big display case of porcelain, just to their left. Zara flinched, swerved to avoid the explosion of glass and china, and stumbled. As she fell headlong, Sam and Marcia lost their hold on her arms and she landed flat out on her chest, skidding along the polished wooden floor, between Ben and Adam, and out through the opening onto the Main Hall's upper gallery.

Then, something absolutely extraordinary happened. One moment, Zara could see the white latticework of the upper gallery's railings, dead ahead as she slid towards them; a split second later, the floor seemed to drop away and the railings flashed past beneath her as, inexplicably, she zoomed over them and out into thin air. She screamed in terror, looking down at the floor of the Main Hall far below, expecting to plummet down towards it. She saw the adults gaping up at her in horror. Then horror turning to disbelief. Then she realized she wasn't plummeting at all: she was floating, out into the centre of the hall and up towards the arching white ribs of the hall's glass roof.

The switch! She'd felt the switch on the harness go click as she'd fallen on her front. As she drifted to a hovering standstill, she realized that the machine on her back was vibrating slightly, emitting a low growl that seemed to buzz through her whole body. And a strange blue aura, just visible in the dimly lit space, seemed to flicker all around her. Maskil Stribnik's anti-gravity machine was working.

Chapter Thirty-Nine

'Move, Zara, or they'll shoot you!'

'Squeeze the handlebars!'

Responding to the urgency in Ben and Sam's voices, Zara grabbed the handlebars, squeezing the little levers as she did so. She instantly shot forward – just in time; she heard a volley of gunfire behind her and heard the bullets shattering the glass roof. But she was hurtling towards the opposite side of the gallery, heading between the pillars, about to crash into the wall behind.

Instinctively, she pulled the handlebars to the left, trying to steer. It worked! She slewed round a pillar and zoomed back out across the hall.

'Aim for the girl; don't damage the machine!' rasped Sir Roland. She could see him now, and the faceless men, standing on the gallery, pointing their guns at her chest. Had to swerve again. *TRRRRRRRRRRRR!* Once more, the bullets missed, but not by much.

Down below, Zara could see armed policemen charging into the Main Hall through the front doors and from other parts of the museum. Chief Commissioner Grayloch was ordering the other adults to evacuate the area. Up on her level, Zara could see Ben, Sam, Marcia and Adam escaping through the archway at the end of the gallery. 'Fly this way!' yelled Ben, looking back.

But she was too late. Sir Roland and the two men had split up around the upper gallery and now had the archway and all the other exits covered by their guns. Her adversaries alternated their shooting, each taking turns to fire at her when she flew near, while the other two fired down at the armed police, and at the stairs, to discourage any attack. The police were firing back up at the gunmen, but without much success, and Zara saw one officer fall, clutching his shoulder.

Zara continued to evade the gunmen's bullets, which were blasting glass display cases to smithereens all around her. At first, her only strategy was to keep moving from one part of the upper gallery to another. But then she began to really get the hang of the controls. By frantic trial and error she discovered that she could soar by moving the handlebars up, dive by moving them down, perform rolls by moving one up and one down together, and make lightning-quick hairpin turns by releasing one or other of the accelerator levers.

She tumbled and flitted all around the Main Hall, weaving in and out of the pillars, soaring and plunging from ceiling to floor at increasingly high speeds. Yet there was a total absence of g-forces acting on her body, just as Gabrielle had predicted when describing anti-gravity flight. The sensation was nothing like the roller-coaster rides Zara had been on, when her head and limbs and stomach had been pushed this way and that at every turn. Instead, her insides felt unaffected, and her arms and legs felt completely weightless. She guessed the blue aura was some sort of electromagnetic field that was shielding her from all gravitational forces.

But Zara was unable to dwell on the science or on the peculiar sensation. She had to get out of the Main Hall and away from Sir Roland and his faceless gunmen. Confident that she now had the speed and manoeuvrability to evade their gunfire, she decided to make a break for the entrance to the Ancient Egypt room which led off from the middle level gallery. From there she would be able to fly through to the back of the museum, where she hoped she'd find more police and the adults. First, she made it look as if she was zooming for the archway at the end of the upper level gallery; then she rolled left and downwards at the last moment.

But she was unlucky or overconfident. Sir Roland let loose a blast of gunfire and Zara felt one of the bullets hit the shell on her back. P*TANG!* It hadn't injured her, but the machine was instantly affected, jerking all over the place before flipping up and coming crashing down on its back on the upper level gallery, near to where Zara had started her flight.

Before Zara could pick herself up, one of the faceless gunmen was grabbing her by the arm. Then his colleague was holding her other arm, and they dragged her to her feet.

'This way! Don't bother to unstrap her; bring her with it,' hissed Sir Roland, who was near the archway at the end of the gallery, firing down on a policeman who had started trying to come up the stairs. *'Get back!'* he rasped. 'Don't follow us or we'll shoot the girl.'

Still strapped into the machine, Zara found herself being half-dragged, half-carried through the archway and along a connecting gallery to the Museum of Scotland side of the complex. Sir Roland ran just behind, turning occasionally to send a blast of discouraging gunfire in the direction of any would-be pursuers.

The machine on Zara's back felt particularly heavy to her now, after her weightless experience. It was emitting a very faint uneven growl from within the shell. The machine was also growing extremely warm. But that was the least of her worries. She didn't know where they were going, but she had little doubt that once Sir Roland got clear of the police with the anti-gravity machine, he would have no reason to keep her alive and every reason to kill her.

From behind a display of historic ships, Ben, Marcia, Adam and Sam watched Zara being dragged past by the two men. 'Come on,' whispered Ben, once Sir Roland had also passed, and the four children followed as silently as they could, through the maze of curved white walls and exhibits.

Zara's heart sank when she saw the sinister shape of StratoSting Two, its underside softly illuminated by the roof terrace's floor lighting. Sir Roland had clearly got his escape very well planned out indeed. She was dragged quickly over to the plane, where she saw Lady Clarissa in the rear seat, glaring at her with undisguised hatred, her face green in the glow from the instruments.

'We now possess Stribnik's invention,' Sir Roland hissed to his mother proudly, as he hurriedly unstrapped the machine from Zara's back. His eyes gleamed. 'It is everything I had hoped for. Once this prototype is developed for our purposes, Noctarma truly shall be invincible. Our destiny will be fulfilled.' He squeezed the invention into the cockpit, in front of Lady Clarissa's seat. 'I had to shoot the machine to prevent this brat from escaping with it,' he explained, 'but no doubt the damage is minor and can be put right by our scientists.'

'What aboot the girl?' asked Creevler, as Sir Roland climbed into the pilot's seat. 'Shall we shoot her noo, afore we go?'

'Shooting's too good for her,' said Lady Clarissa. 'She and her urchin friends attacked me, you know. Teach her to know her place. Throw her over the edge.'

'A splendid idea,' rasped Sir Roland, smirking. 'We will teach our little high-flyer that the power to defy gravity is not for the likes of her. Throw her over the edge, then escape across the roofs the way you came. You two have acquitted yourselves well tonight. There shall be a place for you in Noctarma's new world order.' He shut the canopy and StratoSting Two began to rise from the roof terrace.

As the plane soared silently away, Creevler and Lerkner began dragging Zara to the roof's edge. She screamed for help, but knew it was hopeless: the police in the Main Hall wouldn't have dared to follow too closely with Sir Roland threatening to shoot her; they wouldn't get up here to the roof in time. She struggled and fought, but that was useless too. The men had her arms in a vicelike grip and were impervious to her kicks. They reached the edge. Together, they pulled her back, ready to fling her hard and high enough to clear the parapet and safety rail. This was it, thought Zara, with despair. She was going to die.

Then four figures emerged from the shadows and flung themselves at the two men from behind. Marcia and Ben rugby tackled them at the knees, while Sam and Adam grappled for their guns. As they fell to the floor, the men let go of Zara and she joined the fight, punching Lerkner's grey-masked face in the eyes. Creevler was fighting back hard, however, kicking Ben off, wrestling back control of his gun, aiming it at Adam . . .

But now, half a dozen policemen were throwing themselves on the two men, and the fight was soon over, with Lerkner and Creevler handcuffed and held securely. The children picked themselves up and saw yet more police officers streaming out onto the roof terrace, followed by the two professors, Amy, Gabrielle, George and Chief Commissioner Grayloch.

'Where's Sir Roland?' barked the Chief Commissioner, as soon as he had seen that Zara and the other children were safe.

'He got away in his plane, with Lady Clarissa,' said Zara, pointing into the sky. The sky had begun to turn from black to grey-blue with the approaching dawn, but even so, Zara expected the StratoSting to be visible as no more than a distant dot by now.

However, she was wrong. The black silhouette of the StratoSting could be seen swerving round in a wide banking zoom, low over the city spires. Its missiles were visible beneath the wings.

'He's coming back!' yelled Zara, horrified. Sir Roland or his mother must have turned and seen that Zara had been rescued. They must have seen that all the people who had crossed them were now on the roof: all the people who knew most about Noctorama, and Sir Roland's future plans. The StratoSting was coming back to kill them all.

'Evacuate the roof!' bellowed Chief Commissioner Grayloch. Everyone ran for the door at the top of the stairs, but everyone knew it was too late. The door was narrow and most of them would not even make it that far. The children looked back, to see the StratoSting tearing straight towards them, coming in close for the kill. Sir Roland's thumb would be on the weapons button, ready to fire his missiles into the rooftop . . .

Then suddenly, the StratoSting bucked as if it had been kicked hard from beneath, and tumbled wildly up into the night sky, tail over nose, wing tip over wing tip. Higher and higher it went, up and up at incredible speed, rolling and twisting the whole time, a corona of blue sparks flickering over its surface, and an orange glow radiating from within its cockpit, a glow bright enough to penetrate its black-tinted windows. The anti-gravity machine! Zara remembered the heat she'd felt from it after it had crashed. Sir Roland's bullet had done something worse to the machine than he'd thought. Something that had unleashed chaotic and terrible forces. Now the writhing StratoSting was directly over-head, still ascending, so high that only the blue sparks and orange glow were visible.

Everyone stared up, speechless. The air around them felt strange, tingly and alive. And they all felt a weird, buzzing vibration in their brains. Then they heard a hum-ming noise, rapidly growing in volume, not emanating from above, but from all around them, here on the roof. The railings! The steel safety rails around the roof terrace were vibrating, realized Sam. Looking at the closest rail, he could actually see a slight blurring of its surface. The ends of the horizontal bars almost seemed to be straining to bend upwards. Sam looked back up at the StratoSting. The glow was becoming brighter, turning from orange to yellow.

And then, there was a huge white flash, brighter than lightning, so bright they had to close their eyes. The noise of the explosion reached them a couple of seconds later, a great thunderous *WHAM!* that shook their bones as the shock wave slammed down through them.

For a split second, all was silent. The humming vibrations had stopped; the air was still again. Then every car alarm in the city seemed to go off.

'Look out for falling debris!' yelled Chief Commis-sioner Grayloch and everyone scuttled for the door again, covering their heads with their arms in anticipation of bits of falling metal. But there were no bits of metal. All that anyone heard, saw or felt falling from the sky – all that was left of the StratoSting Two, of Maskil Stribnik's anti-gravity invention, and of Sir Roland and Lady Clarissa Mantlingham – was a fine shower of grey, gritty dust.

Chapter Forty

Without a wisp of cloud surrounding it, the giant dough-nut-shaped airship floated over the centre of Edinburgh, its underhanging circular catwalk and two cabins lit up in the evening sky for all to see.

A week had passed since the shadowy careers of Sir Roland and Lady Clarissa Mantlingham had come to their explosive end. The day after her release from the Château de Lamprey, Professor Sharpe had badgered the Swiss authorities into helping Hank to salvage and repair his stricken airship so he could fly it up off the lake. After the inadequate behaviour of Lieutenant Doltaine, the rest of the police-boat officers on Lake Geneva had been keen to prove their helpfulness and efficiency by overseeing the engineers working on the job, and the airship had been ready to fly again in six days. Part of the airship's side would always look rather dented and patched, but she flew as well as ever. The artificial cloud system had been damaged beyond repair but, as Hank himself pointed out, his airship wasn't exactly a secret now anyway, since the people who lived around the eastern end of Lake Geneva had woken up one morning to find it floating on the water with the wreck of a stealth fighter sticking out of its side.

Now, Marcia, Sam, Zara, Ben, Adam, the six professors, Amy, Gabrielle, George and Chief Commissioner Gray-loch had all joined Hank aboard his newly restored airship for an evening cruise over Edinburgh and for something of a party. He had flown it up to Scotland during the day and picked them all up at Petticraig Bay, using a rope ladder.

They all stood on the catwalk and the platform around the front of Hank's cabin, enjoying the view below. The catwalk had little lamps gleaming all around it, the cabin had had its window shutters removed, and the delicious smell of Hank's chicken stew was emanating from a huge bubbling pan on his stove.

Ben and Zara stood on either side of Professor Ampersand, looking down over the city spread out beneath them. Ben loved Edinburgh at this time of  evening, when the sun had set, and the sky was a deep rich blue, and the buildings were all floodlit. From up here, it looked like a giant map, though one which was three-dimensional and alive. They were low enough to easily see people bustling about below, many of whom looked up at the airship and waved. Zara was looking down at the museum, going over her anti-gravity flight in her mind for the hundredth time, wishing she could have had a go on the machine in less terrifying circumstances.

George, standing next to her, was recalling Zara's flight too. 'It's what I saw as a boy,' he said, his grey eyes looking out into the sky, 'late one night, when my father had sent me back intae the museum tae get something he'd left. I saw Mr Stribnik flying aroond like you were, testing his anti-gravity machine. I only caught a glimpse; he stopped as soon as he realized I was there. But now I know I really saw it. All these years I thought it must have been my imagination.'

Sam was studying one of the airship's big, silent engines with Professor Pottle. Hank had been talking earlier to Professor Ampersand about converting them to electric ones, though Professor Pottle had been telling Sam about his superior scheme for collecting huge quantities of bird droppings on the upper surface of the airship, which could be used as a source of fuel. Everyone, not least Sam and Marcia, had been congratulating Professor Pottle for his courage on the *Bernoulli*, and he had been enjoying the novel experience of telling people about his ideas without interruption or criticism. 'Did you know,' he said to Sam, 'that an average-size flock of migrating red-breasted geese, if they could be persuaded to make a stopover on the airship, would produce enough methane in a single night to power this airship from here to Middlesborough. Did you know that?'

'I didn't,' said Sam.

The existence of Noctarma had been causing something of a stir in the news over the past week. As Interpol got to grips with the extent of Noctarma's secret power and influence, every day seemed to bring a new revelation about a prominent person or business corporation having been involved with the organization.

There had also been considerable media interest in the *Silver Turtle* flying boat and in Professor Ampersand's energy cells and electric motors. As a result, quite a few potential financial backers had come forward to discuss joining Professor Ampersand, Amy, and Professor Hartleigh-Broadbeam in setting up an electric vehicles and aircraft business. Zara and Ben were pretty sure that their financial worries would soon be over.

Amy was telling Hank about their plans. 'Of course, we've still tae do quite a few more tests on the *Silver Turtle*,' she said, 'though Gabrielle and the children have already put her through a pretty testing first test flight.'

'Well, she's a darn fine plane,' said Hank. 'The best of luck to ya all.'

'And the best of luck to you and your future travels in

this marvellous airship,' said Professor Hartleigh-Broad-beam.

'I'm really glad you got your airship back, Hank,' said Marcia. 'Sorry that it lost its cloud cover. Do you miss living in secret?'

'Nope, Marcia,' answered Hank. 'Tell ya the truth, I ain't sure it was good for me livin' alone and in secret for that long. There was always a danger of it makin' me go a little crazy. Overly paranoid about things. Keepin' things secret can make ya start feelin' kinda guilty and furtive, even when ya ain't got nothin' to feel guilty and furtive about, if ya know what I mean.'

'I know what you mean,' said Marcia. She decided that maybe she'd have a go telling her school friends the truth about her parents next term.

'I don't even have to worry 'bout my old employers comin' after me for wreckin' the stuff in the factory and takin' the airship,' added Hank. 'Turns out they've had all sortsa secret dealings with Noctarma in recent years, so they're in too much trouble of their own now. The authorities have told me I can keep the airship, and ol' Gabrielle's got all sortsa grand schemes for it: a travellin' flying school, a mobile aid and rescue centre for disaster zones. She's gonna keep me pretty busy.'

'Someone sane and level-headed's got ter keep an eye on you,' said Gabrielle.

'And of course, we're gonna start rebuildin' Maskil's anti-gravity invention,' continued Hank. 'We've still got his notebook. Might take a good few years, but we'll have a go. And we're gonna do the work in public. Too much important research into this sorta stuff gets done in secret, usually for military purposes. If we ever do make another anti-gravity machine, it's gonna be for everybody.'

'Yes indeed,' said Professor Gadling. 'We wouldn't want to end up like the paranoid armoured bee of the Serengeti.' He paused, waiting for a response.

'Go on, Garrulous,' sighed Professor Sharpe. 'Tell us about the paranoid armoured bee of the Serengeti.'

'As long as you're not expecting me to come on an expedition looking for it,' muttered Professor Gauntraker.

'The paranoid armoured bee of the Serengeti,' said Professor Gadling, 'seems to have evolved from the ordinary honey bee which, as you know, is a species that works together. But the paranoid armoured bee lives singly, in its own hole, building elaborate body armour with tiny bits of bark and thorns, convinced it will need to fight against *other* paranoid armoured bees. However all the other paranoid armoured bees are busy constructing their own armour and staying in *their* holes. Eventually the completely unnecessary armour becomes so elaborate, the bee cannot move from its hole at all. They usually end up dying of hunger.'

'I know just how they feel,' said Hank, opening the cabin door, and ushering everyone through towards the smell of the bubbling chicken stew. 'Let's eat.'